James Baldwin

# GO
# TELL IT
# ON
# THE
# MOUNTAIN

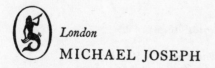

*London*

MICHAEL JOSEPH

*First published in Great Britain by*
MICHAEL JOSEPH LTD
52 *Bedford Square*
*London, W.C.*1
MARCH 1954
SECOND IMPRESSION APRIL 1954
THIRD IMPRESSION JULY 1954
FOURTH IMPRESSION JUNE 1963
FIFTH IMPRESSION JANUARY 1964
SIXTH IMPRESSION APRIL 1966
SEVENTH IMPRESSION NOVEMBER 1970

7181 0161 8

*Printed in Great Britain by Hollen Street Press Ltd*
*at Slough and bound by James Burn at Esher, Surrey*

*For*

MY FATHER AND MOTHER

*They that wait upon the Lord shall renew their strength; they shall mount up with wings like eagles; they shall run and not be weary, they shall walk and not faint.*

# Contents

*Part One*

# THE
# SEVENTH
# DAY

*And the Spirit and the bride say,*
*Come. And let him that heareth say,*
*Come. And let him that is athirst*
*come. And whosoever will, let him*
*take the water of life freely.*

*I looked down the line,*
*And I wondered*

EVERYONE had always said that John would be a preacher when he grew up, just like his father. It had been said so often that John, without ever thinking about it, had come to believe it himself. Not until the morning of his fourteenth birthday did he really begin to think about it, and by then it was already too late.

His earliest memories—which were in a way, his only memories—were of the hurry and brightness of Sunday mornings. They all rose together on that day; his father, who did not have to go to work, and led them in prayer before breakfast; his mother, who dressed up on that day, and looked almost young, with her hair straightened, and on her head the close-fitting white cap that was the uniform of holy women; his younger brother, Roy, who was silent that day because his father was home. Sarah, who wore a red ribbon in her hair that day, and was fondled by her father. And the baby, Ruth, who was dressed in pink and white, and rode in her mother's arms to church.

11

The church was not very far away, four blocks up Lenox Avenue, on a corner not far from the hospital. It was to this hospital that his mother had gone when Roy, and Sarah, and Ruth were born. John did not remember very clearly the first time she had gone, to have Roy; folks said that he had cried and carried on the whole time his mother was away; he remembered only enough to be afraid every time her belly began to swell, knowing that each time the swelling began it would not end until she was taken from him, to come back with a stranger. Each time this happened she became a little more of a stranger herself. She would soon be going away again, Roy said—he knew much more about such things than John. John had observed his mother closely, seeing no swelling yet, but his father had prayed one morning for the 'little voyager soon to be among them,' and so John knew that Roy spoke the truth.

Every Sunday morning, then, since John could remember, they had taken to the streets, the Grimes family on their way to church. Sinners along the avenue watched them—men still wearing their Saturday-night clothes, wrinkled and dusty now, muddy-eyed and muddy-faced; and women with harsh voices and tight, bright dresses, cigarettes between their fingers or held tightly in the corners of their mouths. They talked, and laughed, and fought together, and the women fought like the men. John and Roy, passing these men and women, looked at one another briefly, John embarrassed and Roy amused. Roy would be like them when he grew up, if the Lord did not change his heart. These men and women they passed on Sunday mornings had spent the night in bars, or in cat houses, or on the streets, or on rooftops, or under the stairs. They had been drinking. They had gone from cursing to laughter, to anger, to lust. Once he and Roy had watched a man and woman in the basement of a condemned house.

They did it standing up. The woman had wanted fifty cents, and the man had flashed a razor.

John had never watched again; he had been afraid. But Roy had watched them many times, and he told John he had done it with some girls down the block.

And his mother and father, who went to church on Sundays, they did it too, and sometimes John heard them in the bedroom behind him, over the sound of rat's feet, and rat screams, and the music and cursing from the harlot's house downstairs.

Their church was called the *Temple of the Fire Baptized*. It was not the biggest church in Harlem, nor yet the smallest, but John had been brought up to believe it was the holiest and best. His father was head deacon in this church—there were only two, the other a round, black man named Deacon Braithwaite—and he took up the collection, and sometimes he preached. The pastor, Father James, was a genial, well-fed man with a face like a darker moon. It was he who preached on Pentecost Sundays, and led revivals in the summer-time, and anointed and healed the sick.

On Sunday mornings and Sunday nights the church was always full; on special Sundays it was full all day. The Grimes family arrived in a body, always a little late, usually in the middle of Sunday school, which began at nine o'clock. This lateness was always their mother's fault—at least in the eyes of their father; she could not seem to get herself and the children ready on time, ever, and sometimes she actually remained behind, not to appear until the morning service. When they all arrived together, they separated upon entering the doors, father and mother going to sit in the Adult Class, which was taught by Sister McCandless, Sarah going to the Infants' Class, John and Roy sitting in the Intermediate, which was taught by Brother Elisha.

When he was young, John had paid no attention in

Sunday school, and always forgot the golden text, which earned him the wrath of his father. Around the time of his fourteenth birthday, with all the pressures of church and home uniting to drive him to the altar, he strove to appear more serious and therefore less conspicuous. But he was distracted by his new teacher, Elisha, who was the pastor's nephew and who had but lately arrived from Georgia. He was not much older than John, only seventeen, and he was already saved and was a preacher. John stared at Elisha all during the lesson, admiring the timbre of Elisha's voice, much deeper and manlier than his own, admiring the leanness, and grace, and strength, and darkness of Elisha in his Sunday suit, wondering if he would ever be holy as Elisha was holy. But he did not follow the lesson, and when, sometimes, Elisha paused to ask John a question, John was ashamed and confused, feeling the palms of his hands become wet and his heart pound like a hammer. Elisha would smile and reprimand him gently, and the lesson would go on.

Roy never knew his Sunday school lesson either, but it was different with Roy—no one really expected of Roy what was expected of John. Everyone was always praying that the Lord would change Roy's heart, but it was John who was expected to be good, to be a good example.

When Sunday school service ended there was a short pause before morning service began. In this pause, if it was good weather, the old folks might step outside a moment to talk among themselves. The sisters would almost always be dressed in white from crown to toe. The small children, on this day, in this place, and oppressed by their elders, tried hard to play without seeming to be disrespectful of God's house. But sometimes, nervous or perverse, they shouted, or threw hymn-books, or began to cry, putting their parents, men or women of God, under the necessity of proving—by harsh means or tender—who, in a sanctified household,

ruled. The older children, like John or Roy, might
wander down the avenue, but not too far. Their father
never let John and Roy out of his sight, for Roy had
often disappeared between Sunday school and morning
service and had not come back all day.

The Sunday morning service began when Brother
Elisha sat down at the piano and raised a song. This
moment and this music had been with John, so it seemed,
since he had first drawn breath. It seemed that there had
never been a time when he had not known this moment
of waiting while the packed church paused—the sisters
in white, heads raised, the brothers in blue, heads back;
the white caps of the women seeming to glow in the
charged air like crowns, the kinky, gleaming heads of
the men seeming to be lifted up—and the rustling and
the whispering ceased and the children were quiet; perhaps someone coughed, or the sound of a car horn, or
a curse from the streets came in; then Elisha hit the
keys, beginning at once to sing, and everybody joined
him, clapping their hands, and rising, and beating the
tambourines.

The song might be: *Down at the cross where my
Saviour died!*

Or: *Jesus, I'll never forget how you set me free!*

Or: *Lord, hold my hand while I run this race!*

They sang with all the strength that was in them, and
clapped their hands for joy. There had never been a
time when John had not sat watching the saints rejoice
with terror in his heart, and wonder. Their singing
caused him to believe in the presence of the Lord;
indeed, it was no longer a question of belief, because
they made that presence real. He did not feel it himself,
the joy they felt, yet he could not doubt that it was, for
them, the very bread of life—could not doubt it, that is,
until it was too late to doubt. Something happened to
their faces and their voices, the rhythm of their bodies,

and to the air they breathed; it was as though wherever they might be became the upper room, and the Holy Ghost were riding on the air. His father's face, always awful, became more awful now; his father's daily anger was transformed into prophetic wrath. His mother, her eyes raised to heaven, hands arked before her, moving, made real for John that patience, that endurance, that long suffering, which he had read of in the Bible and found so hard to imagine.

On Sunday mornings the women all seemed patient, all the men seemed mighty. While John watched, the Power struck someone, a man or woman; they cried out, a long, wordless crying, and, arms outstretched like wings, they began the Shout. Someone moved a chair a little to give them room, the rhythm paused, the singing stopped, only the pounding feet and the clapping hands were heard; then another cry, another dancer; then the tambourines began again, and the voices rose again, and the music swept on again, like fire, or flood, or judgment. Then the church seemed to swell with the Power it held, and, like a planet rocking in space, the temple rocked with the Power of God. John watched, watched the faces, and the weightless bodies, and listened to the timeless cries. One day, so everyone said, this Power would possess him; he would sing and cry as they did now, and dance before his King. He watched young Ella Mae Washington, the seventeen-year-old granddaughter of Praying Mother Washington, as she began to dance. And then Elisha danced.

At one moment, head thrown back, eyes closed, sweat standing on his brow, he sat at the piano, singing and playing; and then, like a great black cat in trouble in the jungle, he stiffened and trembled, and cried out. *Jesus, Jesus, oh Lord Jesus!* He struck on the piano one last, wild note, and threw up his hands, palms upward, stretched wide apart. The tambourines raced to fill the vacuum left by his silent piano, and his cry drew answering cries. Then he was on his feet, turning, blind, his face congested, contorted with this rage, and the muscles leaping and swelling in his long, dark neck. It seemed that he could not breathe, that his body could not contain this passion, that he would be, before their eyes, dispersed into the waiting air. His hands, rigid to the very fingertips, moved outward and back against his hips, his sightless eyes looked upward, and he began to dance. Then his hands closed into fists, and his head snapped downward, his sweat loosening the grease that slicked down his hair; and the rhythm of all the others quickened to match Elisha's rhythm; his thighs moved terribly against the cloth of his suit, his heels beat on the floor, and his fists moved beside his body as though he were beating his own drum. And so, for a while, in the centre of the dancers, head down, fists beating, on, on, unbearably, until it seemed the walls of the church would fall for very sound; and then, in a moment, with a cry, head up, arms high in the air, sweat pouring from his forehead, and all his body dancing as though it would never stop. Sometimes he did not stop until he fell—until he dropped like some animal felled by a hammer—moaning, on his face. And then a great moaning filled the church.

There was sin among them. One Sunday, when regular service was over, Father James had uncovered sin in the congregation of the righteous. He had uncovered Elisha and Ella Mae. They had been 'walking disorderly'; they were in danger of straying from the truth. And as Father James spoke of the sin that he knew they had not committed yet, of the unripe fig plucked too early from the tree—to set the children's teeth on edge—John felt himself grow dizzy in his seat and could not look at Elisha where he stood, beside Ella Mae, before the altar. Elisha hung his head as Father James spoke, and the congregation murmured. And Ella Mae was not so beautiful now as she was when she was singing and testifying, but looked like a sullen, ordinary girl. Her full lips were loose and her eyes were black—with shame, or rage, or both. Her grandmother, who had raised her, sat watching quietly, with folded hands. She was one of the pillars of the church, a powerful evangelist and very widely known. She said nothing in Ella Mae's defence, for she must have felt, as the congregation felt, that Father James was only exercising his clear and painful duty; he was responsible, after all, for Elisha, as Praying Mother Washington was responsible for Ella Mae. It was not an easy thing, said Father James, to be the pastor of a flock. It might look easy to just sit up there in the pulpit night after night, year in, year out, but let them remember the awful responsibility placed on his shoulders by almighty God—let them remember that God would ask an accounting of him one day for every soul in his flock. Let them remember this when they thought he was hard, let them remember that the Word was hard, that the way of holiness was a hard way. There was no room in God's army for the coward heart, no crown awaiting him who put mother, or father, sister, or brother, sweetheart, or friend above God's will. Let the church cry amen to this! And they cried: 'Amen! Amen!'

The Lord had led him, said Father James, looking down on the boy and girl before him, to give them a public warning before it was too late. For he knew them to be sincere young people, dedicated to the service of the Lord—it was only that, since they were young, they did not know the pitfalls Satan laid for the unwary. He knew that sin was not in their minds—not yet; yet sin was in the flesh; and should they continue with their walking out alone together, their secrets and laughter, and touching of hands, they would surely sin a sin beyond all forgiveness. And John wondered what Elisha was thinking—Elisha, who was tall and handsome, who played basket-ball, and who had been saved at the age of eleven in the improbable fields down south. *Had* he sinned? Had he been tempted? And the girl beside him, whose white robes now seemed the merest, thinnest covering for the nakedness of breasts and insistent thighs —what was her face like when she was alone with Elisha, with no singing, when they were not surrounded by the saints? He was afraid to think of it, yet he could think of nothing else; and the fever of which they stood accused began also to rage in him.

After this Sunday Elisha and Ella Mae no longer met each other each day after school, no longer spent Saturday afternoons wandering through Central Park, or lying on the beach. All that was over for them. If they came together again it would be in wedlock. They would have children and raise them in the church.

This was what was meant by a holy life, this was what the way of the cross demanded. It was somehow on that Sunday, a Sunday shortly before his birthday, that John first realized that this was the life awaiting him—realized it consciously, as something no longer far off, but imminent, coming closer day by day.

John's birthday fell on a Saturday in March, in 1935. He awoke on this birthday morning with the feeling that there was menace in the air around him—that something irrevocable had occurred in him. He stared at a yellow stain on the ceiling just above his head. Roy was still smothered in the bedclothes, and his breath came and went with a small, whistling sound. There was no other sound anywhere; no one in the house was up. The neighbours' radios were all silent, and his mother hadn't yet risen to fix his father's breakfast. John wondered at his panic, then wondered about the time; and then (while the yellow stain on the ceiling slowly transformed itself into a woman's nakedness) he remembered that it was his fourteenth birthday and that he had sinned.

His first thought, nevertheless, was: 'Will anyone remember?' For it had happened, once or twice, that his birthday had passed entirely unnoticed, and no one had said 'Happy Birthday, Johnny,' or given him anything —not even his mother.

Roy stirred again and John pushed him away, listening to the silence. On other mornings he awoke hearing his mother singing in the kitchen, hearing his father in the bedroom behind him grunting and muttering prayers to himself as he put on his clothes; hearing, perhaps, the chatter of Sarah and the squalling of Ruth, and the radios, the clatter of pots and pans, and the voices of all the folk nearby. This morning not even the cry of a bed-spring disturbed the silence, and John seemed, therefore, to be listening to his own unspeaking doom. He could believe, almost, that he had awakened late on that great getting-up morning; that all the saved had been trans-formed in the twinkling of an eye, and had risen to meet Jesus in the clouds, and that he was left, with his sinful body, to be bound in hell a thousand years.

He had sinned. In spite of the saints, his mother and his father, the warnings he had heard from his earliest beginnings, he had sinned with his hands a sin that was hard to forgive. In the school lavatory, alone, thinking of the boys, older, bigger, braver, who made bets with each other as to whose urine could arch higher, he had watched in himself a transformation of which he would never dare to speak.

And the darkness of John's sin was like the darkness of the church on Saturday evenings; like the silence of the church while he was there alone, sweeping, and running water into the great bucket, and overturning chairs, long before the saints arrived. It was like his thoughts as he moved about the tabernacle in which his life had been spent; the tabernacle that he hated, yet loved and feared. It was like Roy's curses, like the echoes these curses raised in John: he remembered Roy, on some rare Saturday when he had come to help John clean the church, cursing in the house of God, and making obscene gestures before the eyes of Jesus. It was like all this, and it was like the walls that witnessed and the placards on the walls which testified that the wages of sin was death. The darkness of his sin was in the hardheartedness with which he resisted God's power; in the scorn that was often his while he listened to the crying, breaking voices, and watched the black skin glisten while they lifted up their arms and fell on their faces before the Lord. For he had made his decision. He would not be like his father, or his father's fathers. He would have another life.

For John excelled in school, though not, like Elisha, in mathematics or basket-ball, and it was said that he had a Great Future. He might become a Great Leader of His People. John was not much interested in His people and still less in leading them anywhere, but the phrase so often repeated rose in his mind like a great brass gate, opening outward for him on a world where people did not live in the darkness of his father's house, did not pray to Jesus in the darkness of his father's church, where he would eat good food, and wear fine clothes, and go to the movies as often as he wished. In this world John, who was, his father said, ugly, who was always the smallest boy in his class, and who had no friends, became immediately beautiful, tall, and popular. People fell all over themselves to meet John Grimes. He was a poet, or a college president, or a movie star; he drank expensive whisky, and he smoked Lucky Strike cigarettes in the green package.

It was not only coloured people who praised John,

since they could not, John felt, in any case really know; but white people also said it, in fact had said it first and said it still. It was when John was five years old and in the first grade that he was first noticed; and since he was noticed by an eye altogether alien and impersonal, he began to perceive, in wild uneasiness, his individual existence.

They were learning the alphabet that day, and six children at a time were sent to the blackboard to write the letters they had memorized. Six had finished and were waiting for the teacher's judgment when the back door opened and the school principal, of whom everyone was terrified, entered the room. No one spoke or moved. In the silence the principal's voice said:

'Which child is that?'

She was pointing at the blackboard, at John's letters. The possibility of being distinguished by her notice did not enter John's mind, and so he simply stared at her. Then he realized, by the immobility of the other children and by the way they avoided looking at him, that it was he who was selected for punishment.

'Speak up, John,' said the teacher, gently.

On the edge of tears, he mumbled his name and waited. The principal, a woman with white hair and an iron face, looked down at him.

'You're a very bright boy, John Grimes,' she said. 'Keep up the good work.'

Then she walked out of the room.

That moment gave him, from that time on, if not a weapon at least a shield; he apprehended totally, without belief or understanding, that he had in himself a power that other people lacked; that he could use this to save himself, to raise himself; and that, perhaps, with this power he might one day win that love which he so longed for. This was not, in John, a faith subject to death or alteration, nor yet a hope subject to destruction;

it was his identity, and part, therefore, of that wickedness
for which his father beat him and to which he clung in
order to withstand his father. His father's arm, rising and
falling, might make him cry, and that voice might cause
him to tremble; yet his father could never be entirely
the victor, for John cherished something that his father
could not reach. It was his hatred and his intelligence
that he cherished, the one feeding the other. He lived
for the day when his father would be dying and he, John,
would curse him on his death-bed. And this was why,
though he had been born in the faith and had been
surrounded all his life by the saints and by their prayers
and their rejoicing, and though the tabernacle in which
they worshipped was more completely real to him than
the several precarious homes in which he and his family
had lived, John's heart was hardened against the Lord.
His father was God's minister, the ambassador of the
King of Heaven, and John could not bow before the
throne of grace without first kneeling to his father. On
his refusal to do this had his life depended, and John's
secret heart had flourished in its wickedness until the
day his sin first overtook him.

In the midst of all his wonderings he fell asleep again,
and when he woke up this time and got out of bed his
father had gone to the factory, where he would work for
half a day. Roy was sitting in the kitchen, quarrelling
with their mother. The baby, Ruth, sat in her high chair
banging on the tray with an oatmeal-covered spoon.
This meant that she was in a good mood; she would not
spend the day howling, for reasons known only to herself, allowing no one but her mother to touch her. Sarah
was quiet, not chattering to-day, or at any rate not yet,
and stood near the stove, arms folded, staring at Roy
with the flat black eyes, her father's eyes, that made her
look so old.

Their mother, her head tied up in an old rag, sipped black coffee and watched Roy. The pale end-of-winter sunlight filled the room and yellowed all their faces; and John, drugged and morbid and wondering how it was that he had slept again and had been allowed to sleep so long, saw them for a moment like figures on a screen, an effect that the yellow light intensified. The room was narrow and dirty; nothing could alter its dimensions, no labour could ever make it clean. Dirt was in the walls and the floorboards, and triumphed beneath the sink where cockroaches spawned; was in the fine ridges of the pots and pans, scoured daily, burnt black on the bottom, hanging above the stove; was in the wall against which they hung, and revealed itself where the paint had cracked and leaned outwards in stiff squares and fragments, the paper-thin underside webbed with black. Dirt was in every corner, angle, crevice of the monstrous stove, and lived behind it in delirious communion with the corrupted wall. Dirt was in the baseboard that John scrubbed every Saturday, and roughened the cupboard shelves that held the cracked and gleaming dishes. Under this dark weight the walls leaned, under it the ceiling, with a great crack like lightning in its centre, sagged. The windows gleamed like beaten gold or silver, but now John saw, in the yellow light, how fine dust veiled their doubtful glory. Dirt crawled in the grey mop hung out of the windows to dry. John thought with shame and horror, yet in angry hardness of heart: *He who is filthy, let him be filthy still*. Then he looked at his mother, seeing, as though she were someone else, the dark, hard lines running downward from her eyes, and the deep, perpetual scowl in her forehead, and the downturned, tightened mouth, and the strong, thin, brown, and bony hands; and the phrase turned against him like a two-edged sword, for was it not he, in his false pride and his evil imagination, who was filthy? Through a storm of

tears that did not reach his eyes, he stared at the yellow
room; and the room shifted, the light of the sun darkened,
and his mother's face changed. Her face became the face
that he gave her in his dreams, the face that had been
hers in a photograph he had seen once, long ago, a
photograph taken before he was born. This face was
young and proud, uplifted, with a smile that made the
wide mouth beautiful and glowed in the enormous eyes.
It was the face of a girl who knew that no evil could
undo her, and who could laugh, surely, as his mother
did not laugh now. Between the two faces there stretched
a darkness and a mystery that John feared, and that
sometimes caused him to hate her.

Now she saw him and she asked, breaking off her
conversation with Roy: 'You hungry, little sleepyhead?'

'Well! About time you was getting up,' said Sarah.

He moved to the table and sat down, feeling the most
bewildering panic of his life, a need to touch things, the
table and chairs and the walls of the room, to make certain that the room existed and that he was in the room.
He did not look at his mother, who stood up and went
to the stove to heat his breakfast. But he asked, in order
to say something to her, and to hear his own voice:

'What we got for breakfast?'

He realized, with some shame, that he was hoping
she had prepared a special breakfast for him on his
birthday.

'What you *think* we got for breakfast?' Roy asked
scornfully. 'You got a special craving for something?'

John looked at him. Roy was not in a good mood.

'I ain't said nothing to you,' he said.

'Oh, I *beg* your pardon,' said Roy, in the shrill, little-
girl tone he knew John hated.

'What's the *matter* with you to-day?' John asked,
angry, and trying at the same time to lend his voice as
husky a pitch as possible.

'Don't you let Roy bother you,' said their mother. 'He cross as two sticks this morning.'

'Yeah,' said John, 'I reckon.' He and Roy watched each other. Then his plate was put before him: hominy grits and a scrap of bacon. He wanted to cry, like a child: 'But, Mama, it's my birthday!' He kept his eyes on his plate and began to eat.

'You can *talk* about your Daddy all you want to,' said his mother, picking up her battle with Roy, 'but *one* thing you can't say—you can't say he ain't always done his best to be a father to you and to see to it that you ain't never gone hungry.'

'I been hungry plenty of times,' Roy said, proud to be able to score this point against his mother.

'Wasn't *his* fault, then. Wasn't because he wasn't *trying* to feed you. That man shovelled snow in zero weather when he ought've been in bed just to put food in your belly.'

'Wasn't just *my* belly,' said Roy indignantly. 'He got a belly, too, I *know*—it's a *shame* the way that man eats. I sure ain't asked him to shovel no snow for me.' But he dropped his eyes, suspecting a flaw in his argument. 'I just don't want him beating on me all the time,' he said at last. 'I ain't no dog.'

She sighed, and turned slightly away, looking out of the window. 'Your Daddy beats you,' she said, 'because he loves you.'

Roy laughed. 'That ain't the kind of love I understand, old lady. What you reckon he'd do if he didn't love me?'

'He'd let you go right on,' she flashed, 'right on down to hell where it looks like you is just determined to go anyhow! Right on, Mister Man, till somebody puts a knife in you, or takes you off to jail!'

'Mama,' John asked suddenly, 'is Daddy a good man?'

He had not known that he was going to ask the

question, and he watched in astonishment as her mouth
tightened and her eyes grew dark.

'That ain't no kind of question,' she said mildly. 'You
don't know no better men, do you?'

'Looks to me like he's a mighty good man,' said
Sarah. 'He sure is praying all the time.'

'You children is young,' their mother said, ignoring
Sarah and sitting down again at the table, 'and you don't
know how lucky you is to have a father what worries
about you and tries to see to it that you come up right.'

'Yeah,' said Roy, 'we don't know how lucky we *is*
to have a father what don't want you to go to movies,
and don't want you to play in the streets, and don't
want you to have no friends, and he don't want this and
he don't want that, and he don't want you to do *nothing*.
We so *lucky* to have a father who just wants us to go to
church and read the Bible and beller like a fool in front
of the altar and stay home all nice and quiet, like a little
mouse. Boy, we sure is lucky, all right. Don't know what
I done to be so lucky.'

She laughed. 'You going to find out one day,' she
said, 'you mark my words.'

'Yeah,' said Roy.

'But it'll be too late, then,' she said. 'It'll be too late
when you come to be . . . sorry.' Her voice had changed.
For a moment her eyes met John's eyes, and John was
frightened. He felt that her words, after the strange
fashion God sometimes chose to speak to men, were
dictated by Heaven and were meant for him. He was
fourteen—was it too late? And this uneasiness was reinforced by the impression, which at that moment he
realized had been his all along, that his mother was not
saying everything she meant. What, he wondered, did
she say to Aunt Florence when they talked together?
Or to his father? What were her thoughts? Her face
would never tell. And yet, looking down at him in a

moment that was like a secret, passing sign, her face did tell him. Her thoughts were bitter.

'I don't care,' Roy said, rising. 'When *I* have children I ain't going to treat them like this.' John watched his mother; she watched Roy. 'I'm *sure* this ain't no way to be. Ain't got no right to have a houseful of children if you don't know how to treat them.'

'You mighty grown up this morning,' his mother said. 'You be careful.'

'And tell me something else,' Roy said, suddenly leaning over his mother, 'tell me how come he don't never let me talk to him like I talk to you? He's my father, ain't he? But he don't never listen to me—no, I all the time got to listen to him.'

'Your father,' she said, watching him, 'knows best. You listen to your father, I guarantee you you won't end up in no jail.'

Roy sucked his teeth in fury. 'I ain't looking to go to no *jail*. You think that's all that's in the world is jails and churches? You ought to know better than that, Ma.'

'I know,' she said, 'there ain't no safety except you walk humble before the Lord. You going to find it out, too, one day. You go on, hardhead. You going to come to grief.'

And suddenly Roy grinned. 'But you be there, won't you, Ma—when I'm in trouble?'

'You don't know,' she said, trying not to smile, 'how long the Lord's going to let me stay with you.'

Roy turned and did a dance step. 'That's all right,' he said. 'I know the Lord ain't as hard as Daddy. Is he, boy?' he demanded of John, and struck him lightly on the forehead.

'Boy, let me eat my breakfast,' John muttered— though his plate had long been empty, and he was pleased that Roy had turned to him.

'That sure is a crazy boy,' ventured Sarah, soberly.

'Just listen,' cried Roy, 'to the little saint! Daddy ain't never going to have no trouble with her—*that* one, she was born holy. I bet the first words she ever said was: "Thank you, Jesus." Ain't that so, Ma?'

'You stop this foolishness,' she said, laughing, 'and go on about your work. Can't nobody play the fool with you all morning.'

'Oh, is you got work for me to do this morning? Well, I declare,' said Roy, 'what you got for me to do?'

'I got the woodwork in the dining-room for you to do. And you going to do it, too, before you set foot out of *this* house.'

'Now, why you want to talk like that, Ma? Is I said I wouldn't do it? You know I'm a right good worker when I got a mind. After I do it, can I go?'

'You go ahead and do it, and we'll see. You better do it right.'

'I *always* do it right,' said Roy. 'You won't know your old woodwork when *I* get through.'

'John,' said his mother, 'you sweep the front room for me like a good boy, and dust the furniture. I'm going to clean up in here.'

'Yes'm,' he said, and rose. She *had* forgotten about his birthday. He swore he would not mention it. He would not think about it any more.

To sweep the front room meant, principally, to sweep the heavy red and green and purple Oriental-style carpet that had once been that room's glory, but was now so faded that it was all one swimming colour, and so frayed in places that it tangled with the broom. John hated sweeping this carpet, for dust rose, clogging his nose and sticking to his sweaty skin, and he felt that should he sweep it for ever, the clouds of dust would not diminish, the rug would not be clean. It became in his imagination his impossible, lifelong task, his hard trial, like that of a man he had read about somewhere, whose curse it was to push a boulder up a steep hill, only to have the giant who guarded the hill roll the boulder down again—and so on, for ever, throughout eternity; he was still out there, that hapless man, somewhere at the other end of the earth, pushing his boulder up the hill. He had John's entire sympathy, for the longest and hardest part of his Saturday mornings was his voyage with the broom across this endless rug; and, coming to the French doors that ended the living-room and stopped the rug, he felt like an indescribably weary traveller who sees his home at last. Yet for each dustpan he so laboriously filled at the door-sill demons added to the rug twenty more; he saw in the expanse behind him the dust that he had raised settling again into the carpet; and he gritted his teeth, already on edge because of the dust that filled his mouth, and nearly wept to think that so much labour brought so little reward.

Nor was this the end of John's labour; for, having put away the broom and the dustpan, he took from the small bucket under the sink the dust rag and the furniture oil and a damp cloth, and returned to the living-room to excavate, as it were, from the dust that threatened to bury them, his family's goods and gear. Thinking bitterly of his birthday, he attacked the mirror with the cloth, watching his face appear as out of a cloud. With a shock he saw that his face had not changed, that the hand of Satan was as yet invisible. His father had always said that his face was the face of Satan—and was there not something—in the lift of the eyebrow, in the way his rough hair formed a V on his brow—that bore witness to his father's words? In the eye there was a light that was not the light of Heaven, and the mouth trembled, lustful and lewd, to drink deep of the wines of Hell. He stared at his face as though it were, as indeed it soon appeared to be, the face of a stranger, a stranger who held secrets that John could never know. And, having thought of it as the face of a stranger, he tried to look at it as a stranger might, and tried to discover what other people saw. But he saw only details: two great eyes, and a broad, low forehead, and the triangle of his nose, and his enormous mouth, and the barely perceptible cleft in his chin, which was, his father said, the mark of the devil's little finger. These details did not help him, for the principle of their unity was undiscoverable, and he could not tell what he most passionately desired to know: whether his face was ugly or not.

And he dropped his eyes to the mantelpiece, lifting one by one the objects that adorned it. The mantelpiece held, in brave confusion, photographs, greeting cards, flowered mottoes, two silver candlesticks that held no candles, and a green metal serpent, poised to strike. To-day in his apathy John stared at them, not seeing; he began to dust them with the exaggerated care of the profoundly preoccupied. One of the mottoes was pink and blue, and proclaimed in raised letters, which made the work of dusting harder:

> *Come in the evening, or come in the morning,*
> *Come when you're looked for, or come without*
>     *warning,*
> *A thousand welcomes you'll find here before you,*
> *And the oftener you come here, the more we'll*
>     *adore you.*

And the other, in letters of fire against a background of gold, stated:

> *For God so loved the world, that He gave His only*
> *begotten Son, that whosoever should believe in Him should*
> *not perish, but have everlasting life.*
>
>                                            *John iii*, 16

These somewhat unrelated sentiments decorated either side of the mantelpiece, obscured a little by the silver candlesticks. Between these two extremes, the greeting cards, received year after year, on Christmas, or Easter, or birthdays, trumpeted their glad tidings; while the green metal serpent, perpetually malevolent, raised its head proudly in the midst of these trophies, biding the time to strike. Against the mirror, like a procession, the photographs were arranged.

These photographs were the true antiques of the family, which seemed to feel that a photograph should commemorate only the most distant past. The photographs of John and Roy, and of the two girls, which seemed to violate this unspoken law, served only in fact to prove it most iron-hard: they had all been taken in infancy, a time and a condition that the children could not remember. John in his photograph lay naked on a white counterpane, and people laughed and said that it was cunning. But John could never look at it without feeling shame and anger that his nakedness should be here so unkindly revealed. None of the other children was naked; no, Roy lay in his crib in a white gown and grinned toothlessly into the camera, and Sarah, sombre at the age of six months, wore a white bonnet, and Ruth was held in her mother's arms. When people looked at these photographs and laughed, their laughter differed from the laughter with which they greeted the naked John. For this reason, when visitors tried to make advances to John he was sullen, and they, feeling that for some reason he disliked them, retaliated by deciding that he was a 'funny' child.

Among the other photographs there was one of Aunt Florence, his father's sister, in which her hair, in the old-fashioned way, was worn high and tied with a ribbon; she had been very young when this photograph was taken, and had just come North. Sometimes, when she came to visit, she called the photograph to witness that she had indeed been beautiful in her youth. There was

a photograph of his mother, not the one John liked and
had seen only once, but one taken immediately after
her marriage. And there was a photograph of his father,
dressed in black, sitting on a country porch with his
hands folded heavily in his lap. The photograph had
been taken on a sunny day, and the sunlight brutally
exaggerated the planes of his father's face. He stared into
the sun, head raised, unbearable, and though it had been
taken when he was young, it was not the face of a young
man; only something archaic in the dress indicated that
this photograph had been taken long ago. At the time
this picture was taken, Aunt Florence said, he was
already a preacher, and had a wife who was now in
Heaven. That he had been a preacher at that time was
not astonishing, for it was impossible to imagine that
he had ever been anything else; but that he had had a
wife in the so distant past who was now dead filled John
with a wonder by no means pleasant. If she had lived,
John thought, then he would never have been born; his
father would never have come North and met his mother.
And this shadowy woman, dead so many years, whose
name he knew had been Deborah, held in the fastness
of her tomb, it seemed to John, the key to all those
mysteries he so longed to unlock. It was she who had
known his father in a life where John was not, and in a
country John had never seen. When he was nothing,
nowhere, dust, cloud, air, and sun, and falling rain, *not
even thought of*, said his mother, *in Heaven with the angels*,
said his aunt, she had known his father, and shared his
father's house. She had loved his father. She had known
his father when lightning flashed and thunder rolled
through Heaven, and his father said: 'Listen. God is
talking.' She had known him in the mornings of that
far-off country when his father turned on his bed and
opened his eyes, and she had looked into those eyes,
seeing what they held, and she had not been afraid. She

B

had seen him baptized, *kicking like a mule and howling*, and she had seen him weep when his mother died; *he was a right young man then*, Florence said. Because she had looked into those eyes before they had looked on John, she knew what John would never know—the purity of his father's eyes when John was not reflected in their depths. She could have told him—had he but been able from his hiding-place to ask!—how to make his father love him. But now it was too late. She would not speak before the judgment day. And among those many voices, and stammering with his own, John would care no longer for her testimony.

When he had finished and the room was ready for Sunday, John felt dusty and weary and sat down beside the window in his father's easy chair. A glacial sun filled the streets, and a high wind filled the air with scraps of paper and frosty dust, and banged the hanging signs of stores and store-front churches. It was the end of winter, and the garbage-filled snow that had been banked along the edges of pavements was melting now and filling the gutters. Boys were playing stickball in the damp, cold streets; dressed in heavy woollen sweaters and heavy trousers, they danced and shouted, and the ball went *crack* as the stick struck it and sent it speeding through the air. One of them wore a bright-red stocking cap with a great ball of wool hanging down behind that bounced as he jumped, like a bright omen above his head. The cold sun made their faces like copper and brass, and through the closed window John heard their coarse, irreverent voices. And he wanted to be one of them, playing in the streets, unfrightened, moving with such grace and power, but he knew this could not be. Yet, if he could not play their games, he could do something they could not do; he was able, as one of his teachers said, to think. But this brought him little in the way of consolation, for to-day he was terrified of his thoughts. He wanted to be with these boys in the street, heedless and thoughtless, wearing out his treacherous and bewildering body.

But now it was eleven o'clock, and in two hours his father would be home. And then they might eat, and then his father would lead them in prayer, and then he would give them a Bible lesson. By and by it would be evening and he would go to clean the church, and remain for tarry service. Suddenly, sitting at the window, and with a violence unprecedented, there arose in John a flood of fury and tears, and he bowed his head, fists clenched against the window-pane, crying, with teeth on edge: 'What shall I do? What shall I do?'

Then his mother called him; and he remembered that she was in the kitchen washing clothes and probably had something for him to do. He rose sullenly and walked into the kitchen. She stood over the wash-tub, her arms wet and soapy to the elbows and sweat standing on her brow. Her apron, improvised from an old sheet, was wet where she had been leaning over the scrubbing-board. As he came in, she straightened, drying her hands on the edge of the apron.

'You finish your work, John?' she asked.

He said: 'Yes'm,' and thought how oddly she looked at him; as though she were looking at someone else's child.

'That's a good boy,' she said. She smiled a shy, strained smile. 'You know you're your mother's right-hand man?'

He said nothing, and he did not smile, but watched her, wondering to what task this preamble led.

She turned away, passing one damp hand across her forehead, and went to the cupboard. Her back was to him, and he watched her while she took down a bright, figured vase, filled with flowers only on the most special occasions, and emptied the contents into her palm. He heard the chink of money, which meant that she was going to send him to the store. She put the vase back and turned to face him, her palm loosely folded before her.

'I didn't never ask you,' she said, 'what you wanted for your birthday. But you take this, son, and go out and get yourself something you think you want.'

And she opened his palm and put the money into it, warm and wet from her hand. In the moment that he felt the warm, smooth coins and her hand on his, John stared blindly at her face, so far above him. His heart broke and he wanted to put his head on her belly where the wet spot was, and cry. But he dropped his eyes and looked at his palm, at the small pile of coins.

'It ain't much there,' she said.

'That's all right.' Then he looked up, and she bent down and kissed him on the forehead.

'You getting to be,' she said, putting her hand beneath his chin and holding his face away from her, 'a right big boy. You going to be a mighty fine man, you know that? Your mama's counting on you.'

And he knew again that she was not saying everything she meant; in a kind of secret language she was telling him to-day something that he must remember and understand to-morrow. He watched her face, his heart swollen with love for her and with an anguish, not yet his own, that he did not understand and that frightened him.

'Yes, Ma,' he said, hoping that she would realize, despite his stammering tongue, the depth of his passion to please her.

'I know,' she said, with a smile, releasing him and rising, 'there's a whole lot of things you don't understand. But don't you fret. The Lord'll reveal to you in His own good time everything He wants you to know. You put your faith in the Lord, Johnny, and He'll surely bring you out. Everything works together for good for them that love the Lord.'

He had heard her say this before—it was her text, as *Set thine house in order* was his father's—but he knew that to-day she was saying it to him especially; she was trying to help him because she knew he was in trouble. And this trouble was also her own, which she would never tell to John. And even though he was certain that they could not be speaking of the same things—for then, surely, she would be angry and no longer proud of him—this perception on her part and this avowal of her love for him lent to John's bewilderment a reality that terrified and a dignity that consoled him. Dimly, he felt that he ought to console her, and he listened, astounded, at the words that now fell from his lips:

'Yes, Mama. I'm going to try to love the Lord.'

At this there sprang into his mother's face something startling, beautiful, unspeakably sad—as though she were looking far beyond him at a long, dark road, and seeing on that road a traveller in perpetual danger. Was it he, the traveller? or herself? or was she thinking of the cross of Jesus? She turned back to the wash-tub, still with this strange sadness on her face.

'You better go on now,' she said, 'before your daddy gets home.'

In Central Park the snow had not yet melted on his favourite hill. This hill was in the centre of the park, after he had left the circle of the reservoir, where he always found, outside the high wall of crossed wire, ladies, white, in fur coats, walking their great dogs, or old, white gentlemen with canes. At a point that he knew by instinct and by the shape of the buildings surrounding the park, he struck out on a steep path overgrown with trees, and climbed a short distance until he reached the clearing that led to the hill. Before him, then, the slope stretched upward, and above it the brilliant sky, and beyond it, cloudy, and far away, he saw the skyline of New York. He did not know why, but there arose in him an exultation and a sense of power, and he ran up the hill like an engine, or a madman, willing to throw himself headlong into the city that glowed before him.

But when he reached the summit he paused; he stood on the crest of the hill, hands clasped beneath his chin, looking down. Then he, John, felt like a giant who might crumble this city with his anger; he felt like a tyrant who might crush this city beneath his heel; he felt like a long-awaited conqueror at whose feet flowers would be strewn, and before whom multitudes cried, Hosanna! He would be, of all, the mightiest, the most beloved, the Lord's anointed; and he would live in this shining city which his ancestors had seen with longing from far away. For it was his; the inhabitants of the city had told him it was his; he had but to run down, crying, and they would take him to their hearts and show him wonders his eyes had never seen.

And still, on the summit of that hill he paused. He remembered the people he had seen in that city, whose eyes held no love for him. And he thought of their feet so swift and brutal, and the dark grey clothes they wore, and how when they passed they did not see him, or, if they saw him, they smirked. And how their lights, unceasing, crashed on and off above him, and how he was a stranger there. Then he remembered his father and his mother, and all the arms stretched out to hold him back, to save him from this city where, they said, his soul would find perdition.

And certainly perdition sucked at the feet of the people who walked there; and cried in the lights, in the gigantic towers; the marks of Satan could be found in the faces of the people who waited at the doors of movie houses; his words were printed on the great movie posters that invited people to sin. It was the roar of the damned that

filled Broadway, where motor-cars and buses and the
hurrying people disputed every inch with death. *Broadway:* the way that led to death *was* broad, and many
could be found thereon; but narrow was the way that
led to life eternal, and few there were who found it. But
he did not long for the narrow way, where all his people
walked; where the houses did not rise, piercing, as it
seemed, the unchanging clouds, but huddled, flat, ignoble,
close to the filthy ground, where the streets and the
hallways and the rooms were dark, and where the uncon-
querable odour was of dust, and sweat, and urine, and
home-made gin. In the narrow way, the way of the
cross, there awaited him only humiliation for ever; there
awaited him, one day, a house like his father's house, and
a church like his father's, and a job like his father's, where
he would grow old and black with hunger and toil. The
way of the cross had given him a belly filled with wind
and had bent his mother's back; they had never worn
fine clothes, but here, where the buildings contested
God's power and where the men and women did not fear
God, here he might eat and drink to his heart's content
and clothe his body with wondrous fabrics, rich to the
eye and pleasing to the touch. And then what of his
soul, which would one day come to die and stand naked
before the judgment bar? What would his conquest of
the city profit him on that day? To hurl away, for a
moment of ease, the glories of eternity!

These glories were unimaginable—but the city was
real. He stood for a moment on the melting snow, distracted, and then began to run down the hill, feeling
himself fly as the descent became more rapid, and thinking: 'I can climb back up. If it's wrong, I can always
climb back up.' At the bottom of the hill, where the
ground abruptly levelled off on to a gravel path, he
nearly knocked down an old white man with a white
beard, who was walking very slowly and leaning on his

cane. They both stopped, astonished, and looked at one another. John struggled to catch his breath and apologize, but the old man smiled. John smiled back. It was as though he and the old man had between them a great secret; and the old man moved on. The snow glittered in patches all over the park. Ice, under the pale, strong sun, melted slowly on the branches and the trunks of trees.

He came out of the park at Fifth Avenue where, as always, the old-fashioned horse-carriages were lined along the kerb, their drivers sitting on the high seats with rugs around their knees, or standing in twos and threes near the horses, stamping their feet and smoking pipes and talking. In summer he had seen people riding in these carriages, looking like people out of books, or out of movies in which everyone wore old-fashioned clothes and rushed at nightfall over frozen roads, hotly pursued by their enemies who wanted to carry them back to death. '*Look back, look back,*' had cried a beautiful woman with long blonde curls, '*and see if we are pursued!*'—and she had come, as John remembered, to a terrible end. Now he stared at the horses, enormous and brown and patient, stamping every now and again a polished hoof, and he thought of what it would be like to have one day a horse of his own. He would call it Rider, and mount it at morning when the grass was wet, and from the horse's back look out over great, sun-filled fields, his own. Behind him stood his house, great and rambling and very new, and in the kitchen his wife, a beautiful woman, made breakfast, and the smoke rose out of the chimney, melting into the morning air. They had children, who called him Papa and for whom at Christmas he bought electric trains. And he had turkeys and cows and chickens and geese, and other horses besides Rider. They had a closet full of whisky and wine; they had cars—but what church did they go to and what would he teach his children when they gathered around him in the evening? He looked straight ahead, down Fifth Avenue, where graceful women in fur coats walked, looking into the windows that held silk dresses, and watches, and rings. What church did they go to? And what were their houses like when in the evening they took off these coats, and these silk dresses, and put their jewellery in a box, and leaned back in soft beds to think for a moment before they slept of the day gone by? Did they read a verse from the Bible every night and fall on their knees to pray? But no, for their thoughts were not of God, and their way was not God's way. They were in the world, and of the world, and their feet laid hold on Hell.

Yet in school some of them had been nice to him, and it was hard to think of them burning in Hell for ever, they who were so gracious and beautiful now. Once, one winter when he had been very sick with a heavy cold that would not leave him, one of his teachers had bought him a bottle of cod-liver oil, especially prepared with heavy syrup so that it did not taste so bad: this was surely a Christian act. His mother had said that God would bless that woman; and he had got better. They were kind—he was sure that they were kind—and on the day that he would bring himself to their attention they would surely love and honour him. This was not his father's opinion. His father said that all white people were wicked, and that God was going to bring them low. He said that white people were never to be trusted, and that they told nothing but lies, and that not one of them had ever loved a nigger. He, John, was a nigger, and he would find out, as soon as he got a little older, how evil white people could be. John had read about the things white people did to coloured people; how, in the South, where his parents came from, white people cheated them of their wages, and burned them, and shot them—

and did worse things, said his father, which the tongue could not endure to utter. He had read about coloured men being burned in the electric chair for things they had not done; how in riots they were beaten with clubs; how they were tortured in prisons; how they were the last to be hired and the first to be fired. Niggers did not live on these streets where John now walked; it was forbidden; and yet he walked here, and no one raised a hand against him. But did he dare to enter this shop out of which a woman now casually walked, carrying a great round box? Or this apartment before which a white man stood, dressed in a brilliant uniform? John knew he did not dare, not to-day, and he heard his father's laugh: '*No, nor to-morrow neither!*' For him there was the back door, and the dark stairs, and the kitchen or the basement. This world was not for him. If he refused to believe, and wanted to break his neck trying, then he could try until the sun refused to shine; they would never let him enter. In John's mind then, the people and the avenue underwent a change, and he feared them and knew that one day he could hate them if God did not change his heart.

He left Fifth Avenue and walked west towards the movie houses. Here on 42nd Street it was less elegant but no less strange. He loved this street, not for the people or the shops but for the stone lions that guarded the great main building of the Public Library, a building filled with books and unimaginably vast, and which he had never yet dared to enter. He might, he knew, for he was a member of the branch in Harlem and was entitled to take books from any library in the city. But he had never gone in because the building was so big that it must be full of corridors and marble steps, in the maze of which he would be lost and never find the book he wanted. And then everyone, all the white people inside, would know that he was not used to great build-

ings, or to many books, and they would look at him with
pity. He would enter on another day, when he had read
all the books uptown, an achievement that would, he
felt, lend him the poise to enter any building in the
world. People, mostly men, leaned over the stone parapets
of the raised park that surrounded the library, or walked
up and down and bent to drink water from the public
drinking-fountains. Silver pigeons lighted briefly on the
heads of the lions or the rims of fountains, and strutted
along the walks. John loitered in front of Woolworth's
staring at the candy display, trying to decide what candy
to buy—and buying none, for the store was crowded
and he was certain that the salesgirl would never notice
him—and before a vendor of artificial flowers, and
crossed Sixth Avenue where the Automat was, and the
parked taxis, and the shops, which he would not look
at to-day, that displayed in their windows dirty post-
cards and practical jokes. Beyond Sixth Avenue the
movie houses began, and now he studied the stills carefully, trying to decide which of all these theatres he
should enter. He stopped at last before a gigantic,
coloured poster that represented a wicked woman, half
undressed, leaning in a doorway, apparently quarrelling
with a blond man who stared wretchedly into the street.
The legend above their heads was: 'There's a fool like
him in every family—and a woman next door to take
him over!' He decided to see this, for he felt identified
with the blond young man, the fool of his family, and he
wished to know more about his so blatantly unkind fate.

And so he stared at the price above the ticket-seller's
window and, showing her his coins, received the piece
of paper that was charged with the power to open doors.
Having once decided to enter, he did not look back at
the street again for fear that one of the saints might be
passing and, seeing him, might cry out his name and lay
hands on him to drag him back. He walked very quickly

across the carpeted lobby, looking at nothing, and pausing only to see his ticket torn, half of it thrown into a silver box and half returned to him. And then the usherette opened the doors of this dark palace and with a flashlight held behind her took him to his seat. Not even then, having pushed past a wilderness of knees and feet to reach his designated seat, did he dare to breathe; nor, out of a last, sick hope for forgiveness, did he look at the screen. He stared at the darkness around him, and at the profiles that gradually emerged from this gloom, which was so like the gloom of Hell. He waited for this darkness to be shattered by the light of the second coming, for the ceiling to crack upwards, revealing, for every eye to see, the chariots of fire on which descended a wrathful God and all the host of Heaven. He sank far down in his seat, as though his crouching might make him invisible and deny his presence there. But then he thought: 'Not yet. The day of judgment is not yet,' and voices reached him, the voices no doubt of the hapless man and the evil woman, and he raised his eyes helplessly and watched the screen.

The woman was most evil. She was blonde and pasty white, and she had lived in London, which was in England, quite some time ago, judging from her clothes, and she coughed. She had a terrible disease, tuberculosis, which he had heard about. Someone in his mother's family had died of it. She had a great many boy friends, and she smoked cigarettes and drank. When she met the young man, who was a student and who loved her very much, she was very cruel to him. She laughed at him because he was a cripple. She took his money and she went out with other men, and she lied to the student—who was certainly a fool. He limped about, looking soft and sad, and soon all John's sympathy was given to this violent and unhappy woman. He understood her when she raged and shook her hips and threw back her head in laughter so furious that it seemed the veins of her neck would burst. She walked the cold, foggy streets, a little woman and not pretty, with a lewd, brutal swagger, saying to the whole world: 'You can kiss my arse.' Nothing tamed or broke her, nothing touched her, neither kindness, nor scorn, nor hatred, nor love. She had never thought of prayer. It was unimaginable that she would ever bend her knees and come crawling along a dusty floor to anybody's altar, weeping for forgiveness. Perhaps her sin was so extreme that it could not be forgiven; perhaps her pride was so great that she did not need forgiveness. She had fallen from that high estate which God had intended for men and women, and she made her fall glorious because it was so complete. John could not have found in his heart, had he dared to search it, any wish for her redemption. He wanted to be like her, only more powerful, more thorough, and more cruel; to make those around him, all who hurt him, suffer as she made the student suffer, and laugh in their faces when they asked pity for their pain. *He* would have asked no pity, and his pain was greater than theirs. Go on, girl, he whispered, as the student, facing her implacable ill-will, sighed and wept. Go on, girl. One day he would talk like that, he would face them and tell them how much he hated them, how they had made him suffer, how he would pay them back!

Nevertheless, when she came to die, which she did eventually, looking more grotesque than ever, as she deserved, his thoughts were abruptly arrested, and he was chilled by the expression on her face. She seemed to stare endlessly outward and down, in the face of a wind more piercing than any she had felt on earth, feeling herself propelled with speed into a kingdom where nothing could help her, neither her pride, nor her courage, nor her glorious wickedness. In the place where she was going, it was not these things that mattered but something else, for which she had no name, only a cold intimation, something that she could not alter in any degree, and that she had never thought of. She began to cry, her depraved face breaking into an infant's grimace; and they moved away from her, leaving her dirty in a dirty room, alone to face her Maker. The scene faded out and she was gone; and though the movie went on, allowing the student to marry another girl, darker, and very sweet, but by no means so arresting, John thought of this woman and her dreadful end. Again, had the thought not been blasphemous, he would have thought that it was the Lord who had led him into this theatre to show him an example of the wages of sin. The movie ended and people stirred around him; the newsreel came on, and while girls in bathing suits paraded before him and boxers growled and fought, and baseball players ran home safe and presidents and kings of countries that were only names to him moved briefly across the flickering square of light, John thought of Hell, of his soul's redemption, and struggled to find a compromise between the way that led to life everlasting and the way that ended in the pit. But there was none, for he had been raised in the truth. He could not claim, as African savages might be able to claim, that no one had brought him the gospel. His father and mother and all the saints had taught him from his earliest childhood what was the will of God. Either he arose from this theatre, never to return, putting behind him the world and its pleasures, its honours, and its glories, or he remained here with the wicked and partook of their certain punishment. Yes, it was a narrow way—and John stirred in his seat, not daring to feel it God's injustice that he must make so cruel a choice.

As John approached his home again in the late afternoon, he saw little Sarah, her coat unbuttoned, come

flying out of the house and run the length of the street
away from him into the far drug-store. Instantly, he was
frightened; he stopped a moment, staring blankly down
the street, wondering what could justify such hysterical
haste. It was true that Sarah was full of self-importance,
and made any errand she ran seem a matter of life or
death; nevertheless, she had been sent on an errand, and
with such speed that her mother had not had time to
make her button up her coat.

Then he felt weary; if something had really happened
it would be very unpleasant upstairs now, and he did not
want to face it. But perhaps it was simply that his mother
had a headache and had sent Sarah to the store for some
aspirin. But if this were true, it meant that he would
have to prepare supper, and take care of the children,
and be naked under his father's eyes all the evening long.
And he began to walk more slowly.

There were some boys standing on the verandah. They
watched him as he approached, and he tried not to look
at them and to approximate the swagger with which they
walked. One of them said, as he mounted the short, stone
steps and started into the hall: 'Boy, your brother was
hurt real bad to-day.'

He looked at them in a kind of dread, not daring to
ask for details; and he observed that they, too, looked
as though they had been in a battle; something hangdog
in their looks suggested that they had been put to flight.
Then he looked down, and saw that there was blood at
the threshold, and blood spattered on the tile floor of
the vestibule. He looked again at the boys, who had not
ceased to watch him, and hurried up the stairs.

The door was half open—for Sarah's return, no doubt
—and he walked in, making no sound, feeling a confused
impulse to flee. There was no one in the kitchen, though
the light was burning—the lights were on all through
the house. On the kitchen table stood a shopping-bag

filled with groceries, and he knew that his Aunt Florence had arrived. The wash-tub, where his mother had been washing earlier, was open still, and filled the kitchen with a sour smell.

There were drops of blood on the floor here too, and there had been small, smudged coins of blood on the stairs as he walked up.

All this frightened him terribly. He stood in the middle of the kitchen, trying to imagine what had happened, and preparing himself to walk into the living-room, where all the family seemed to be. Roy had been in trouble before, but this new trouble seemed to be the beginning of the fulfilment of a prophecy. He took off his coat, dropping it on a chair, and was about to start into the living-room when he heard Sarah running up the steps.

He waited, and she burst through the door, carrying a clumsy parcel.

'What happened?' he whispered.

She stared at him in astonishment, and a certain wild joy. He thought again that he really did not like his sister. Catching her breath, she blurted out, triumphantly: 'Roy got stabbed with a knife!' and rushed into the living-room.

Roy got stabbed with a knife. Whatever this meant, it was sure that his father would be at his worst to-night. John walked slowly into the living-room.

His father and mother, a small basin of water between them, knelt by the sofa where Roy lay, and his father was washing the blood from Roy's forehead. It seemed that his mother, whose touch was so much more gentle, had been thrust aside by his father, who could not bear to have anyone else touch his wounded son. And now she watched, one hand in the water, the other, in a kind of anguish, at her waist, which was circled still by the improvised apron of the morning. Her face, as she watched, was full of pain and fear, of tension barely supported, and of pity that could scarcely have been expressed had she filled all the world with her weeping. His father muttered sweet, delirious things to Roy, and his hands, when he dipped them again in the basin and wrung out the cloth, were trembling. Aunt Florence, still wearing her hat and carrying her handbag, stood a little removed, looking down at them with a troubled, terrible face.

Then Sarah bounded into the room before him, and his mother looked up, reached out for the package, and saw him. She said nothing, but she looked at him with a strange, quick intentness, almost as though there were a warning on her tongue which at the moment she did not dare to utter. His Aunt Florence looked up, and said: 'We been wondering where you was, boy. This bad brother of yours done gone out and got hisself hurt.'

But John understood from her tone that the fuss was, possibly, a little greater than the danger—Roy was not, after all, going to die. And his heart lifted a little. Then his father turned and looked at him.

'Where you been, boy,' he shouted, 'all this time? Don't you know you's needed here at home?'

More than his words, his face caused John to stiffen instantly with malice and fear. His father's face was terrible in anger, but now there was more than anger in it. John saw now what he had never seen there before, except in his own vindictive fantasies: a kind of wild, weeping terror that made the face seem younger, and yet at the same time unutterably older and more cruel. And John knew, in the moment his father's eyes swept over him, that he hated John because John was not lying on the sofa where Roy lay. John could scarcely meet his father's eyes, and yet, briefly, he did, saying nothing, feeling in his heart an odd sensation of triumph, and hoping in his heart that Roy, to bring his father low, would die.

His mother had unwrapped the package and was opening a bottle of peroxide. 'Here,' she said, 'you better wash it with this now.' Her voice was calm and dry; she looked at his father briefly, her face unreadable, as she handed him the bottle and the cotton.

'This going to hurt,' his father said—in such a different voice, so sad and tender!—turning again to the sofa. 'But you just be a little man and hold still; it ain't going to take long.'

John watched and listened, hating him. Roy began to moan. Aunt Florence moved to the mantelpiece and put her handbag down near the metal serpent. From the room behind him, John heard the baby begin to whimper.

'John,' said his mother, 'go and pick her up like a good boy.' Her hands, which were not trembling, were still busy: she had opened the bottle of iodine and was cutting up strips of bandage.

John walked into his parents' bedroom and picked up the squalling baby, who was wet. The moment Ruth felt him lift her up she stopped crying and stared at him with a wide-eyed, pathetic stare, as though she knew that there was trouble in the house. John laughed at her so ancient-seeming distress—he was very fond of his baby sister—and whispered in her ear as he started back to the living-room: 'Now, you let your big brother tell you something, baby. Just as soon as you's able to stand on your feet, you run away from *this* house, run far away.' He did not quite know why he said this, or where he wanted her to run, but it made him feel instantly better.

His father was saying, as John came back into the room: 'I'm sure going to be having some questions to ask you in a minute, old lady. I'm going to be wanting to know just how come you let this boy go out and get half killed.'

'Oh, no, you ain't,' said Aunt Florence. 'You ain't going to be starting none of that mess this evening. You know right doggone well that Roy don't never ask *nobody* if he can do *nothing*—he just go right ahead and do like he pleases. Elizabeth sure can't put no ball and chain on him. She got her hands full right here in this house, and it ain't her fault if Roy got a head just as hard as his father's.'

'You got a awful lot to say, look like for once you could keep from putting your mouth in my business.' He said this without looking at her.

'It ain't my fault,' she said, 'that you was born a fool, and always done been a fool, and ain't never going to change. I swear to my Father you'd try the patience of Job.'

'I done told you before,' he said—he had not ceased working over the moaning Roy, and was preparing now to dab the wound with iodine—'that I didn't want you coming in here and using that gutter language in front of my children.'

'Don't you worry about my language, brother,' she said with spirit, 'you better start worrying about your *life*. What these children hear ain't going to do them near as much harm as what they *see*.'

'What they *see*,' his father muttered, 'is a poor man trying to serve the Lord. *That's* my life.'

'Then I guarantee *you*,' she said, 'that they going to do their best to keep it from being *their* life. *You* mark my words.'

He turned and looked at her, and intercepted the look that passed between the two women. John's mother, for reasons that were not at all his father's reasons, wanted Aunt Florence to keep still. He looked away, ironically. John watched his mother's mouth tighten bitterly as she dropped her eyes. His father, in silence, began bandaging Roy's forehead.

'It's just the mercy of God,' he said at last, 'that this boy didn't lose his eye. Look here.'

His mother leaned over and looked into Roy's face with a sad, sympathetic murmur. Yet, John felt, she had seen instantly the extent of the danger to Roy's eye and to his life, and was beyond that worry now. Now she was merely marking time, as it were, and preparing herself against the moment when her husband's anger would turn, full force, against her.

His father now turned to John, who was standing near the French doors with Ruth in his arms.

'You come here, boy,' he said, 'and see what them white folks done done to your brother.'

John walked over to the sofa, holding himself as proudly beneath his father's furious eyes as a prince approaching the scaffold.

'Look here,' said his father, grasping him roughly by one arm, 'look at your brother.'

John looked down at Roy, who gazed at him with almost no expression in his dark eyes. But John knew by the weary, impatient set of Roy's young mouth that his brother was asking that none of this be held against him. It wasn't his fault, or John's, Roy's eyes said, that they had such a crazy father.

His father, with the air of one forcing the sinner to look down into the pit that is to be his portion, moved away slightly so that John could see Roy's wound.

Roy had been gashed by a knife, luckily not very sharp, from the centre of his forehead where his hair began, downward to the bone just above his left eye: the wound described a kind of crazy half-moon and ended in a violent, fuzzy tail that was the ruin of Roy's eyebrow. Time would darken the half-moon wound into Roy's dark skin, but nothing would bring together again the so violently divided eyebrow. This crazy lift, this question, would remain with him for ever, and emphasize for ever something mocking and sinister in Roy's face. John felt a sudden impulse to smile, but his father's eyes were on him and he fought the impulse back. Certainly the wound was now very ugly, and very red, and must, John felt, with a quickened sympathy towards Roy, who had not cried out, have been very painful. He could imagine the sensation caused when Roy staggered into the house, blinded by his blood; but just the same, he wasn't dead, he wasn't changed, he would be in the streets again the moment he was better.

'You see?' came now from his father. 'It was white folks, some of them white folks *you* like so much that tried to cut your brother's throat.'

John thought, with immediate anger and with a curious contempt for his father's inexactness, that only a blind man, however white, could possibly have been aiming at Roy's throat; and his mother said with a calm insistence:

'And he was trying to cut theirs. Him and them bad boys.'

'Yes,' said Aunt Florence, 'I ain't heard you ask that boy nary a question about how all this happened. Look like you just determined to raise Cain any*how* and make everybody in this house suffer because something done happened to the apple of your eye.'

'I done asked you,' cried his father in a fearful exasperation, 'to stop running your *mouth*. Don't none of this concern you. This is *my* family and this is my house. You want me to slap you side of the head?'

'You slap me,' she said, with a placidity equally fearful, 'and I *do* guarantee you you won't do no more slapping in a hurry.'

'Hush now,' said his mother, rising, 'ain't no need for all this. What's done is done. We ought to be on our knees, thanking the Lord it weren't no worse.'

'Amen to that,' said Aunt Florence, '*tell* that foolish nigger something.'

'You can tell that foolish *son* of yours something,' he said to his wife with venom, having decided, it seemed, to ignore his sister, 'him standing there with them big buck-eyes. You can tell him to take this like a warning from the Lord. *This* is what white folks does to niggers. I been telling you, now you see.'

'*He* better take it like a warning?' shrieked Aunt Florence. '*He* better take it? Why, Gabriel, it ain't *him* went half-way across this city to get in a fight with white boys. This boy on the sofa went *deliberately*, with a whole lot of other boys, all the way to the west side, just *looking* for a fight. I declare, I do wonder what goes on in your head.'

'You know right well,' his mother said, looking directly at his father, 'that Johnny don't travel with the same class of boys as Roy goes with. You done beat Roy too many times, here, in this very room for going out with them bad boys. Roy got hisself hurt this afternoon because he was out doing something he didn't have no business doing, and that's the end of it. You ought to be thanking your Redeemer he ain't dead.'

'And for all the care you take of him,' he said, 'he might as well be dead. Don't look like you much care whether he lives, or dies.'

'*Lord*, have mercy,' said Aunt Florence.

'He's my son, too,' his mother said, with heat. 'I carried him in my belly for nine months and I know him just like I know his daddy, and they's just *exactly* alike. Now. You ain't got no *right* in the world to talk to me like that.'

'I reckon you *know*,' he said, choked, and breathing hard, 'all about a mother's love. I sure reckon on you telling me how a woman can sit in the house all day and let her own flesh and blood go out and get half butchered. Don't you tell me you don't know no way to stop him, because I remember *my* mother, God rest her soul, and *she'd* have found a way.'

'She was my mother, too,' said Aunt Florence, 'and

I recollect, if you don't, you being brought home many a time more dead than alive. She didn't find no way to stop *you*. She wore herself out beating on you, just like you been wearing yourself out beating on this boy here.'

'My, my, *my*,' he said, 'you got a lot to say.'

'I ain't doing a thing,' she said, 'but trying to talk some sense into your big, black, hard head. You better stop trying to blame everything on Elizabeth and look to your own wrongdoings.'

'Never mind, Florence,' his mother said, 'it's all over and done with now.'

'I'm out of this house,' he shouted, 'every day the Lord sends, working to put the food in these children's mouths. Don't you think I got a right to ask the mother of these children to look after them and see that they don't break their necks before I get back home?'

'You ain't got but one child,' she said, 'that's liable to go out and break his neck, and that's Roy, and you know it. And I don't know how in the world you expect me to run this house, and look after these children, and keep running around the block after Roy. *No*, I can't stop him, I done told you that, and you can't stop him neither. You don't know *what* to do with this boy, and that's why you all the time trying to fix the blame on somebody. Ain't nobody to *blame*, Gabriel. You just better pray God to stop him before somebody puts another knife in him and puts him in his grave.'

They stared at each other a moment in an awful pause, she with a startled, pleading question in her eyes. Then, with all his might, he reached out and slapped her across the face. She crumpled at once, hiding her face with one thin hand, and Aunt Florence moved to hold her up. Sarah watched all this with greedy eyes. Then Roy sat up, and said in a shaking voice:

'Don't you slap my mother. That's my *mother*. You

slap her again, you black bastard, and I swear to God I'll kill you.'

In the moment that these words filled the room, and hung in the room like the infinitesimal moment of hanging, jagged light that precedes an explosion, John and his father were staring into each other's eyes. John thought for that moment that his father believed the words had come from him, his eyes were so wild and depthlessly malevolent, and his mouth was twisted into such a snarl of pain. Then, in the absolute silence that followed Roy's words, John saw that his father was not seeing him, was not seeing anything unless it were a vision. John wanted to turn and flee, as though he had encountered in the jungle some evil beast, crouching and ravenous, with eyes like Hell unclosed; and exactly as though, on a road's turning, he found himself staring at certain destruction, he found that he could not move. Then his father turned and looked down at Roy.

'What did you say?' his father asked.

'I told you,' said Roy, 'not to touch my mother.'

'You cursed me,' said his father.

Roy said nothing; neither did he drop his eyes.

'Gabriel,' said his mother, 'Gabriel. Let us pray. . . .'

His father's hands were at his waist, and he took off his belt. Tears were in his eyes.

'Gabriel,' cried Aunt Florence, 'ain't you done playing the fool for to-night?'

Then his father raised his belt, and it fell with a whistling sound on Roy, who shivered, and fell back, his face to the wall. But he did not cry out. And the belt was raised again, and again. The air rang with the whistling, and the *crack!* against Roy's flesh. And the baby, Ruth, began to scream.

'*My Lord, my Lord,*' his father whispered, '*my Lord, my Lord.*'

He raised the belt again. but Aunt Florence caught

it from behind, and held it. His mother rushed over to the sofa and caught Roy in her arms, crying as John had never seen a woman, or anybody, cry before. Roy caught his mother around the neck and held on to her as though he were drowning.

His Aunt Florence and his father faced each other.

'Yes, Lord,' Aunt Florence said, 'you was born wild, and you's going to die wild. But ain't no use to try to take the whole world with you. You can't change nothing, Gabriel. You ought to know that by now.'

John opened the church door with his father's key at six o'clock. Tarry service officially began at eight, but it could begin at any time, whenever the Lord moved one of the saints to enter the church and pray. It was seldom, however, that anyone arrived before eight-thirty, the Spirit of the Lord being sufficiently tolerant to allow the saints time to do their Saturday-night shopping, clean their houses, and put their children to bed.

John closed the door behind him and stood in the narrow church aisle, hearing behind him the voices of children playing, and ruder voices, the voices of their elders, cursing and crying in the streets. It was dark in the church; street lights had been snapping on all around him on the populous avenue; the light of the day was gone. His feet seemed planted on this wooden floor; they did not wish to carry him one step further. The darkness and silence of the church pressed on him, cold as judgment, and the voices crying from the window might have been crying from another world. John moved forward, hearing his feet crack against the sagging wood, to where the golden cross on the red field of the altar cloth glowed like smothered fire, and switched on one weak light.

In the air of the church hung, perpetually, the odour of dust and sweat; for, like the carpet in his mother's living-room, the dust of this church was invincible; and when the saints were praying or rejoicing, their bodies gave off an acrid, steamy smell, a marriage of the odours of dripping bodies and soaking, starched white linen. It was a store-front church and had stood, for John's lifetime, on the corner of this sinful avenue, facing the hospital to which criminal wounded and dying were carried almost every night. The saints, arriving, had rented this abandoned store and taken out the fixtures; had painted the walls and built a pulpit, moved in a piano and camp chairs, and bought the biggest Bible they could find. They put white curtains in the show window, and painted across this window TEMPLE OF THE FIRE BAPTIZED. Then they were ready to do the Lord's work.

And the Lord, as He had promised to the two or three first gathered together, sent others; and these brought others and created a church. From this parent branch, if the Lord blessed, other branches might grow and a mighty work he begun throughout the city and throughout the land. In the history of the Temple the Lord had raised up evangelists and teachers and prophets, and called them out into the field to do His work; to go up and down the land carrying the gospel, or to raise other temples—in Philadelphia, Georgia, Boston, or Brooklyn. Wherever the Lord led, they followed. Every now and again one of them came home to testify of the wonders the Lord had worked through him, or her. And sometimes on a special Sunday they all visited one of the nearest churches of the Brotherhood.

There had been a time, before John was born, when his father had also been in the field; but now, having to earn for his family their daily bread, it was seldom that he was able to travel further away than Philadelphia, and then only for a very short time. His father no longer, as he had once done, led great revival meetings, his name printed large on placards that advertised the coming of a man of God. His father had once had a mighty reputation; but all this, it seemed, had changed since he had left the South. Perhaps he ought now to have a church of his own—John wondered if his father wanted that; he ought, perhaps, to be leading, as Father James now led, a great flock to the Kingdom. But his father was only a caretaker in the house of God. He was responsible for the replacement of burnt-out light bulbs, and for the cleanliness of the church, and the care of the Bibles, and the hymn-books, and the placards on the walls. On Friday night he conducted the Young Ministers' Service and preached with them. Rarely did he bring the message on a Sunday morning; only if there was no one else to speak was his father called upon. He was a kind of fill-in speaker, a holy handyman.

Yet he was treated, so far as John could see, with great respect. No one, none of the saints in any case, had ever reproached or rebuked his father, or suggested that his life was anything but spotless. Nevertheless, this man, God's minister, had struck John's mother, and John had wanted to kill him—and wanted to kill him still.

John had swept one side of the church and the chairs were still piled in the space before the altar when there was a knocking at the door. When he opened the door he saw that it was Elisha, come to help him.

'Praise the Lord,' said Elisha, standing on the door-step, grinning.

'Praise the Lord,' said John. This was the greeting always used among the saints.

Brother Elisha came in, slamming the door behind him and stamping his feet. He had probably just come from a basket-ball court; his forehead was polished with recent sweat and his hair stood up. He was wearing his green woollen sweater, on which was stamped the letter of his high school, and his shirt was open at the throat.

'You ain't cold like that?' John asked, staring at him.

'No, little brother, I ain't cold. You reckon everybody's frail like you?'

'It ain't only the little ones gets carried to the graveyard,' John said. He felt unaccustomedly bold and lighthearted; the arrival of Elisha had caused his mood to change.

Elisha, who had started down the aisle towards the back room, turned to stare at John with astonishment and menace. 'Ah,' he said, 'I see you fixing to be sassy with Brother Elisha to-night—I'm going to have to give you a little correction. You just wait till I wash my hands.'

'Ain't no need to wash your hands if you come here to work. Just take hold of that mop and put some soap and water in the bucket.'

'Lord,' said Elisha, running water into the sink, and talking, it seemed, to the water, 'that sure is a sassy nigger out there. I sure hope he don't get hisself hurt one of these days, running his mouth thataway. Look like he just *won't* stop till somebody busts him in the eye.' He sighed deeply, and began to lather his hands. 'Here I come running all the way so he wouldn't bust a gut lifting one of them chairs, and all he got to say is "put some water in the bucket." Can't do nothing with a nigger nohow.' He stopped and turned to face John. 'Ai'nt you got no manners, boy? You better learn how to talk to old folks.'

'You better get out here with that mop and pail. We ain't got all night.'

'Keep on,' said Elisha. 'I see I'm going to have to give you your lumps to-night.'

He disappeared. John heard him in the toilet, and then over the thunderous water he heard him knocking things over in the back room.

'*Now* what you doing?'

'Boy, leave me alone. I'm fixing to work.'

'It sure sounds like it.' John dropped his broom and

walked into the back. Elisha had knocked over a pile of
camp chairs, folded in the corner, and stood over them
angrily, holding the mop in his hand.

'I keep telling you not to hide that mop back there.
Can't nobody get at it.'

'I always get at it. Ain't everybody as clumsy as you.'

Elisha let fall the stiff grey mop and rushed at John,
catching him off balance and lifting him from the floor
With both arms tightening around John's waist he tried
to cut John's breath, watching him meanwhile with a
smile that, as John struggled and squirmed, became
a set, ferocious grimace. With both hands John pushed
and pounded against the shoulders and biceps of Elisha,
and tried to thrust with his knees against Elisha's belly.
Usually such a battle was soon over, since Elisha was so
much bigger and stronger and as a wrestler so much
more skilled; but to-night John was filled with a determination not to be conquered, or at least to make the
conquest dear. With all the strength that was in him he
fought against Elisha, and he was filled with a strength
that was almost hatred. He kicked, pounded, twisted,
pushed, using his lack of size to confound and exasperate
Elisha, whose damp fists, joined at the small of John's
back, soon slipped. It was a deadlock; he could not
tighten his hold, John could not break it. And so they
turned, battling in the narrow room, and the odour of
Elisha's sweat was heavy in John's nostrils. He saw the
veins rise on Elisha's forehead and in his neck; his breath
became jagged and harsh, and the grimace on his face
became more cruel; and John, watching these manifesta-
tions of his power, was filled with a wild delight. They
stumbled against the folding-chairs, and Elisha's foot
slipped and his hold broke. They stared at each other,
half grinning. John slumped to the floor, holding his
head between his hands.

'I didn't hurt you none, did I?' Elisha asked.

John looked up. 'Me?' No, I just want to catch my breath.'

Elisha went to the sink, and splashed cold water on his face and neck. 'I reckon you going to let me work now,' he said.

'It wasn't *me* that stopped you in the first place.' He stood up. He found that his legs were trembling. He looked at Elisha, who was drying himself on the towel. 'You teach me wrestling one time, okay?'

'No, boy,' Elisha said, laughing. 'I don't want to wrestle with *you*. You too strong for me.' And he began to run hot water into the great pail.

John walked past him to the front and picked up his broom. In a moment Elisha followed and began mopping near the door. John had finished sweeping, and he now mounted to the pulpit to dust the three throne-like chairs, purple, with white linen squares for the head-pieces and for the massive arms. It dominated all, the pulpit: a wooden platform raised above the congregation, with a high stand in the centre for the Bible, before which the preacher stood. There faced the congregation, flowing downwards from this height, the scarlet altar cloth that bore the golden cross and the legend: JESUS SAVES. The pulpit was holy. None could stand so high unless God's seal was on him.

He dusted the piano and sat down on the piano stool to wait until Elisha had finished mopping one side of the church and he could replace the chairs. Suddenly Elisha said, without looking at him:

'Boy, ain't it time you was thinking about your soul?'

'I guess so,' John said with a quietness that terrified him.

'I know it looks hard,' said Elisha, 'from the outside, especially when you young. But you believe me, boy, you can't find no greater joy than you find in the service of the Lord.'

John said nothing. He touched a black key on the piano and it made a dull sound, like a distant drum.

'You got to remember,' Elisha said, turning now to look at him, 'that you think about it with a carnal mind. You still got Adam's mind, boy, and you keep thinking about your friends, you want to do what they do, and you want to go to the movies, and I bet you think about girls, don't you, Johnny? Sure you do,' he said, half smiling, finding his answer in John's face, 'and you don't want to give up all that. But when the Lord saves you He burns out all that old Adam, He gives you a new mind and a new heart, and then you don't find no pleasure in the world, you get all your joy in walking and talking with Jesus every day.'

He stared in a dull paralysis of terror at the body of Elisha. He saw him standing—had Elisha forgotten?—beside Ella Mae before the altar while Father James rebuked him for the evil that lived in the flesh. He looked into Elisha's face, full of questions he would never ask. And Elisha's face told him nothing.

'People say it's hard,' said Elisha, bending again to his mop, 'but, let me tell you, it ain't as hard as living in this wicked world and all the sadness of the world where there ain't no pleasure nohow, and then dying and going to Hell. Ain't nothing as hard as that.' And he looked back at John. 'You see how the Devil tricks people into losing their souls?'

'Yes,' said John at last, sounding almost angry, unable to bear his thoughts, unable to bear the silence in which Elisha looked at him.

Elisha grinned. 'They got girls in the school I go to' —he was finished with one side of the church and he motioned to John to replace the chairs—'and they nice girls, but their minds ain't on the Lord, and I try to tell them the time to repent ain't to-morrow, it's to-day. They think ain't no sense to worrying now, they can sneak into Heaven on their deathbed. But I tell them, honey, ain't everybody lies down to die—people going all the time, just like that, to-day you see them and to-morrow you don't. Boy, they don't know what to make of old Elisha because he don't go to movies, and he don't dance, and he don't play cards, and he don't go with them behind the stairs.' He paused and stared at John, who watched him helplessly, not knowing what to say. 'And boy, some of them is real nice girls, I mean *beautiful* girls, and when you got so much power that *they* don't tempt you then you know you saved sure enough. I just look at them and I tell them Jesus saved me one day, and I'm going to go all the way with *Him*. Ain't no woman, no, nor no man neither going to make me change my mind.' He paused again, and smiled and dropped his eyes. 'That Sunday,' he said, 'that Sunday, you remember?—when Father got up in the pulpit and called me an Ella Mae down because he thought we was about to commit sin—well, boy, I don't want to tell no lie, I was mighty hot against the old man that Sunday. But I thought about it, and the Lord made me to see that he was right. Me and Ella Mae, we didn't have nothing on our minds at all, but look like the Devil is just everywhere—sometime the Devil he put his hand on you and look like you just can't breathe. Look like you just a-burning up, and you got to do something, and you can't do nothing; I been on my knees many a time, weeping and wrestling before the Lord—*crying*, Johnny—and calling on Jesus' name. That's the only name that's got power over Satan. That's the way it's been with *me* sometime, and I'm *saved*. What you think it's going to be like for you, boy?' He looked at John, who, head down, was putting the chairs in order. 'Do you want to be saved, Johnny?'

'I don't know,' John said.

'Will you try him? Just fall on your knees one day and ask him to help you to pray?'

John turned away, and looked out over the church, which now seemed like a vast, high field, ready for the harvest. He thought of a First Sunday, a Communion Sunday not long ago when the saints, dressed all in white, ate flat, unsalted Jewish bread, which was the body of the Lord, and drank red grape juice, which was His blood. And when they rose from the table, prepared especially for this day, they separated, the men on the one side, and the women on the other, and two basins were filled with water so that they could wash each other's feet, as Christ had commanded His disciples to do. They knelt before each other, woman before woman, and man before man, and washed and dried each other's feet. Brother Elisha had knelt before John's father. When the service was over they had kissed each other with a holy kiss. John turned again and looked at Elisha.

Elisha looked at him and smiled. 'You think about what I said, boy.'

When they were finished Elisha sat down at the piano and played to himself. John sat on a chair in the front row and watched him.

'Don't look like nobody's coming to-night,' he said after a long while. Elisha did not arrest his playing of a mournful song: 'Oh, Lord, have mercy on me.'

'They'll be here,' said Elisha.

And as he spoke there was a knocking on the door. Elisha stopped playing. John went to the door, where two sisters stood, Sister McCandless and Sister Price.

'Praise the Lord, son,' they said.

'Praise the Lord,' said John.

They entered, heads bowed and hands folded before them around their Bibles. They wore the black cloth coats that they wore all week and they had old felt hats on their heads. John felt a chill as they passed him, and he closed the door.

C

Elisha stood up, and they cried again: 'Praise the Lord!' Then the two women knelt for a moment before their seats to pray. This was also passionate ritual. Each entering saint, before he could take part in the service, must commune for a moment alone with the Lord. John watched the praying women. Elisha sat again at the piano and picked up his mournful song. The women rose, Sister Price first, and then Sister McCandless, and looked around the church.

'Is we the first?' asked Sister Price. Her voice was mild, her skin was copper. She was younger than Sister McCandless by several years, a single woman who had never, as she testified, known a man.

'No, Sister Price,' smiled Brother Elisha, 'Brother Johnny here was the first. Him and me cleaned up this evening.'

'Brother Johnny is mighty faithful,' said Sister McCandless. 'The Lord's going to work with him in a mighty way, you mark my words.'

There were times—whenever, in fact, the Lord had shown His favour by working through her—when whatever Sister McCandless said sounded like a threat. To-night she was still very much under the influence of the sermon she had preached the night before. She was an enormous woman, one of the biggest and blackest God had ever made, and He had blessed her with a mighty voice with which to sing and preach, and she was going out soon into the field. For many years the Lord had pressed Sister McCandless to get up, as she said, and move; but she had been of timid disposition and feared to set herself above others. Not until He laid her low, before this very altar, had she dared to rise and preach the gospel. But now she had buckled on her travelling shoes. She would cry aloud and spare not, and lift up her voice like a trumpet in Zion.

'Yes,' said Sister Price, with her gentle smile, 'He

says that he that is faithful in little things shall be made chief over many.'

John smiled back at her, a smile that, despite the shy gratitude it was meant to convey, did not escape being ironic, or even malicious. But Sister Price did not see this, which deepened John's hidden scorn.

'Ain't but you two who cleaned the church?' asked Sister McCandless with an unnerving smile—the smile of the prophet who sees the secrets hidden in the hearts of men.

'Lord, Sister McCandless,' said Elisha, 'look like it ain't never but us two. I don't know what the other young folks does on Saturday nights, but they don't come nowhere near here.'

Neither did Elisha usually come anywhere near the church on Saturday evenings; but as the pastor's nephew he was entitled to certain freedoms; in him it was a virtue that he came at all.

'It sure is time we had a revival among our young folks,' said Sister McCandless. 'They cooling off something terrible. The Lord ain't going to bless no church what lets its young people get so lax, no sir. He said, because you ain't neither hot or cold I'm going to spit you outen my mouth. That's the Word.' And she looked around sternly, and Sister Price nodded.

'And Brother Johnny here ain't even saved yet,' said Elisha. 'Look like the saved young people would be ashamed to let him be more faithful in the house of God than they are.'

'He said that the first shall be last and the last shall be first,' said Sister Price with a triumphant smile.

'Indeed, He did,' agreed Sister McCandless. 'This boy going to make it to the Kingdom before any of them, you wait and see.'

'Amen,' said Brother Elisha, and he smiled at John.

'Is Father going to come and be with us to-night?' asked Sister McCandless after a moment.

Elisha frowned and thrust out his lower lip. 'I don't reckon so, Sister,' he said. 'I believe he going to try to stay home to-night and preserve his strength for the morning service. The Lord's been speaking to him in visions and dreams and he ain't got much sleep lately.'

'Yes,' said Sister McCandless, 'that sure is a praying man. I tell you, it ain't every shepherd tarries before the Lord for his flock like Father James does.'

'Indeed, that is the truth,' said Sister Price, with animation. 'The Lord sure done blessed us with a good shepherd.'

'He mighty hard sometimes,' said Sister McCandless, 'but the Word is hard. The way of holiness ain't no joke.'

'He done made me to know that,' said Brother Elisha with a smile.

Sister McCandless stared at him. Then she laughed. 'Lord,' she cried, 'I *bet* you can say so!'

'And I loved him for that,' said Sister Price. 'It ain't every pastor going to set down his own nephew—in front of the whole church, too. And Elisha hadn't committed no big fault.'

'Ain't no such thing,' said Sister McCandless, 'as a little fault or a big fault. Satan get his foot in the door, he ain't going to rest till he's in the room. You is in the Word or you *ain't*—ain't no half-way with God.'

'You reckon we ought to start?' asked Sister Price doubtfully, after a pause. 'Don't look to me like nobody else is coming.'

'Now, don't you sit there,' laughed Sister McCandless, 'and be of little faith like that. I just believe the Lord's going to give us a great service to-night.' She turned to John. 'Ain't your daddy coming out to-night?'

'Yes'm,' John replied, 'he said he was coming.'

'There!' said Sister McCandless. 'And your mama— is she coming out, too?'

'I don't know,' John said. 'She mighty tired.'

'She ain't so tired she can't come out and pray a *little* while,' said Sister McCandless.

For a moment John hated her, and he stared at her fat, black profile in anger. Sister Price said:

'But I declare, it's a wonder how that woman works like she does, and keeps those children looking so neat and clean and all, and gets out to the house of God almost every night. Can't be nothing but the Lord that bears her up.'

'I reckon we might have a little song,' said Sister McCandless, 'just to warm things up. I sure hate to walk in a church where folks is just sitting and talking. Look like it takes all my spirit away.'

'Amen,' said Sister Price.

Elisha began a song: 'This may be my last time,' and they began to sing:

> *This may be the last time I pray with you,*
> *This may be my last time, I don't know.'*

As they sang, they clapped their hands, and John saw that Sister McCandless looked about her for a tambourine. He rose and mounted the pulpit steps, and took from the small opening at the bottom of the pulpit three tambourines. He gave one to Sister McCandless, who nodded and smiled, not breaking her rhythm, and he put the rest on a chair near Sister Price.

> *This may be the last time I sing with you*
> *This may be my last time, I don't know.'*

He watched them, singing with them—because otherwise they would force him to sing—and trying not to hear the words that he forced outwards from his throat. And he thought to clap his hands, but he could not; they remained tightly folded in his lap. If he did not sing they would be upon him, but his heart told him that he had no right to sing or to rejoice.

> '*Oh, this*
> *May be my last time*
> *This*
> *May be my last time*
> *Oh, this*
> *May be my last time . . .*'

And he watched Elisha, who was a young man in the Lord; who, a priest after the order of Melchizedek, had been given power over death and Hell. The Lord had lifted him up, and turned him around, and set his feet on the shining way. What were the thoughts of Elisha when night came, and he was alone where no eye could see, and no tongue bear witness, save only the trumpet-like tongue of God? Were his thoughts, his bed, his body foul? What were his dreams?

> '*This may be my last time,*
> *I don't know.*'

Behind him the door opened and the wintry air rushed in. He turned to see, entering the door, his father, his mother, and his aunt. It was only the presence of his aunt that shocked him, for she had never entered this church before: she seemed to have been summoned to witness a bloody act. It was in all her aspect, quiet with a dreadful quietness, as she moved down the aisle behind his mother and knelt for a moment beside his mother and father to pray. John knew that it was the hand of the Lord that had led her to this place, and his heart grew cold. The Lord was riding on the wind to-night. What might that wind have spoken before the morning came?

*Part Two*

# THE
# PRAYERS
# OF THE
# SAINTS

*And they cried with a loud voice, saying, How long, O Lord, holy and true, dost thou not judge and avenge our blood on them that dwell on the earth?*

# 1  FLORENCE'S PRAYER

*Light and life to all He brings,*
*Risen with healing in His wings!*

FLORENCE raised her voice in the only song she could remember that her mother used to sing:

> *'It's me, it's me, it's me, oh, Lord,*
> *Standing in the need of prayer.'*

Gabriel turned to stare at her, in astonished triumph that his sister should at last be humbled. She did not look at him. Her thoughts were all on God. After a moment, the congregation and the piano joined her:

> *'Not my father, not my mother,*
> *But it's me, oh, Lord.'*

She knew that Gabriel rejoiced, not that her humility might lead her to grace, but only that some private anguish had brought her low: her song revealed that she was suffering, and this her brother was glad to see. This had always been his spirit. Nothing had ever changed it; nothing ever would. For a moment her pride stood up; the resolution that had brought her to this place to-night faltered, and she felt that if Gabriel was the Lord's anointed, she would rather die and endure Hell for all eternity than bow before His altar. But she strangled her pride, rising to stand with them in the holy space before the altar, and still singing:

*'Standing in the need of prayer.'*

Kneeling as she had not knelt for many years, and in this company before the altar, she gained again from the song the meaning it had held for her mother, and gained a new meaning for herself. As a child, the song had made her see a woman, dressed in black, standing in infinite mists alone, waiting for the form of the Son of God to lead her through that white fire. This woman now returned to her, more desolate; it was herself, not knowing where to put her foot; she waited, trembling, for the mists to be parted that she might walk in peace. That long road, her life, which she had followed for sixty groaning years, had led her at last to her mother's starting-place, the altar of the Lord. For her feet stood on the edge of that river which her mother, rejoicing, had crossed over. And would the Lord now reach out His hand to Florence and heal and save? But, going down before the scarlet cloth at the foot of the golden cross, it came to her that she had forgotten how to pray.

Her mother had taught her that the way to pray was to forget everything and everyone but Jesus; to pour out of the heart, like water from a bucket, all evil thoughts, all thoughts of self, all malice for one's enemies; to come boldly, and yet more humbly than a little child, before the Giver of all good things. Yet, in Florence's heart to-night hatred and bitterness weighed like granite, pride refused to abdicate from the throne it had held so long. Neither love nor humility had led her to the altar, but only fear. And God did not hear the prayers of the fearful, for the hearts of the fearful held no belief. Such prayers could rise no higher than the lips that uttered them.

Around her she heard the saints' voices, a steady, charged murmur, with now and again the name of *Jesus* rising above, sometimes like the swift rising of a bird into the air of a sunny day, sometimes like the slow rising of the mist from swamp ground. Was this the way to pray? In the church that she had joined when she first came North one knelt before the altar once only, in the beginning, to ask forgiveness of sins; and this accomplished, one was baptized and became a Christian, to kneel no more thereafter. Even if the Lord should lay some great burden on one's back—as He had done, but never so heavy a burden as this she carried now—one prayed in silence. It was indecent, the practice of common niggers to cry aloud at the foot of the altar, tears streaming for all the world to see. She had never done it, not even as a girl down home in the church they had gone to in those days. Now perhaps it was too late, and the Lord would suffer her to die in the darkness in which she had lived so long.

In the olden days God had healed His children. He had caused the blind to see, the lame to walk, and He had raised dead men from the grave. But Florence remembered one phrase, which now she muttered against the knuckles that bruised her lips: 'Lord, help my unbelief.'

For the message had come to Florence that had come to Hezekiah: *Set thine house in order, for thou shalt die and not live.* Many nights ago, as she turned on her bed, this message came to her. For many days and nights the message was repeated; there had been time, then, to turn to God. But she had thought to evade him, seeking among the women she knew for remedies; and then, because the pain increased, she had sought doctors; and when the doctors did no good she had climbed stairs all over town to rooms where incense burned and where

men or women in traffic with the devil gave her white
powders, or herbs to make tea, and cast spells upon her
to take the sickness away. The burning in her bowels
did not cease—that burning which, eating inward, took
the flesh visibly from her bones and caused her to vomit
up her food. Then one night she found death standing in
the room. Blacker than night, and gigantic, he filled one
corner of her narrow room, watching her with eyes like
the eyes of a serpent when his head is lifted to strike.
Then she screamed and called on God, turning on the
light. And death departed, but she knew he would be
back. Every night would bring him a little closer to her
bed.

And after death's first silent vigil her life came to her
bedside to curse her with many voices. Her mother, in
rotting rags and filling the room with the stink of the
grave, stood over her to curse the daughter who had
denied her on her deathbed. Gabriel came, from all his
times and ages, to curse the sister who had held him to
scorn and mocked his ministry. Deborah, black, her
body as shapeless and hard as iron, looked on with veiled,
triumphant eyes, cursing the Florence who had mocked
her in her pain and barrenness. Frank came, even he,
with that same smile, the same tilt of his head. Of them
all she would have begged forgiveness, had they come
with ears to hear. But they came like many trumpets;
even if they had come to hear and not to testify it was
not they who could forgive her, but only God.

The piano had stopped. All around her now were only
the voices of the saints.


'Dear Father'—it was her mother praying—'we come
before You on our knees this evening to ask You to
watch over us and hold back the hand of the destroying
angel. Lord, sprinkle the doorpost of this house with
the blood of the Lamb to keep all the wicked men away.

Lord, we praying for every mother's son and daughter
everywhere in the world but we want You to take special
care of this girl here to-night, Lord, and don't let no evil
come nigh her. We know you's able to do it, Lord, in
Jesus' name, Amen.'

This was the first prayer Florence heard, the only
prayer she was ever to hear in which her mother demanded the protection of God more passionately for her
daughter than she demanded it for her son. It was night,
the windows were shut tightly with the shades drawn,
and the great table was pushed against the door. The
kerosene lamps burned low and made great shadows
on the newspaper-covered wall. Her mother, dressed in
the long, shapeless, colourless dress that she wore every
day but Sunday, when she wore white, and with her
head tied up in a scarlet cloth, knelt in the centre of the
room, her hands hanging loosely folded before her, her
black face lifted, her eyes shut. The weak, unsteady light
placed shadows under her mouth and in the sockets of
her eyes, making the face impersonal with majesty, like
the face of a prophetess, or like a mask. Silence filled the
room after her 'Amen,' and in the silence they heard,
far up the road, the sound of a horse's hoofs. No one
moved. Gabriel, from his corner near the stove, looked
up and watched his mother.

'I ain't afraid,' said Gabriel.

His mother turned, one hand raised. 'You hush, now!'

Trouble had taken place in town to-day. Their neigh-
bour Deborah, who was sixteen, three years older than
Florence, had been taken away into the fields the night
before by many white men, where they did things to her
to make her cry and bleed. To-day, Deborah's father had
gone to one of the white men's houses, and said that he
would kill him and all the other white men he could
find. They had beaten him and left him for dead. Now,
everyone had shut their doors, praying and waiting, for

it was said that the white folks would come to-night and set fire to all the houses, as they had done before.

In the night that pressed outside they heard only the horse's hoofs, which did not stop; there was not the laughter they would have heard had there been many coming on this road, and no calling out of curses, and no one crying for mercy to white men, or to God. The hoofbeats came to the door and passed, and rang, while they listened, ever more faintly away. Then Florence realized how frightened she had been. She watched her mother rise and walk to the window. She peered out through a corner of the blanket that covered it.

'They's gone,' she said, 'whoever they was.' Then: 'Blessed be the name of the Lord,' she said.

Thus had her mother lived and died; and she had often been brought low, but she had never been forsaken. She had always seemed to Florence the oldest woman in the world, for she often spoke of Florence and Gabriel as the children of her old age, and she had been born, innumerable years ago, during slavery, on a plantation in another state. On this plantation she had grown up as one of the field-workers, for she was very tall and strong; and by and by she had married and raised children, all of whom had been taken from her, one by sickness and two by auction; and one, whom she had not been allowed to call her own, had been raised in the master's house. When she was a woman grown, well past thirty as she reckoned it, with one husband buried —but the master had given her another—armies, plundering and burning, had come from the North to set them free. This was in answer to the prayers of the faithful, who had never ceased, both day and night, to cry out for deliverance.

For it had been the will of God that they should hear, and pass thereafter, one to another, the story of the Hebrew children who had been held in bondage in the

land of Egypt; and how the Lord had heard their groaning, and how His heart was moved; and how He bid
them wait but a little season till He should send
deliverance. Florence's mother had known this story,
so it seemed, from the day that she was born. And
while she lived—rising in the morning before the sun
came up, standing and bending in the fields when the
sun was high, crossing the fields homeward while the
sun went down at the gates of Heaven far away, hearing
the whistle of the foreman and his eerie cry across the
fields; in the whiteness of winter when hogs and turkeys
and geese were slaughtered, and lights burned bright in
the big house, and Bathsheba, the cook, sent over in a
napkin bits of ham and chicken and cakes left over by
the white folks—in all that befell: in her joys, her pipe
in the evening, her man at night, the children she
suckled, and guided on their first short steps; and in her
tribulations, death, and parting, and the lash, she did
not forget that deliverance was promised and would
surely come. She had only to endure and trust in God.
She knew that the big house, the house of pride where
the white folks lived, would come down; it was written
in the Word of God. They, who walked so proudly now,
had not fashioned for themselves or their children so
sure a foundation as was hers. They walked on the edge
of a steep place and their eyes were sightless—God
would cause them to rush down, as the herd of swine
had once rushed down, into the sea. For all that they
were so beautiful, and took their ease, she knew them,
and she pitied them, who would have no covering in the
great day of His wrath.

Yet, she told her children, God was just, and He
struck no people without first giving many warnings.
God gave men time, but all the times were in His hand,
and one day the time to forsake evil and do good would
all be finished: then only the whirlwind, death riding

on the whirlwind, awaited those people who had forgotten God. In all the days that she was growing up, signs failed not, but none heeded. 'Slaves done ris,' was whispered in the cabin and at the master's gate: slaves in another county had fired the masters' houses and fields and dashed their children to death against the stones. 'Another slave in hell,' Bathsheba might say one morning, shooing the piccaninnies away from the great porch: a slave had killed his master, or his overseer, and had gone down to Hell to pay for it. 'I ain't got long to stay here,' someone crooned beside her in the fields, someone who would be gone by morning on his journey north. All these signs, like the plagues with which the Lord had afflicted Egypt, only hardened the hearts of these people against the Lord. They thought the lash would save them, and they used the lash; or the knife, or the gallows, or the auction block; they thought that kindness would save them, and the master and mistress came down, smiling, to the cabins, making much of the piccaninnies and bearing gifts. These were great days, and they all, black and white, seemed happy together. But when the Word has gone forth from the mouth of God nothing can turn it back.

The Word was fulfilled one morning, before she was awake. Many of the stories her mother told meant nothing to Florence; she knew them for what they were, tales told by an old black woman in a cabin in the evening to distract her children from their cold and hunger. But the story of this day she was never to forget; it was a day for which she lived. There was a great running and shouting, said her mother, everywhere outside, and, as she opened her eyes to the light of that day, so bright, she said, and cold, she was certain that the judgment trumpet had sounded. While she still sat, amazed, and wondering what, on the judgment day, would be the best behaviour, in rushed Bathsheba, and behind her many tumbling children and field hands and house niggers, all together, and Bathsheba shouted: 'Rise up, rise up, Sister Rachel, and see the Lord's deliverance! He done brought us out of Egypt, just like He promised, and we's free at last!' Bathsheba grabbed her, tears running down her face; she, dressed in the clothes in which she had slept, walked to the door to look out on the new day God had given them.

On that day she saw the proud house humbled; green silk and velvet blowing out of windows, and the garden trampled by many horsemen, and the big gate open. The master and mistress, and their kin, and one child she had borne were in that house—which she did not enter. Soon it occurred to her that there was no longer any reason to tarry here. She tied her things in a cloth that she put on her head, and walked out through the big gate, never to see that country any more.

And this became Florence's deep ambition: to walk out one morning through the cabin door, never to return. Her father, whom she scarcely remembered, had departed that way one morning not many months after the birth of Gabriel. And not only her father; every day she heard that another man or woman had said farewell to this iron earth and sky, and started on the journey north. But her mother had no wish to go North where, she said, wickedness dwelt and Death rode mighty through the streets. She was content to stay in this cabin and do washing for the white folks, though she was old and her back was sore. And she wanted Florence, also, to be content—helping with the washing, and fixing meals and keeping Gabriel quiet.

Gabriel was the apple of his mother's eye. If he had never been born, Florence might have looked forward to a day when she would be released from her unrewarding round of labour, when she might think of her own future and go out to make it. With the birth of Gabriel, which occurred when she was five, her future was swallowed up. There was only one future in that house, and it was Gabriel's—to which, since Gabriel was a man-child, all else must be sacrificed. Her mother did not, indeed, think of it as sacrifice, but as logic: Florence was a girl, and would by and by be married, and have children of her own, and all the duties of a woman; and this being so, her life in the cabin was the best possible preparation for her future life. But Gabriel was a man; he would go out one day into the world to do a man's work, and he needed, therefore, meat, when there was any in the house, and clothes, whenever clothes could be bought, and the strong indulgence of his womenfolk, so that he would know how to be with women when he had a wife. And he needed the education that Florence desired far more than he, and that she might have got if he had not been born. It was Gabriel who was slapped and scrubbed each morning and sent off to the one-room schoolhouse—which he hated, and where he managed to learn, so far as Florence could discover, almost nothing at all. And often he was not at school, but getting into mischief with other boys. Almost all of their neighbours, and even some of the white folks, came at one time or another to complain of Gabriel's wrongdoing. Their mother would walk out into the yard and cut a switch from a tree and beat him—beat him, it seemed to Florence, until any other boy would have fallen down dead; and so often that any other boy would have ceased his wickedness. Nothing stopped Gabriel, though he made Heaven roar with his howling, though he screamed aloud, as his mother approached, that he would never be such a bad boy again. And, after the beating, his pants still down around his knees and his face wet with tears and mucus, Gabriel was made to kneel down while his mother prayed. She asked Florence to pray, too, but in her heart Florence never prayed. She hoped that Gabriel

would break his neck. She wanted the evil against which
their mother prayed to overtake him one day.

In those days Florence and Deborah, who had become
close friends after Deborah's 'accident,' hated all men.
When men looked at Deborah they saw no further than
her unlovely and violated body. In their eyes lived perpetually a lewd, uneasy wonder concerning the night she
had been taken in the fields. That night had robbed her
of the right to be considered a woman. No man would
approach her in honour because she was a living reproach,
to herself and to all black women and to all black men.
If she had been beautiful, and if God had not given her
a spirit so demure, she might, with ironic gusto, have
acted out that rape in the fields for ever. Since she could
not be considered a woman, she could only be looked
on as a harlot, a source of delights more bestial and
mysteries more shaking than any a proper woman could
provide. Lust stirred in the eyes of men when they looked
at Deborah, lust that could not be endured because it
was so impersonal, limiting communion to the area of
her shame. And Florence, who was beautiful but did not
look with favour on any of the black men who lusted
after her, not wishing to exchange her mother's cabin
for one of theirs and to raise their children and so go
down, toil-blasted, into, as it were, a common grave,
reinforced in Deborah the terrible belief against which
no evidence had ever presented itself: that all men were
like this, their thoughts rose no higher, and they lived
only to gratify on the bodies of women their brutal and
humiliating needs.

One Sunday at a camp-meeting, when Gabriel was
twelve years old and was to be baptized, Deborah and
Florence stood on the banks of a river along with all the
other folks and watched him. Gabriel had not wished to
be baptized. The thought had frightened and angered
him, but his mother insisted that Gabriel was now of an

age to be responsible before God for his sins—she would not shirk the duty, laid on her by the Lord, of doing everything within her power to bring him to the throne of grace. On the banks of a river, under the violent light of noon, confessed believers and children of Gabriel's age waited to be led into the water. Standing out, waist-deep and robed in white, was the preacher, who would hold their heads briefly under water, crying out to Heaven as the baptized held his breath: 'I indeed have baptized you with water: but He shall baptize you with the Holy Ghost.' Then, as they rose sputtering and blinded and were led to the shore, he cried out again: 'Go thou and sin no more.' They came up from the water, visibly under the power of the Lord, and on the shore the saints awaited them, beating their tambourines. Standing near the shore were the elders of the church, holding towels with which to cover the newly baptized, who were then led into the tents, one for either sex, where they could change their clothes.

At last, Gabriel, dressed in an old white shirt and short linen pants, stood on the edge of the water. Then he was slowly led into the river, where he had so often splashed naked, until he reached the preacher. And the moment that the preacher threw him down, crying out the words of John the Baptist, Gabriel began to kick and sputter, nearly throwing the preacher off balance; and though at first they thought that it was the power of the Lord that worked in him, they realized as he rose, still kicking and with his eyes tightly shut, that it was only fury, and too much water in his nose. Some folks smiled, but Florence and Deborah did not smile. Though Florence had also been indignant, years before when the slimy water entered her incautiously open mouth, she had done her best not to sputter, and she had not cried out. But now, here came Gabriel, floundering and furious up the bank, and what she looked at, with an anger more violent than any she had felt before, was his nakedness. He was drenched, and his thin, white clothes clung like another skin to his black body. Florence and Deborah looked at one another, while the singing rose to cover Gabriel's howling, and Deborah looked away.

Years later, Deborah and Florence had stood on Deborah's porch at night and watched a vomit-covered Gabriel stagger up the moonlit road, and Florence had cried out: 'I hate him! I hate him! Big, black, prancing tomcat of a nigger!' And Deborah had said, in that heavy voice of hers: 'You know, honey, the Word tell us to hate the sin but not the sinner.'

In nineteen hundred, when she was twenty-six, Florence walked out through the cabin door. She had thought to wait until her mother, who was so ill now that she no longer stirred out of bed, should be buried— but suddenly she knew that she would wait no longer, the time had come. She had been working as cook and serving-girl for a large white family in town, and it was on the day her master proposed that she become his concubine that she knew her life among these wretched people had come to its destined end. She left her employment that same day (leaving behind her a most vehement conjugal bitterness), and with part of the money that with cunning, cruelty, and sacrifice she had saved over a period of years, bought a railroad ticket to New York. When she bought it, in a kind of scarlet rage, she held like a talisman at the back of her mind the thought: 'I can give it back, I can sell it. This don't mean I got to go.' But she knew that nothing could stop her.

And it was this leave-taking that came to stand, in Florence's latter days, and with many another witness, at her bedside. Grey clouds obscured the sun that day, and outside the cabin window she saw that mist still covered the ground. Her mother lay in bed, awake; she was pleading with Gabriel, who had been out drinking the night before, and who was not really sober now, to mend his ways and come to the Lord. And Gabriel, full of the confusion, and pain, and guilt that were his whenever he thought of how he made his mother suffer, but that became nearly insupportable when she taxed him with it, stood before the mirror, head bowed, buttoning his shirt. Florence knew that he could not unlock his lips to speak; he could not say yes to his mother, and to the Lord; and he could not say no.

'Honey,' their mother was saying, 'don't you *let* your old mother die without you look her in the eye and tell her she going to see you in glory. You hear me, boy?'

In a moment, Florence thought with scorn, tears would fill his eyes, and he would promise to 'do better.' He had been promising to 'do better' since the day he had been baptized.

She put down her bag in the centre of the hateful room.

'Ma,' she said, 'I'm going. I'm a-going this morning.'

Now that she had said it, she was angry with herself for not having said it the night before, so that they would have had time to be finished with their weeping and their arguments. She had not trusted herself to withstand the night before; but now there was almost no time left. The centre of her mind was filled with the image of the great, white clock at the railway station, on which the hands did not cease to move.

'You going where?' her mother asked sharply. But she knew that her mother had understood, had indeed long before this moment known that this time would come. The astonishment with which she stared at Florence's bag was not altogether astonishment, but a startled, wary attention. A danger imagined had become present and real, and her mother was already searching for a way to break Florence's will. All this Florence knew in a moment, and it made her stronger. She watched her mother, waiting.

But at the tone of his mother's voice Gabriel, who had scarcely heard Florence's announcement, so grateful had he been that something had occurred to distract from him his mother's attention, dropped his eyes and saw Florence's travelling-bag. And he repeated his mother's question in a stunned, angry voice, understanding it only as the words hit the air:

'Yes, girl. Where you think you going?'

'I'm going,' she said, 'to New York. I got my ticket.'

And her mother watched her. For a moment no one said a word. Then, Gabriel, in a changed and frightened voice, asked:

'And when you done decide that?'

She did not look at him, nor answer his question. She continued to watch her mother. 'I got my ticket,' she repeated. 'I'm going on the morning train.'

'Girl,' asked her mother, quietly, 'is you sure you know what you's doing?'

She stiffened, seeing in her mother's eyes a mocking pity. 'I'm a woman grown,' she said. 'I know what I'm doing.'

'And you going,' cried Gabriel, 'this morning—just like that? And you going to walk off and leave your mother—just like that?'

'You hush,' she said, turning to him for the first time, 'she got you, ain't she?'

This was indeed, she realized as he dropped his eyes, the bitter, troubling point. He could not endure the thought of being left alone with his mother, with nothing whatever to put between himself and his guilty love. With Florence gone, time would have swallowed up all his mother's children, except himself; and *he*, then, must make amends for all the pain that she had borne, and sweeten her last moments with all his proofs of love.

And his mother required of him one proof only, that he tarry no longer in sin. With Florence gone, his stammering time, his playing time, contracted with a bound to the sparest interrogative second, when he must stiffen himself, and answer to his mother, and all the host of Heaven, yes or no.

Florence smiled inwardly a small, malicious smile, watching his slow bafflement, and panic, and rage; and she looked at her mother again. 'She got you,' she repeated. 'She don't need me.'

'You going north,' her mother said, then. 'And when you reckon on coming back?'

'I don't reckon on coming back,' she said.

'You come crying back soon enough,' said Gabriel, with malevolence, 'soon as they whip your butt up there four or five times.'

She looked at him again. 'Just don't you try to hold your breath till then, you hear?'

'Girl,' said her mother, 'you mean to tell me the Devil's done made your heart so hard you can just leave your mother on her dying bed, and you don't care if you don't never see her in this world no more? Honey, you can't tell me you done got so evil as all that?'

She felt Gabriel watching her to see how she would take this question—the question that, for all her determination, she had dreaded most to hear. She looked away from her mother, and straightened, catching her breath, looking outwards through the small, cracked window. There, outside, beyond the slowly rising mist, and farther off than her eyes could see, her life awaited her. The woman on the bed was old, her life was fading as the mist rose. She thought of her mother as already in the grave; and she would not let herself be strangled by the hands of the dead.

'I'm going, Ma,' she said. 'I got to go.'

Her mother leaned back, face upward to the light

and began to cry. Gabriel moved to Florence's side and grabbed her arm. She looked up into his face and saw that his eyes were full of tears.

'You can't go,' he said. 'You can't go. You can't go and leave your mother thisaway. She need a woman, Florence, to help look after her. What she going to do here, all alone with me?'

She pushed him from her and moved to stand over her mother's bed.

'Ma,' she said, 'don't be like that. Ain't a blessed thing for you to cry about so. Ain't a thing can happen to me up North can't happen to me here. God's everywhere, Ma. Ain't no need to worry.'

She knew that she was mouthing words; and she realized suddenly that her mother scorned to dignify these words with her attention. She had granted Florence the victory—with a promptness that had the effect of making Florence, however dimly and unwillingly, wonder if her victory was real. She was not weeping for her daughter's future, she was weeping for the past, and weeping in an anguish in which Florence had no part. And all of this filled Florence with a terrible fear, which was immediately transformed into anger. 'Gabriel can take care of you,' she said, her voice shaking with malice. 'Gabriel ain't never going to leave you. Is you, boy?' and she looked at him. He stood, stupid with bewilderment and grief, a few inches from the bed. 'But me,' she said, 'I got to go.' She walked to the centre of the room again, and picked up her bag.

'Girl,' Gabriel whispered, 'ain't you got no feelings at *all*?'

'*Lord!*' her mother cried; and at the sound her heart turned over; she and Gabriel, arrested, stared at the bed. 'Lord, Lord, Lord! Lord, have mercy on my sinful daughter! Stretch out your hand and hold her back from the lake that burns forever! Oh, my Lord, my Lord!'

and her voice dropped, and broke, and tears ran down her face. 'Lord, I done my best with all the children what you give me. Lord, have mercy on my children, and my children's children.'

'Florence,' said Gabriel, 'please don't go. Please don't go. You ain't really fixing to go and leave her like this?'

Tears stood suddenly in her own eyes, though she could not have said what she was crying for. 'Leave me be,' she said to Gabriel, and picked up her bag again. She opened the door; the cold, morning air came in. 'Good-bye,' she said. And then to Gabriel: 'Tell her I said good-bye.' She walked through the cabin door and down the short steps into the frosty yard. Gabriel watched her, standing frozen between the door and the weeping bed. Then, as her hand was on the gate, he ran before her, and slammed the gate shut.

'Girl, where you going? What you doing? You reckon on finding some men up North to dress you in pearls and diamonds?'

Violently, she opened the gate and moved out into the road. He watched her with his jaw hanging, and his lips loose and wet. 'If you ever see me again,' she said, 'I won't be wearing rags like yours.'

All over the church there was only the sound, more awful than the deepest silence, of the prayers of the saints of God. Only the yellow, moaning light shone above them, making their faces gleam like muddy gold. Their faces, and their attitudes, and their many voices rising as one voice made John think of the deepest valley, the longest night, of Peter and Paul in the dungeon cell, one praying while the other sang; or of endless, depth-less, swelling water, and no dry land in sight, the true believer clinging to a spar. And, thinking of to-morrow, when the church would rise up, singing, under the booming Sunday light, he thought of the light for which they tarried, which, in an instant, filled the soul, causing (throughout those iron-dark, unimaginable ages before John had come into the world) the new-born in Christ to testify: Once I was blind and now I see.

And then they sang: 'Walk in the light, the beautiful light. Shine all around me by day and by night, Jesus, the light of the world.' And they sang: Oh, Lord, Lord, I want to be ready, I want to be ready. I want to be ready to walk in Jerusalem just like John.'

*To walk in Jerusalem just like John.* To-night, his mind was awash with visions: nothing remained. He was ill with doubt and searching. He longed for a light that would teach him, forever and forever, and beyond all question, the way to go; for a power that would bind him, forever and forever, and beyond all crying, to the love of God. Or else he wished to stand up now, and leave this tabernacle and never see these people any more. Fury and anguish filled him, unbearable, unanswerable; his mind was stretched to breaking. For it was time that filled his mind, time that was violent with the mysterious love of God. And his mind could not contain the terrible stretch of time that united twelve men fishing by the shores of Galilee, and black men weeping on their knees to-night, and he, a witness.

*My soul is a witness for my Lord.* There was an awful silence at the bottom of John's mind, a dreadful weight, a dreadful speculation. And not even a speculation, but a deep, deep turning, as of something huge, black, shapeless, for ages dead on the ocean floor, that now felt its rest disturbed by a faint, far wind, which bid it: 'Arise.' And this weight began to move at the bottom of John's mind, in a silence like the silence of the void before creation, and he began to feel a terror he had never felt before.

And he looked around the church, at the people praying there. Praying Mother Washington had not come in until all of the saints were on their knees, and now she stood, the terrible, old, black woman, above his Aunt Florence, helping her to pray. Her granddaughter, Ella Mae, had come in with her, wearing a mangy fur jacket over her everyday clothes. She knelt heavily in a corner near the piano, under the sign that spoke of the wages of sin, and now and again she moaned. Elisha had not looked up when she came in, and he prayed in silence: sweat stood on his brow. Sister McCandless and Sister Price cried out every now and again: 'Yes, Lord!' or: 'Bless your name, Jesus!' And his father prayed, his head lifted up and his voice going on like a distant mountain stream.

But his Aunt Florence was silent; he wondered if she slept. He had never seen her praying in a church before. He knew that different people prayed in different ways: had his aunt always prayed in such a silence? His mother, too, was silent, but he had seen her pray before, and her silence made him feel that she was weeping. And why did she weep? And why did they come here, night after night after night, calling out to a God who cared nothing for them—if, above this flaking ceiling, there was any God at all? Then he remembered that the fool has said in his heart, There is no God—and he dropped his eyes, seeing that over his Aunt Florence's head Praying Mother Washington was looking at him.

Frank sang the blues, and he drank too much. His skin was the colour of caramel candy. Perhaps for this reason she always thought of him as having candy in his mouth, candy staining the edges of his straight, cruel teeth. For a while he wore a tiny moustache, but she made him shave it off, for it made him look, she thought, like a half-breed gigolo. In details such as this he was always very easy—he would always put on a clean shirt, or get his hair cut, or come with her to Uplift meetings where they heard speeches by prominent Negroes about the future and duties of the Negro race. And this had given her, in the beginning of their marriage, the impression that she controlled him. This impression had been entirely and disastrously false.

When he had left her, more than twenty years before, and after more than ten years of marriage, she had felt for that moment only an exhausted exasperation and a vast relief. He had not been home for two days and three nights, and when he did return they quarrelled with more than their usual bitterness. All of the rage she had accumulated during their marriage was told him in that evening as they stood in their small kitchen. He was still wearing overalls, and he had not shaved, and his face was muddy with sweat and dirt. He had said nothing for a long while, and then he had said: 'All right, baby. I guess you don't never want to see me no more, not a miserable, black sinner like me.' The door closed behind him, and she heard his feet echoing down the long hall, away. She stood alone in the kitchen, holding the empty coffee-pot that she had been about to wash. She thought: 'He'll come back, and he'll come back drunk.' And then she had thought, looking about the kitchen: 'Lord, wouldn't it be a blessing if he didn't never come back no more.' The Lord had given her what she said she wanted, as was often, she had found, His bewildering method of answering prayer. Frank never did come back. He lived for a long while with another woman, and when the war came he died in France.

Now, somewhere at the other end of the earth, her husband lay buried. He slept in a land his fathers had never seen. She wondered often if his grave was marked —if there stood over it, as in pictures she had seen, a small white cross. If the Lord had ever allowed her to cross that swelling ocean she would have gone, among all the millions buried there, to seek out his grave. Wearing deep mourning, she would have laid on it, perhaps, a wreath of flowers, as other women did; and stood for a moment, head bowed, considering the un-speaking ground. How terrible it would be for Frank to rise on the day of judgment so far from home! And he surely would not scruple, even on that day, to be angry at the Lord. 'Me and the Lord,' he had often said, 'don't always get along so well. He running the world like He thinks I ain't got good sense.' How had he died? Slow or sudden? Had he cried out? Had death come creeping on him from behind, or faced him like a man? She knew nothing about it, for she had not known that he was dead until long afterwards, when boys were coming home and she had begun searching for Frank's face in the streets. It was the woman with whom he had lived who had told her, for Frank had given this woman's name as his next-of-kin. The woman, having told her, had not known what else to say, and she stared at Florence in simple-minded pity. This made Florence furious, and she barely murmured: 'Thank you,' before she turned away. She hated Frank for making this woman official witness to her humiliation. And she wondered again what Frank had seen in this woman, who, though she was younger than Florence, had never been so pretty, and who drank all the time, and who was seen with many men.

But it had been from the first her great mistake—to meet him, to marry him, to love him as she so bitterly had. Looking at his face, it sometimes came to her that all women had been cursed from the cradle; all, in one fashion or another, being given the same cruel destiny, born to suffer the weight of men. Frank claimed that she got it all wrong side up: it was men who suffered because they had to put up with the ways of women—and this from the time that they were born until the day they died. But it was she who was right, she knew; with Frank she had always been right; and it had not been

her fault that Frank was the way he was, determined to
live and die a common nigger.

But he was always swearing that he would do better;
it was, perhaps, the brutality of his penitence that had
kept them together for so long. There was something in
her which loved to see him bow—when he came home,
stinking with whisky, and crept with tears into her arms.
Then he, so ultimately master, was mastered. And holding him in her arms while, finally, he slept, she thought
with the sensations of luxury and power: 'But there's
lots of good in Frank. I just got to be patient and he'll
come along all right.' To 'come along' meant that he
would change his ways and consent to be the husband she
had travelled so far to find. It was he who, unforgivably,
taught her that there are people in the world for whom
'coming along' is a perpetual process, people who are
destined never to arrive. For ten years he came along,
but when he left her he was the same man she had
married. He had not changed at all.

He had never made enough money to buy the home
she wanted, or anything else she really wanted, and this
had been part of the trouble between them. It was not
that he could not make money, but that he would not
save it. He would take half a week's wages and go out
and buy something he wanted, or something he thought
she wanted. He would come home on Saturday afternoons, already half drunk, with some useless object,
such as a vase, which, it had occurred to him, she would
like to fill with flowers—she who never noticed flowers
and who would certainly never have bought any. Or a
hat, always too expensive or too vulgar, or a ring that
looked as though it had been designed for a whore.
Sometimes it occurred to him to do the Saturday shopping
on his way home, so that she would not have to do it; in
which case he would buy a turkey, the biggest and most
expensive he could find, and several pounds of coffee, it

being his belief that there was never enough in the house, and enough breakfast cereal to feed an army for a month. Such foresight always filled him with such a sense of his own virtue that, as a kind of reward, he would also buy himself a bottle of whisky; and—lest she should think that he was drinking too much—invite some ruffian home to share it with him. Then they would sit all afternoon in her parlour, playing cards and telling indecent jokes, and making the air foul with whisky and smoke. She would sit in the kitchen, cold with rage and staring at the turkey, which, since Frank always bought them unplucked and with the head on, would cost her hours of exasperating, bloody labour. Then she would wonder what on earth had possessed her to undergo such hard trials and travel so far from home, if all she had found was a two-room apartment in a city she did not like, and a man yet more childish than any she had known when she was young.

Sometimes from the parlour where he and his visitor sat he would call her:

'Hey, Flo!'

And she would not answer. She hated to be called 'Flo,' but he never remembered. He might call her again, and when she did not answer he would come into the kitchen.

'What's the matter with you, girl? Don't you hear me a-calling you?'

And once when she still made no answer, but sat perfectly still, watching him with bitter eyes, he was forced to make verbal recognition that there was something wrong.

'What's the matter, old lady? You mad at me?'

And when in genuine bewilderment he stared at her, head to one side, the faintest of smiles on his face, something began to yield in her, something she fought, standing up and snarling at him in a lowered voice so that the visitor might not hear:

'I wish you'd tell me just how you think we's going to live all week on a turkey and five pounds of coffee?'

'Honey, I ain't bought nothing we didn't *need!*'

She sighed in helpless fury, and felt tears springing to her eyes.

'I done told you time and again to give *me* the money when you get paid, and let *me* do the shopping—'cause you ain't got the sense that you was born with.'

'Baby, I wasn't doing a thing in the world but trying to help you out. I thought maybe you wanted to go somewhere to-night and you didn't want to be bothered with no shopping.'

'Next time you want to do me a favour, you tell me first, you hear? And how you expect me to go to a show when you done brought this bird home for me to clean?'

'Honey, I'll clean it. It don't take no time at all.'

He moved to the table where the turkey lay and looked at it critically, as though he were seeing it for the first time. Then he looked at her and grinned. 'That ain't nothing to get mad about.'

She began to cry. 'I declare I don't know what gets into you. Every week the Lord sends you go out and do some more foolishness. How do you expect us to get enough money to get away from here if you all the time going to be spending your money on foolishness?'

When she cried, he tried to comfort her, putting his great hand on her shoulder and kissing her where the tears fell.

'Baby, I'm sorry. I thought it'd be a nice surprise.'

'The only surprise I want from you is to learn some sense! *That'd* be a surprise! You think I want to stay around here the rest of my life with these dirty niggers you all the time bring home?'

'Where you expect us to live, honey, where we ain't going to be with niggers?'

Then she turned away, looking out of the kitchen

D

window. It faced an elevated train that passed so close she always felt that she might spit in the faces of the flying, staring people.

'I just don't like all that ragtag . . . looks like you think so much of.'

Then there was silence. Although she had turned her back to him, she felt that he was no longer smiling and that his eyes, watching her, had darkened.

'And what kind of man you think you married?'

'I thought I married a man with some get up and go to him, who didn't just want to stay on the bottom all his life!'

'And what you want me to do, Florence? You want me to turn white?'

This question always filled her with an ectasy of hatred. She turned and faced him, and, forgetting that there was someone sitting in the parlour, shouted:

'You ain't got to be white to have some self-respect! You reckon I slave in this house like I do so you and them common niggers can sit here every afternoon throwing ashes all over the floor?'

'And who's common now, Florence?' he asked, quietly, in the immediate and awful silence in which she recognized her error. 'Who's acting like a common nigger now? What you reckon my friend is sitting there a-thinking? I declare, I wouldn't be surprised none if he wasn't a-thinking: "Poor Frank, he sure found him a common wife." Anyway, he ain't putting his ashes on the floor— he putting them in the ashtray, just like he knew what a ashtray was.' She knew that she had hurt him, and that he was angry, by the habit he had at such a moment of running his tongue quickly and incessantly over his lower lip. 'But we's a-going now, so you can sweep up the parlour and sit there, if you want to, till the judgment day.'

And he left the kitchen. She heard murmurs in the

parlour, and then the slamming of the door. She remembered, too late, that he had all his money with him. When he came back, long after nightfall, and she put him to bed and went through his pockets, she found nothing, or almost nothing, and she sank helplessly to the parlour floor and cried.

When he came back at times like this he would be petulant and penitent. She would not creep into bed until she thought that he was sleeping. But he would not be sleeping. He would turn as she stretched her legs beneath the blankets, and his arm would reach out, and his breath would be hot and sour-sweet in her face.

'Sugar-plum, what you want to be so evil with your baby for? Don't you know you done made me go out and get drunk, and I wasn't a-fixing to do that? I wanted to take you out somewhere to-night.' And, while he spoke, his hand was on her breast, and his moving lips brushed her neck. And this caused such a war in her as could scarcely be endured. She felt that everything in existence between them was part of a mighty plan for her humiliation. She did not want his touch, and yet she did: she burned with longing and froze with rage. And she felt that he knew this and inwardly smiled to see how easily, on this part of the battlefield, his victory could be assured. But at the same time she felt that his tenderness, his passion, and his love were real.

'Let me alone, Frank. I want to go to sleep.'

'No you don't. You don't want to go to sleep so soon. You want me to talk to you a little. You know how your baby loves to talk. Listen.' And he brushed her neck lightly with his tongue. 'You hear that?'

He waited. She was silent.

'Ain't you got nothing more to say than that? I better tell you something else.' And then he covered her face with kisses; her face, neck, arms, and breasts.

'You stink of whisky. Let me alone.'

'Ah. I ain't the only one got a tongue. What you got to say to this?' And his hand stroked the inside of her thigh.

'Stop.'

'I ain't going to stop. This is sweet talk, baby.'

Ten years. Their battle never ended; they never bought a home. He died in France. To-night she remembered details of those years which she thought she had forgotten, and at last she felt the stony ground of her heart break up; and tears, as difficult and slow as blood, began to trickle through her fingers. This the old woman above her somehow divined, and she cried: 'Yes, honey. You just let go, honey. Let Him bring you low so He can raise you up.' And was this the way she should have gone? Had she been wrong to fight so hard? Now she was an old woman, and all alone, and she was going to die. And she had nothing for all her battles. It had all come to this: she was on her face before the altar, crying to God for mercy. Behind her she heard Gabriel cry: 'Bless your name, Jesus!' and, thinking of him and the high road of holiness he had travelled, her mind swung like a needle, and she thought of Deborah.

Deborah had written her, not many times, but in a rhythm that seemed to remark each crisis in her life with Gabriel, and once, during the time she and Frank were still together, she had received from Deborah a letter that she had still: it was locked to-night in her handbag, which lay on the altar. She had always meant to show this letter to Gabriel one day, but she never had. She had talked with Frank about it late one night while he lay in bed whistling some ragtag tune and she sat before the mirror and rubbed bleaching cream into her skin. The letter lay open before her and she sighed loudly, to attract Frank's attention.

He stopped whistling in the middle of a phrase;

mentally, she finished it. 'What you got there, sugar?'
he asked, lazily.

'It's a letter from my brother's wife.' She stared at
her face in the mirror, thinking angrily that all these
skin creams were a waste of money, they never did any
good.

'What's them niggers doing down home? It ain't no
bad news, is it?' Still he hummed, irrepressibly, deep in
his throat.

'No . . . well, it ain't no good news neither, but it
ain't nothing to surprise *me* none. She say she think my
brother's got a bastard living right there in the same
town what he's scared to call his own.'

'No? And I thought you said your brother was a
preacher.'

'Being a preacher ain't never stopped a nigger from
doing his dirt.'

Then he laughed. 'You sure don't love your brother
like you should. How come his wife found out about this
kid?'

She picked up the letter and turned to face him.
'Sound to *me* like she *been* knowing about it but she
ain't never had the nerve to say nothing.' She paused,
then added, reluctantly: 'Of course, she ain't really
what you might call *sure*. But she ain't a woman to go
around thinking things. She mighty worried.'

'Hell, what she worried about it now for? Can't
nothing be done about it *now*.'

'She wonder if she ought to ask him about it.'

'And do she reckon if she ask him, he going to be fool
enough to say yes?'

She sighed again, more genuinely this time, and
turned back to the mirror. 'Well . . . he's a preacher.
And if Deborah's right, he ain't got no right to be a
preacher. He ain't no better'n nobody else. In *fact*, he
ain't no better than a murderer.'

He had begun to whistle again; he stopped. 'Murderer? How so?'

'Because he done let this child's mother go off and die when the child was born. That's how so.' She paused. 'And it sound just like Gabriel. He ain't never thought a minute about nobody in this world but himself.'

He said nothing, watching her implacable back. Then: 'You going to answer this letter?'

'I reckon.'

'And what you going to say?'

'I'm going to tell her she ought to let him know she know about his wickedness. Get up in front of the congregation and tell them too, if she has to.'

He stirred restlessly, and frowned. 'Well, you know more about it than me. But I don't see where that's going to do no good.'

'It'll do *her* some good. It'll make him treat her better. You don't know my brother like I do. There ain't but one way to get along with him, you got to scare him half to death. That's all. He ain't *got* no right to go around running his mouth about how holy he is if he done turned a trick like that.'

There was silence; he whistled again a few bars of his song; and then he yawned, and said: 'Is you coming to bed, old lady? Don't know why you keep wasting all your time and *my* money on all them old skin whiteners. You as black now as you was the day you was born.'

'You wasn't there the day I was born. And I know you don't want a coal-black woman.' But she rose from the mirror, and moved towards the bed.

'I ain't never said nothing like that. You just kindly turn out that light and I'll make you to know that black's a mighty pretty colour.'

She wondered if Deborah had ever spoken; and she wondered if she would give to Gabriel the letter that she carried in her handbag to-night. She had held it all these years, awaiting some savage opportunity. What this opportunity would have been she did not know; at this moment she did not want to know. For she had always thought of this letter as an instrument in her hands which could be used to complete her brother's destruction. When he was completely cast down she would prevent him from ever rising again by holding before him the evidence of his blood-guilt. But now she thought she would not live to see this patiently awaited day. She was going to be cut down.

And the thought filled her with terror and rage; the tears dried on her face and the heart within her shook, divided between a terrible longing to surrender and a desire to call God into account. Why had he preferred her mother and her brother, the old, black woman, and the low, black man, while she, who had sought only to walk upright, was come to die, alone and in poverty, in a dirty, furnished room? She beat her fists heavily against the altar. He, *he* would live, and, smiling, watch her go down into the grave! And her mother would be there, leaning over the gates of Heaven, to see her daughter burning in the pit.

As she beat her fists on the altar, the old woman above her laid hands on her shoulders, crying: 'Call on Him, daughter! Call on the Lord!' And it was as though she had been hurled outwards into time, where no boundaries were, for the voice was the voice of her mother but the hands were the hands of death. And she cried aloud, as she had never in all her life cried before, falling on her face on the altar, at the feet of the old, black woman. Her tears came down like burning rain. And the hands of death caressed her shoulders, the voice whispered and whispered in her ear: 'God's got your number, knows where you live, death's got a warrant out for you.'

# 2 GABRIEL'S PRAYER

*Now I been introduced*
*To the Father and the Son,*
*And I ain't*
*No stranger now.*

WHEN Florence cried, Gabriel was moving outward in fiery darkness, talking to the Lord. Her cry came to him from afar, as from unimaginable depths; and it was not his sister's cry he heard, but the cry of the sinner when he is taken in his sin. This was the cry he had heard so many days and nights, before so many altars, and he cried to-night, as he had cried before: 'Have your way, Lord! Have your way!'

Then there was only silence in the church. Even Praying Mother Washington had ceased to moan. Soon someone would cry again, and the voices would begin again; there would be music by and by, and shouting, and the sound of the tambourines. But now in this waiting, burdened silence it seemed that all flesh waited—paused, transfixed by something in the middle of the air—for the quickening power.

104

This silence, continuing like a corridor, carried
Gabriel back to the silence that had preceded his birth
in Christ. Like a birth indeed, all that had come before
this moment was wrapped in darkness, lay at the bottom
of the sea of forgetfulness, and was not now counted
against him, but was related only to that blind, and
doomed, and stinking corruption he had been before he
was redeemed.

The silence was the silence of the early morning, and
he was returning from the harlot's house. Yet all around
him were the sounds of the morning: of birds, invisible,
praising God; of crickets in the vines, frogs in the
swamp, of dogs miles away and close at hand, roosters
on the porch. The sun was not yet half awake; only the
utmost tops of trees had begun to tremble at his turning;
and the mist moved sullenly before Gabriel and all
around him, falling back before the light that rules by
day. Later, he said of that morning that his sin was on
him; then he knew only that he carried a burden and
that he longed to lay it down. This burden was heavier
than the heaviest mountain and he carried it in his
heart. With each step that he took his burden grew
heavier, and his breath became slow and harsh, and, of
a sudden, cold sweat stood out on his brow and drenched
his back.

All alone in the cabin his mother lay waiting; not only
for his return this morning, but for his surrender to the
Lord. She lingered only for this, and he knew it, even
though she no longer exhorted him as she had in days
but shortly gone by. She had placed him in the hands of
the Lord, and she waited with patience to see how He
would work the matter.

For she would live to see the promise of the Lord
fulfilled. She would not go to her rest until her son, the
last of her children, he who would place her in the
winding-sheet, should have entered the communion of

the saints. Now she, who had been impatient once, and violent, who had cursed and shouted and contended like a man, moved into silence, contending only, and with the last measure of her strength, with God. And this, too, she did like a man: knowing that she had kept the faith, she waited for Him to keep His promise. Gabriel knew that when he entered she would not ask him where he had been; she would not reproach him; and her eyes, even when she closed her lids to sleep, would follow him everywhere.

Later, since it was Sunday, some of the brothers and sisters would come to her, to sing and pray around her bed. And she would pray for him, sitting up in bed unaided, her head lifted, her voice steady; while he, kneeling in a corner of the room, trembled and almost wished that she would die; and trembled again at this testimony to the desperate wickedness of his heart; and prayed without words to be forgiven. For he had no words when he knelt before the throne. And he feared to make a vow before Heaven until he had the strength to keep it. And yet he knew that until he made the vow he would never find the strength.

For he desired in his soul, with fear and trembling, all the glories that his mother prayed he should find. Yes, he wanted power—he wanted to know himself to be the Lord's anointed, His well-beloved, and worthy, nearly, of that snow-white dove which had been sent down from Heaven to testify that Jesus was the son of God. He wanted to be master, to speak with that authority which could only come from God. It was later to become his proud testimony that he hated his sins— even as he ran towards sin, even as he sinned. He hated the evil that lived in his body, and he feared it, as he feared and hated the lions of lust and longing that prowled the defenceless city of his mind. He was later to say that this was a gift bequeathed him by his mother, that

it was God's hand on him from his earliest beginnings;
but then he knew only that when each night came, chaos
and fever raged in him; the silence in the cabin between
his mother and himself became something that could not
be borne; not looking at her, facing the mirror as he
put on his jacket, and trying to avoid his face there, he
told her that he was going to take a little walk—he
would be back soon.

Sometimes Deborah sat with his mother, watching
him with eyes that were no less patient and reproachful.
He would escape into the starry night and walk until
he came to a tavern, or to a house that he had marked
already in the long daytime of his lust. And then he
drank until hammers rang in his distant skull; he cursed
his friends and his enemies, and fought until blood ran
down; in the morning he found himself in mud, in clay,
in strange beds, and once or twice in jail; his mouth
sour, his clothes in rags, from all of him arising the
stink of his corruption. Then he could not even weep.
He could not even pray. He longed, nearly, for death,
which was all that could release him from the cruelty of
his chains.

And through all this his mother's eyes were on him;
her hand, like fiery tongs, gripped the lukewarm ember
of his heart; and caused him to feel, at the thought of
death, another, colder terror. To go down into the
grave, unwashed, unforgiven, was to go down into the
pit for ever, where terrors awaited him greater than any
the earth, for all her age and groaning, had ever borne.
He would be cut off from the living, for ever; he would
have no name for ever. Where he had been would be
silence only, rock, stubble, and no seed; for him, forever,
and for his, no hope of glory. Thus, when he came to the
harlot, he came to her in rage, and he left her in vain
sorrow—feeling himself to have been, once more, most
foully robbed, having spent his holy seed in a forbidden

darkness where it could only die. He cursed the betray-
ing lust that lived in him, and he cursed it again in
others. But: 'I remember,' he was later to say, 'the day
my dungeon shook and my chains fell off.'

And he walked homeward, thinking of the night
behind him. He had seen the woman at the very beginning of the evening, but she had been with many others,
men and women, and so he had ignored her. But later,
when he was on fire with whisky, he looked again
directly at her, and saw immediately that she had also
been thinking of him. There were not so many people
with her—it was as though she had been making room
for him. He had already been told that she was a widow
from the North, in town for only a few days to visit her
people. When he looked at her she looked at him and, as
though it were part of the joking conversation she was
having with her friends, she laughed aloud. She had the
lie-gap between her teeth, and a big mouth; when she
laughed, she belatedly caught her lower lip in her teeth,
as though she were ashamed of so large a mouth, and
her breasts shook. It was not like the riot that occurred
when big, fat women laughed—her breasts rose and fell
against the tight cloth of her dress. She was much older
than he—around Deborah's age, perhaps thirty-odd—
and she was not really pretty. Yet the distance between
them was abruptly charged with her, and her smell was in
his nostrils. Almost, he felt those moving breasts beneath
his hand. And he drank again, allowing, unconsciously,
or nearly, his face to fall into the lines of innocence and
power which his experience with women had told him
made their love come down.

Well (walking homewards, cold and tingling) yes,
they did the thing. Lord, how they rocked in their bed
of sin, and how she cried and shivered; Lord how her
love came down! Yes (walking homewards through the

fleeing mist, with the cold sweat standing on his brow),
yet, in vanity and the pride of conquest, he thought of
her, of her smell, the heat of her body beneath his hands,
of her voice, and her tongue, like the tongue of a cat,
and her teeth, and her swelling breasts, and how she
moved for him, and held him, and laboured with him,
and how they fell, trembling and groaning, and locked
together, into the world again. And, thinking of this, his
body freezing with his sweat, and yet altogether violent
with the memory of lust, he came to a tree on a gentle
rise, beyond which, and out of sight, lay home, where
his mother lay. And there leaped into his mind, with
the violence of water that has burst the dams and covered
the banks, rushing uncontrolled toward the doomed,
immobile houses—on which, on rooftops and windows,
the sun yet palely shivers—the memory of all the mornings he had mounted here and passed this tree, caught
for a moment between sins committed and sins to be
committed. The mist on this rise had fled away, and
he felt that he stood, as he faced the lone tree, beneath
the naked eye of Heaven. Then, in a moment, there was
silence, only silence, everywhere—the very birds had
ceased to sing, and no dogs barked, and no rooster
crowed for day. And he felt that this silence was God's
judgment; that all creation had been stilled before the
just and awful wrath of God, and waited now to see the
sinner—*he* was the sinner—cut down and banished from
the presence of the Lord. And he touched the tree,
hardly knowing that he touched it, out of an impulse to
be hidden; and then he cried: 'Oh, Lord, have mercy!
Oh, Lord, have mercy on me!'

And he fell against the tree, sinking to the ground and
clutching the roots of the tree. He had shouted into
silence and only silence answered—and yet, when he
cried, his cry had caused a ringing to the outermost
limits of the earth. This ringing, his lone cry rolling

through creation, frightening the sleeping fish and fowl, awakening echoes everywhere, river, and valley, and mountain wall, caused in him a fear so great that he lay for a moment silent and trembling at the base of the tree, as though he wished to be buried there. But that burdened heart of his would not be still, would not let him keep silence—would not let him breathe until he cried again. And so he cried again; and his cry returned again; and still the silence waited for God to speak.

And his tears began—such tears as he had not known were in him. 'I wept,' he said later, 'like a little child.' But no child had ever wept such tears as he wept that morning on his face before Heaven, under the mighty tree. They came from deeps no child discovers, and shook him with an ague no child endures. And presently, in his agony, he was screaming, each cry seeming to tear his throat apart, and stop his breath, and force the hot tears down his face, so that they splashed his hands and wet the root of the tree: 'Save me! Save me!' And all creation rang, but did not answer. 'I couldn't hear nobody pray.'

Yes, he was in that valley where his mother had told him he would find himself, where there was no human help, no hand outstretched to protect or save. Here nothing prevailed save the mercy of God—here the battle was fought between God and the Devil, between death and everlasting life. And he had tarried too long, he had turned aside in sin too long, and God would not hear him. The appointed time had passed and God had turned His face away.

'Then,' he testified, 'I heard my mother singing. She was a-singing for me. She was a-singing low and sweet, right there beside me, like she knew if she just called Him, the Lord would come.' When he heard this singing, which filled all the silent air, which swelled until it filled all the waiting earth, the heart within him broke, and yet began to rise, lifted of its burden; and his throat unlocked; and his tears came down as though the listening skies had opened. 'Then I praised God, Who had brought me out of Egypt and set my feet on the solid rock.' When at last he lifted up his eyes he saw a new Heaven and a new Earth; and he heard a new sound of singing, for a sinner had come home. 'I looked at my hands and my hands were new. I looked at my feet and my feet were new. And I opened my mouth to the Lord that day and Hell won't make me change my mind.' And, yes, there was singing everywhere; the birds and the crickets and the frogs rejoiced, the distant dogs leaping and sobbing, circled in their narrow yards, and roosters cried from every high fence that here was a new beginning, a blood-washed day!

And this was the beginning of his life as a man. He was just past twenty-one; the century was not yet one year old. He moved into town, into the room that awaited him at the top of the house in which he worked, and he began to preach. He married Deborah in that same year. After the death of his mother, he began to see her all the time. They went to the house of God together, and because there was no one, any more, to look after him, she invited him often to her home for meals, and kept his clothes neat, and after he had preached they discussed his sermons; that is, he listened while she praised.

He had certainly never intended to marry her; such an idea was no more in his mind, he would have said, than the possibility of flying to the moon. He had known her all his life; she had been his older sister's older friend, and then his mother's faithful visitor; she had never, for Gabriel, been young. So far as he was concerned, she might have been born in her severe, her sexless, long and shapeless habit, always black or grey.

She seemed to have been put on earth to visit the sick, and to comfort those who wept, and to arrange the last garments of the dying.

Again, there was her legend, her history, which would have been enough, even had she not been so wholly unattractive, to put her for ever beyond the gates of any honourable man's desire. This, indeed, in her silent, stolid fashion, she seemed to know: where, it might be, other women held as their very charm and secret the joy that they could give and share, she contained only the shame that she had borne—shame, unless a miracle of human love delivered her, was all she had to give. And she moved, therefore, through their small community like a woman mysteriously visited by God, like a terrible example of humility, or like a holy fool. No ornaments ever graced her body; there was about her no tinkling, no shining, and no softness. No ribbon falsified her blameless and implacable headgear; on her woollen head there was only the barest minimum of oil. She did not gossip with the other women—she had nothing, indeed, to gossip about—but kept her communication to yea and nay, and read her Bible, and prayed. There were people in the church, and even men carrying the gospel, who mocked Deborah behind her back; but their mockery was uneasy; they could never be certain but that they might be holding up to scorn the greatest saint among them, the Lord's peculiar treasure and most holy vessel.

'You sure is a godsend to me, Sister Deborah,' Gabriel would sometimes say. 'I don't know what I'd do without you.'

For she sustained him most beautifully in his new condition; with her unquestioning faith in God, and her faith in him, she, even more than the sinners who came crying to the altar after he had preached, bore earthly witness to his calling; and speaking, as it were, in the

speech of men she lent reality to the mighty work that
the Lord had appointed to Gabriel's hands.

And she would look up at him with her timid smile.
'You hush, Reverend. It's me that don't never kneel
down without I thank the Lord for *you*.'

Again: she never called him Gabriel or 'Gabe,' but
from the time that he began to preach she called him
Reverend, knowing that the Gabriel whom she had
known as a child was no more, was a new man in Christ
Jesus.

'You ever hear from Florence?' she sometimes asked.

'Lord, Sister Deborah, it's me that ought to be asking
*you*. That girl don't hardly never write to me.'

'I ain't heard from her real lately.' She paused. Then:
'I don't believe she so happy up there.'

'And serve her right, too—she ain't had no business
going away from here like she did, just like a crazy
woman.' And then he asked, maliciously: 'She tell you
if she married yet?'

She looked at him quickly, and looked away. 'Florence
ain't thinking about no husband,' she said.

He laughed. 'God bless you for your pure heart,
Sister Deborah. But if that girl ain't gone away from
here a-looking for a husband, my name ain't Gabriel
Grimes.'

'If she'd a-wanted a husband look to me like she could
a-just picked one out right here. You don't mean to tell
me she done travelled all the way North just for that?'
And she smiled strangely, a smile less gravely impersonal.
He, seeing this, thought that it certainly did a strange
thing to her face: it made her look like a frightened
girl.

'You know,' he said, watching her with more attention, 'Florence ain't never thought none of these niggers
around here was good enough for her.'

'I wonder,' she ventured, 'if she *ever* going to find a

man good enough for her. She so proud—look like she just won't let nobody come near her.'

'Yes,' he said, frowning, 'she so proud the Lord going to bring her low one day. You mark my words.'

'Yes,' she sighed, 'the Word sure do tell us that pride goes before destruction.'

'And a haughty spirit before a fall. That's the Word.'

'Yes,' and she smiled again, 'ain't no shelter against the Word of God, is there, Reverend? You is just got to be in it, that's all—'cause every word is true, and the gates of Hell ain't going to be able to stand against it.'

He smiled, watching her, and felt a great tenderness fill his heart. 'You just *stay* in the Word, little sister. The windows of Heaven going to open up and pour down blessings on you till you won't know where to put them.'

When she smiled now it was with a heightened joy. 'He done blessed me already, Reverend. He blessed me when He saved your soul and sent you out to preach His gospel.'

'Sister Deborah,' he said, slowly, 'all that sinful time —was you a-praying for me?'

Her tone dropped ever so slightly. 'We sure was, Reverend. Me and your mother, we was a-praying all the time.'

And he looked at her, full of gratitude and a sudden, wild conjecture: he had been real for her, she had watched him, and prayed for him during all those years when she, for him, had been nothing but a shadow. And she was praying for him still; he would have her prayers to aid him all his life long—he saw this, now, in her face. She said nothing, and she did not smile, only looked at him with her grave kindness, now a little questioning, a little shy.

'God bless you, sister,' he said at last.

It was during this dialogue, or hard on the heels of

it, that the town was subjected to a monster revival meeting. Evangelists from all the surrounding counties, from as far south as Florida and as far north as Chicago, came together in one place to break the bread of life. It was called the Twenty-Four Elders Revival Meeting, and it was the great occasion of that summer. For there were twenty-four of them, each one given his night to preach—to shine, as it were, before men, and to glorify his Heavenly Father. Of these twenty-four, all of them men of great experience and power, and some of them men of great fame, Gabriel, to his astonished pride, was asked to be one. This was a great, a heavy honour for one so young in the faith and in years—who had but only yesterday been lying, vomit-covered, in the gutters of sin—and Gabriel felt his heart shake with fear as this invitation came to him. Yet he felt that it was the hand of God that had called him out so early to prove himself before such mighty men.

He was to preach on the twelfth night. It was decided, in view of his possible failure to attract, to support him on either side with a nearly equal number of war horses. He would have, thus, the benefit of the storm they would certainly have stirred up before him; and should he fail to add substantially to the effect they had created, there would be others coming after him to obliterate his performance.

But Gabriel did not want his performance—the most important of his career so far, and on which so much depended—to be obliterated; he did not want to be dismissed as a mere boy who was scarcely ready to be counted in the race, much less to be considered a candidate for the prize. He fasted on his knees before God and did not cease, daily and nightly, to pray that God might work through him a mighty work and cause all men to see that, indeed, God's hand was on him, that he was the Lord's anointed.

Deborah, unasked, fasted with him, and prayed, and took his best black suit away, so that it would be clean and mended and freshly pressed for the great day. And she took it away again, immediately afterwards, so that it would be no less splendid on the Sunday of the great dinner that was officially to punctuate the revival. This Sunday was to be a feast day for everyone, but more especially for the twenty-four elders, who were, that day, to be gloriously banqueted at the saints' expense and labour.

On the evening when he was to preach, he and Deborah walked together to the great, lighted, lodge hall that had but lately held a dance band, and that the saints had rented for the duration of the revival. The service had already begun; lights spilled outward into the streets, music filled the air, and passers-by paused to listen and to peek in through the half-open doors. He wanted all of them to enter; he wanted to run through the streets and drag all sinners in to hear the Word of God. Yet, as they approached the doors, the fear held in check so many days and nights rose in him again, and he thought how he would stand to-night, so high, and all alone, to vindicate the testimony that had fallen from his lips, that God had called him to preach.

'Sister Deborah,' he said, suddenly, as they stood before the doors, 'you sit where I can see you?'

'I sure will do that, Reverend,' she said. 'You go on up there. Trust God.'

Without another word he turned, leaving her in the door, and walked up the long aisle to the pulpit. They were all there already, big, comfortable, ordained men; they smiled and nodded as he mounted the pulpit steps; and one of them said, nodding towards the congregation, which was as spirited as any evangelist could wish: 'Just getting these folks warmed up for you, boy. Want to see you make them *holler* to-night.'

He smiled in the instant before he knelt down at his throne-like chair to pray; and thought again, as he had been thinking for eleven nights, that there was about his elders an ease in the holy place, and a levity, that made *his* soul uneasy. While he sat, waiting, he saw that Deborah had found a seat in the very front of the congregation, just below the pulpit, and sat with her Bible folded on her lap.

When, at last, the Scripture lesson read, the testimonies in, the songs sung, the collection taken up, he was introduced—by the elder who had preached the night before—and found himself on his feet, moving towards the pulpit where the great Bible awaited him, and over that sheer drop the murmuring congregation; he felt a giddy terror that he stood so high, and with this, immediately, a pride and joy unspeakable that God had placed him there.

He did not begin with a 'shout' song, or with a fiery testimony; but in a dry, matter-of-fact voice, which trembled only a little, asked them to look with him at the sixth chapter of Isaiah, and the fifth verse; and he asked Deborah to read it aloud for him.

And she read, in a voice unaccustomedly strong: ' "Then said I, Woe is me! for I am undone; because I am a man of unclean lips, and I dwell in the midst of a people of unclean lips: for mine eyes have seen the King, the Lord of hosts." '

Silence filled the lodge hall after she had read this sentence. For a moment Gabriel was terrified by the eyes on him, and by the elders at his back, and could not think how to go on. Then he looked at Deborah, and began.

These words had been uttered by the prophet Isaiah, who had been called the Eagle-eyed because he had looked down the dark centuries and foreseen the birth of Christ. It was Isaiah also who had prophesied that a

man should be as a hiding-place from the wind and
tempest, Isaiah who had described the way of holiness,
saying that the parched ground should become a pool,
and the thirsty land springs of water: the very desert
should rejoice, and blossom as the rose. It was Isaiah
who had prophesied, saying: 'Unto us a child is born,
unto us a son is given; and the government shall be
upon His shoulder.' This was a man whom God had
raised in righteousness, whom God had chosen to do
many mighty works, yet this man, beholding the vision
of God's glory, had cried out: 'Woe is me!'

'Yes!' cried a woman. *'Tell it!'*

'There is a lesson for us all in this cry of Isaiah's, a
meaning for us all, a hard saying. If we have never cried
this cry then we have never known salvation; if we fail
to live with this cry, hourly, daily, in the midnight hour,
and in the light of the noonday sun, then salvation has
left us and our feet have laid hold on Hell. Yes, bless our
God forever! When we cease to tremble before Him we
have turned out of the way.'

'Amen!' cried a voice from far away. 'Amen! You
preach it, boy!'

He paused for only a moment and mopped his brow,
the heart within him great with fear and trembling, and
with power.

'For let us remember that the wages of sin is death;
that it is written, and cannot fail, the soul that sinneth,
it shall die. Let us remember that we are born in sin, in
sin did our mothers conceive us—sin reigns in all our
members, sin is the foul heart's natural liquid, sin looks
out of the eye, amen, and leads to lust, sin is in the hearing of the ear, and leads to folly, sin sits on the tongue,
and leads to murder. Yes! Sin is the only heritage of the
natural man, sin bequeathed us by our natural father,
that fallen Adam, whose apple sickens and will sicken all
generations living, and generations yet unborn! It was

sin that drove the son of the morning out of Heaven, sin that drove Adam out of Eden, sin that caused Cain to slay his brother, sin that built the tower of Babel, sin that caused the fire to fall on Sodom—sin, from the very foundations of the world, living and breathing in the heart of man, that causes women to bring forth their children in agony and darkness, bows down the backs of men with terrible labour, keeps the empty belly empty, keeps the table bare, sends our children, dressed in rags, out into the whore houses and dance halls of the world!'

'Amen! Amen!'

'Ah. Woe is me. Woe is *me*. Yes, beloved—there is no righteousness in man. All men's hearts are evil, all men are liars—only God is true. Hear David's cry: "The Lord is my rock, and my fortress, and my deliverer; my God, my strength, in whom I will trust; my buckler, and the horn of my salvation, and my high tower." Hear Job, sitting in dust and ashes, his children dead, his substance gone, surrounded by false comforters: "Yea, though He slay me, yet will I trust Him." And hear Paul, who had been Saul, a persecutor of the redeemed, struck down on the road to Damascus, and going forth to preach the gospel: "And if ye be Christ's, then ye are Abraham's seed, and heirs according to the promise!" '

'Oh, yes,' cried one of the elders, 'bless our God forever!'

'For God had a plan. He would not suffer the soul of man to die, but had prepared a plan for his salvation. In the beginning, way back there at the laying of the foundations of the world, God had a plan, *amen!*, to bring all flesh to a knowledge of the truth. In the beginning was the Word and the Word was with God and the Word was God—yes, and in Him was life, *hallelujah!* and this life was the light of men. Dearly beloved, when God saw how men's hearts waxed evil, how they turned aside, each to his own way, how they married and gave in marriage, how they feasted on ungodly meat and drink, and lusted, and blasphemed, and lifted up their hearts in sinful pride against the Lord —oh, then, the Son of God, the blessed lamb that taketh away the sins of the world, this Son of God who was the Word made flesh, the fulfilment of the promise—oh, then, He turned to His Father, crying: "Father, prepare me a body and I'll go down and redeem sinful man." '

'So *glad* this evening, praise the Lord!'

'Fathers, here to-night, have you ever had a son who went astray? Mothers, have you seen your daughters cut down in the pride and fullness of youth? Has any man here heard the command which came to Abraham, that he must make his son a living sacrifice on God's altar? Fathers, think of your sons, how you tremble for them, and try to lead them right, try to feed them so they'll grow up strong; think of your love for *your* son, and how any evil that befalls him cracks up the heart, and think of the pain that *God* has borne, sending down His only begotten Son, to dwell among men on the sinful earth, to be persecuted, to suffer, to bear the cross and *die*—not for His *own* sins, like our natural sons, but for the sins of *all* the world, to take away the sins of *all* the world—that we might have the joy bells ringing deep in our hearts to-night!'

'Praise Him!' cried Deborah, and he had never heard her voice so loud.

'Woe is me, for when God struck the sinner, the sinner's eyes were opened, and he saw himself in all his foulness naked before God's glory. Woe is me! For the moment of salvation is a blinding light, cracking down into the heart from Heaven—Heaven so high, and the sinner so low. *Woe is me!* For unless God raised the sinner, he would never rise again!'

'Yes, Lord! I was there!'

How many here to-night had fallen where Isaiah fell?

How many had cried—as Isaiah cried? How many could testify, as Isaiah testified, 'Mine eyes have seen the King, the Lord of hosts'? Ah, whosoever failed to have this testimony should never see His face, but should be told, on that great day: 'Depart from me, ye that work iniquity,' and be hurled for ever into the lake of fire prepared for Satan and all his angels. Oh, would the sinner rise to-night, and walk the little mile to his salvation, here to the mercy seat?

And he waited. Deborah watched him with a calm, strong smile. He looked out over their faces, their faces all upturned to him. He saw joy in those faces, and holy excitement, and belief—and they all looked up to him. Then, far in the back, a boy rose, a tall, dark boy, his white shirt open at the neck and torn, his trousers dusty and shabby and held up with an old necktie, and he looked across the immeasurable, dreadful, breathing distance up to Gabriel, and began to walk down the long, bright aisle. Someone cried: 'Oh, bless the Lord!' and tears filled Gabriel's eyes. The boy knelt, sobbing, at the mercy seat, and the church began to sing.

Then Gabriel turned away, knowing that this night he had run well, and that God had used him. The elders all were smiling, and one of them took him by the hand, and said: 'That was mighty fine, boy. Mighty fine.'

Then came the Sunday of the spectacular dinner that was to end the revival—for which dinner, Deborah and all the other women, had baked, roasted, fried, and boiled for many days beforehand. He jokingly suggested, to repay her a little for her contention that he was the best preacher of the revival, that she was the best cook among the women. She timidly suggested that he was here at a flattering disadvantage, for she had heard all of the preachers, but he had not, for a very long time, eaten another woman's cooking.

When the Sunday came, and he found himself once

more among the elders, about to go to the table, Gabriel
felt a drop in his happy, proud anticipation. He was not
comfortable with these men—that was it—it was difficult for him to accept them as his elders and betters in
the faith. They seemed to him so lax, so nearly worldly;
they were not like those holy prophets of old who grew
thin and naked in the service of the Lord. These, God's
ministers, had indeed grown fat, and their dress was
rich and various. They had been in the field so long that
they did not tremble before God any more. They took
God's power as their due, as something that made the
more exciting their own assured, special atmosphere.
They each had, it seemed, a bagful of sermons often
preached; and knew, in the careless lifting of an eye,
which sermon to bring to which congregation. Though
they preached with great authority, and brought souls
low before the altar—like so many ears of corn lopped
off by the hired labourer in his daily work—they did not
give God the glory, nor count it as glory at all; they
might as easily have been, Gabriel thought, highly paid
circus-performers, each with his own special dazzling
gift. Gabriel discovered that they spoke, jokingly, of the
comparative number of souls each of them had saved, as
though they were keeping score in a pool-room. And
this offended him and frightened him. He did not want,
ever, to hold the gift of God so lightly.

They, the ministers, were being served alone in the
upper room of the lodge hall—the less-specialized workers
in Christ's vineyard were being fed at a table downstairs—and the women kept climbing up and down the
stairs with loaded platters to see that they ate their fill.
Deborah was one of the serving-women, and though she
did not speak, and despite his discomfort, he nearly burst
each time she entered the room, with the pride he knew
she felt to see him sitting there, so serene and manly,
among all these celebrated others, in the severe black

and white that was his uniform. And if only, he felt, his mother could be there to see—her Gabriel, mounted so high!

But, near the end of the dinner, when the women had brought up the pies, and coffee, and cream, and when the talk around the table had become more jolly and more good-naturedly loose than ever, the door had but barely closed behind the women when one of the elders, a heavy, cheery, sandy-haired man, whose face, testifying no doubt to the violence of his beginnings, was splashed with freckles like dried blood, laughed and said, referring to Deborah, that there was a holy woman, all right! She had been choked so early on white men's milk, and it remained so sour in her belly yet, that she would never be able, now, to find a nigger who would let her taste his richer, sweeter substance. Everyone at the table roared, but Gabriel felt his blood turn cold that God's ministers should be guilty of such abominable levity, and that that woman sent by God to comfort him, and without whose support he might already have fallen by the wayside, should be held in such dishonour. They felt, he knew, that among themselves a little rude laughter could do no harm; they were too deeply rooted in the faith to be made to fall by such an insignificant tap from Satan's hammer. But he stared at their boisterous, laughing faces, and felt that they would have much to answer for on the day of judgment, for they were stumbling-stones in the path of the true believer.

Now the sandy-haired man, struck by Gabriel's bitter, astounded face, bit his laughter off, and said: 'What's the matter, son? I hope I ain't said nothing to offend you?'

'She read the Bible for you the night you preached, didn't she?' asked another of the elders, in a conciliatory tone.

'That woman,' said Gabriel, feeling a roaring in his head, 'is my sister in the Lord.'

'Well, Elder Peters here, he just didn't know that,' said someone else. 'He sure didn't mean no harm.'

'Now, you ain't going to get mad?' asked Elder Peters, kindly—yet there remained, to Gabriel's fixed attention, something mocking in his face and voice. 'You ain't going to spoil our little dinner?'

'I don't think it's right,' said Gabriel, 'to talk evil about *no*body. The Word tell me it ain't right to hold nobody up to scorn.'

'Now you just remember,' Elder Peters said, as kindly as before, 'you's talking to your *elders*.'

'Then it seem to me,' he said, astonished at his boldness, 'that if I got to look to you for a example, you ought to *be* a example.'

'Now, you know,' said someone else, jovially, 'you ain't fixing to make that woman your wife or nothing like that—so ain't no need to get all worked up and spoil our little gathering. Elder Peters didn't mean no harm. If *you* don't never say nothing worse than that, you can count yourself already up there in the Kingdom with the chosen.'

And at this a small flurry of laughter swept over the table; they went back to their eating and drinking, as though the matter were finished.

Yet Gabriel felt that he had surprised them; he had found them out and they were a little ashamed and confounded before his purity. And he understood suddenly the words of Christ, where it was written: 'Many are called but few are chosen.' Yes, and he looked around the table, already jovial again, but rather watchful now, too, of him—and he wondered who, of all these, would sit in glory at the right hand of the Father?

And then, as he sat there, remembering again Elder Peters's boisterous, idle remark, this remark shook together in him all those shadowy doubts and fears, those hesitations and tendernesses, which were his in

relation to Deborah, and the sum of which he now
realized was his certainty that there was in that relation-
ship something fore-ordained. It came to him that, as the
Lord had given him Deborah, to help him to stand, so
the Lord had sent him to her, to raise her up, to release
her from that dishonour which was hers in the eyes of
men. And this idea filled him, in a moment, wholly, with
the intensity of a vision: What better woman could be
found? *She* was not like the mincing daughters of Zion!
She was not to be seen prancing lewdly through the
streets, eyes sleepy and mouth half-open with lust, or
to be found mewing under midnight fences, uncovered,
uncovering some black boy's hanging curse! No, their
married bed would be holy, and their children would continue the line of the faithful, a royal line. And, fired with
this, a baser fire stirred in him also, rousing a slumbering
fear, and he remembered (as the table, the ministers, the
dinner, and the talk all burst in on him again) that Paul
had written: 'It is better to marry than to burn.'

Yet, he thought, he would hold his peace awhile; he
would seek to know more clearly the Lord's mind in this
matter. For he remembered how much older she was
than he—eight years; and he tried to imagine, for the
first time in his life, that dishonour to which Deborah
had been forced so many years ago by white men: her
skirts above her head, her secrecy discovered—by white
men. How many? How had she borne it? Had she
screamed? Then he thought (but it did not really trouble
him, for if Christ to save him could be crucified, he, for
Christ's greater glory, could well be mocked) of what
smiles would be occasioned, what filthy conjecture,
barely sleeping now, would mushroom upward overnight like Jonah's gourd, when people heard that he and
Deborah were going to be married. She, who had been
the living proof and witness of their daily shame, and
who had become their holy fool—and he, who had been

the untamable despoiler of their daughters, and thief of
their women, their walking prince of darkness! And he
smiled, watching the elders' well-fed faces and their
grinding jaws—unholy pastors all, unfaithful stewards;
he prayed that he would never be so fat, or so lascivious,
but that God should work through him a mighty work:
to ring, it might be, through ages yet unborn, as sweet,
solemn, mighty proof of His everlasting love and mercy.
He trembled with the presence that surrounded him
now; he could scarcely keep his seat. He felt that light
shone down on him from Heaven, on him, the chosen;
he felt as Christ must have felt in the temple, facing His
so utterly confounded elders; and he lifted up his eyes,
not caring for their glances, or their clearing of throats,
and the silence that abruptly settled over the table,
thinking: 'Yes. God works in many mysterious ways
His wonders to perform.'

'Sister Deborah,' he said, much later that night as he
was walking her to her door, 'the Lord done laid something on my heart and I want you to help me to pray
over it and ask Him to lead me right.'

He wondered if she could divine what was in his
mind. In her face there was nothing but patience, as she
turned to him, and said: 'I'm praying all the time. But
I sure will pray extra hard this week if you want me to.'

And it was during this praying time that Gabriel had
a dream.

He could never afterwards remember how the dream
began, what had happened, or who he was with in
the dream; or any details at all. For there were really
two dreams, the first like a dim, blurred, infernal
foreshadowing of the second. Of this first dream, the
overture, he remembered only the climate, which had
been like the climate of his day—heavy, with danger
everywhere, Satan at his shoulder trying to bring him
down. That night as he tried to sleep, Satan sent demons

to his bedside—old friends he had had, but whom he saw no more, and drinking and gambling scenes that he had thought would never rise to haunt him again, and women he had known. And the women were so real that he could nearly touch them; and he heard again their laughter and their sighs, and felt beneath his hands again their thighs and breasts. Though he closed his eyes and called on Jesus—calling over and over again the name of Jesus—his pagan body stiffened and flamed and the women laughed. And they asked him why he remained in this narrow bed alone when they waited for him; why he had bound his body in the armour of chastity while they sighed and turned on their beds for him. And he sighed and turned, every movement torture, each touch of the sheets a lewd caress—and more abominable, then, in his imagination, than any caress he had received in life. And he clenched his fists and began to plead the blood, to exorcise the hosts of Hell, but even this motion was like another motion, and at length he fell on his knees to pray. By and by he fell into a troublous sleep—it seemed that he was going to be stoned, and then he was in battle, and then shipwrecked in the water—and suddenly he awoke, knowing that he must have dreamed, for his loins were covered with his own white seed.

Then, trembling, he got out of bed again and washed himself. It was a warning, and he knew it, and he seemed to see before him the pit dug by Satan—deep and silent, waiting for him. He thought of the dog returned to his vomit, of the man who had been cleansed, and who fell, and who was possessed by seven devils, the last state of that man being worse than his first. And he thought at last, kneeling by his cold bedside, but with the heart within him almost too sick for prayer, of Onan, who had scattered his seed on the ground rather than continue his brother's line. *Out of the house of David, the son of*

*Abraham.* And he called again on the name of Jesus; and fell asleep again.

And he dreamed that he was in a cold, high place, like a mountain. He was high, so high that he walked in mist and cloud, but before him stretched the blank ascent, the steep side of the mountain. A voice said: 'Come higher.' And he began to climb. After a little, clinging to the rock, he found himself with only clouds above him and mist below—and he knew that beyond the wall of mist reigned fire. His feet began to slip; pebbles and rocks began ringing beneath his feet; he looked up, trembling, in terror of death, and he cried: 'Lord, I can't come no higher.' But the voice repeated after a moment, quiet and strong and impossible to deny: 'Come on, son. Come higher.' Then he knew that, if he would not fall to death, he must obey the voice. He began to climb again, and his feet slipped again; and when he thought that he would fall there suddenly appeared before him green, spiny leaves; and he caught on to the leaves, which hurt his hand, and the voice said again: 'Come higher.' And so Gabriel climbed, the wind blowing through his clothes, and his feet began to bleed, and his hands were bleeding; and still he climbed, and he felt that his back was breaking; and his legs were growing numb and they were trembling, and he could not control them; and still before him there was only cloud, and below him the roaring mist. How long he climbed in this dream of his, he did not know. Then, of a sudden, the clouds parted, he felt the sun like a crown of glory, and he was in a peaceful field.

He began to walk. Now he was wearing long, white robes. He heard singing: 'Walked in the valley, it looked so fine, I asked my Lord was all this mine.' But he knew that it was his. A voice said: 'Follow me.' And he walked, and he was again on the edge of a high place, but bathed and blessed and glorified in the blazing sun, so that he stood like God, all golden, and looked down, down, at the long race he had run, at the steep side of the mountain he had climbed. And now up this mountain, in white robes, singing, the elect came. 'Touch them not,' the voice said, 'my seal is on them.' And Gabriel turned and fell on his face, and the voice said again: 'So shall thy seed be.' Then he awoke. Morning was at the window, and he blessed God, lying on his bed, tears running down his face, for the vision he had seen.

When he went to Deborah and told her that the Lord had led him to ask her to be his wife, his holy helpmeet, she looked at him for a moment in what seemed to be speechless terror. He had never seen such an expression on her face before. For the first time since he had known her he touched her, putting his hands on her shoulders, thinking what untender touch these shoulders had once known, and how she would be raised now in honour. And he asked: 'You ain't scared, is you, Sister Deborah? You ain't got nothing to be scared of?'

Then she tried to smile, and began, instead, to weep. With a movement at once violent and hesitant, she let her head fall forward on his breast.

'No,' she brought out, muffled in his arms, 'I ain't scared.' But she did not stop weeping.

He stroked her coarse, bowed head. 'God bless you, little girl,' he said, helplessly. 'God bless you.'

The silence in the church ended when Brother Elisha, kneeling near the piano, cried out and fell backward under the power of the Lord. Immediately, two or three others cried out also, and a wind, a foretaste of that great downpouring they awaited, swept the church. With this cry, and the echoing cries, the tarry service moved from its first stage of steady murmuring, broken by moans and now and again an isolated cry, into that stage of tears and groaning, of calling aloud and singing, which

was like the labour of a woman about to be delivered of
her child. On this threshing-floor the child was the soul
that struggled to the light, and it was the church that
was in labour, that did not cease to push and pull, calling
on the name of Jesus. When Brother Elisha cried out
and fell back, crying, Sister McCandless rose and stood
over him to help him to pray. For the rebirth of the soul
was perpetual; only rebirth every hour could stay the
hand of Satan.

Sister Price began to sing:

> *'I want to go through, Lord,*
> *I want to go through.*
> *Take me through, Lord,*
> *Take me through.'*

A lone voice, joined by others, among them, waver-
ingly, the voice of John. Gabriel recognized the voice.
When Elisha cried, Gabriel was brought back in an
instant to this present time and place, fearing that it
was John he heard, that it was John who lay astonished
beneath the power of the Lord. He nearly looked up and
turned around; but then he knew it was Elisha, and his
fear departed.

> *'Have your way, Lord,*
> *Have your way.'*

Neither of his sons was here to-night, had ever cried
on the threshing-floor. One had been dead for nearly
fourteen years—dead in a Chicago tavern, a knife kicking in his throat. And the living son, the child, Roy, was
headlong already, and hardhearted: he lay at home,
silent now, and bitter against his father, a bandage on
his forehead. They were not here. Only the son of the
bond-woman stood where the rightful heir should stand.

> *'I'll obey, Lord,*
> *I'll obey.'*

He felt that he should rise and pray over Elisha—when a man cried out, it was right that another man should be his intercessor. And he thought how gladly he would rise, and with what power he would pray if it were only his son who lay crying on the floor to-night. But he remained, bowed low, on his knees. Each cry that came from the fallen Elisha tore through him. He heard the cry of his dead son and his living son; one who cried in the pit forever, beyond the hope of mercy; and one who would cry one day when mercy would be finished.

Now Gabriel tried, with the testimony he had held, with all the signs of His favour that God had shown him, to put himself between the living son and the darkness that waited to devour him. The living son had cursed him—*bastard*—and his heart was far from God; it could not be that the curse he had heard to-night falling from Roy's lips was but the curse repeated, so far, so long resounding, that the mother of his first son had uttered as she thrust the infant from her—herself immediately departing, this curse yet on her lips, into eternity. Her curse had devoured the first Royal; he had been begotten in sin, and he had perished in sin; it was God's punishment, and it was just. But Roy had been begotten in the marriage bed, the bed that Paul described as holy, and it was to him the Kingdom had been promised. It could not be that the living son was cursed for the sins of his father; for God, after much groaning, after many years, had given him a sign to make him know he was forgiven. And yet, it came to him that this living son, this headlong, living Royal, might be cursed for the sin of his mother, whose sin had never been truly repented; for that the living proof of her sin, he who knelt to-night, a very interloper among the saints, stood between her soul and God.

Yes, she was hardhearted, stiff-necked, and hard to

bend, this Elizabeth whom he had married: she had not seemed so, years ago, when the Lord had moved in his heart to lift her up, she and her nameless child, who bore his name to-day. And he was exactly like her, silent, watching, full of evil pride—they would be cast out, one day, into the outer darkness.

Once he had asked Elizabeth—they had been married a long while, Roy was a baby, and she was big with Sarah—if she had truly repented of her sin.

And she had looked at him, and said: 'You done asked me that before. And I done told you, yes.'

But he did not believe her; and he asked: 'You mean you wouldn't do it again? If you was back there, where you was, like you was then—would you do it again?'

She looked down; then, with impatience, she looked into his eyes again: 'Well, if I was back there, Gabriel, and I was the same girl! . . .'

There was a long silence, while she waited. Then, almost unwillingly, he asked: 'And . . . would you let *him* be born again?'

She answered, steadily: 'I know you ain't asking me to say I'm sorry I brought Johnny in the world. Is you?' And when he did not answer: 'And listen, Gabriel. I ain't going to let you *make* me sorry. Not you, nor nothing, nor nobody in this world. We is got *two* children, Gabriel, and soon we's going to have *three*; and I ain't going to make no difference amongst them and you ain't going to make none neither.'

But how could there not be a difference between the son of a weak, proud woman and some careless boy, and the son that God had promised him, who would carry down the joyful line his father's name, and who would work until the day of the second coming to bring about His Father's Kingdom? For God had promised him this so many years ago, and he had lived only for this— forsaking the world and its pleasures, and the joys of his own life, he had tarried all these bitter years to see the promise of the Lord fulfilled. He had let Esther die, and Royal had died, and Deborah had died barren—but he had held on to the promise; he had walked before God in true repentance and waited on the promise. And the time of fulfilment was surely at hand. He had only to possess his soul in patience and wait before the Lord.

And his mind, dwelling bitterly on Elizabeth, yet moved backwards to consider once again Esther, who had been the mother of the first Royal. And he saw her, with the dumb, pale, startled ghosts of joy and desire hovering in him yet, a thin, vivid, dark-eyed girl, with something Indian in her cheekbones and her carriage and her hair; looking at him with that look in which were blended mockery, affection, desire, impatience, and scorn; dressed in the flame-like colours that, in fact, she had seldom worn, but that he always thought of her as wearing. She was associated in his mind with flame; with fiery leaves in the autumn, and the fiery sun going down in the evening over the farthest hill, and with the eternal fires of Hell.

She had come to town very shortly after he and Deborah were married, and she took a job as serving-girl with the same white family for which he worked. He saw her, therefore, all the time. Young men were always waiting for her at the back door when her work was done: Gabriel used to watch her walk off in the dusk on a young man's arm, and their voices and their laughter floated back to him like a mockery of his condition. He knew that she lived with her mother and stepfather, sinful people, given to drinking and gambling and ragtime music and the blues, who never, except at Christmas-time or Easter, appeared in church.

He began to pity her, and one day when he was to preach in the evening he invited her to come to church. This invitation marked the first time she ever really looked at him—he realized it then, and was to remember that look for many days and nights.

'You really going to preach to-night? A pretty man like you?'

'With the Lord's help,' he said, with a gravity so extreme that it was almost hostility. At the same time, at her look and voice something leaped in him that he thought had been put down for ever.

'Well, I be mighty delighted,' she said after a moment, seeming to have briefly regretted the impetuosity that had led her to call him a 'pretty' man.

'Can you make yourself free to come to-night?' he could not prevent himself from asking.

And she grinned, delighted at what she took to be an oblique compliment. 'Well, I don't know, Reverend. But I'll try.'

When the day was ended, she disappeared on the arm of yet another boy. He did not believe that she would come. And this so strangely depressed him that he could scarcely speak to Deborah at dinner, and they walked all the way to church in silence. Deborah watched him out of the corner of her eye, as was her silent and exasperating habit. It was her way of conveying respect for his calling; and she would have said, had it ever occurred to him to tax her with it, that she did not wish to distract him when the Lord had laid something on his heart. To-night, since he was to preach, it could not be doubted that the Lord was speaking more than usual; and it behoved her, therefore, as the helpmeet of the Lord's anointed, as the caretaker, so to speak, of the sanctified temple, to keep silence. Yet, in fact, he would have liked to talk. He would have liked to ask her—so many things; to have listened to her voice, and watched her face while she told him of her day, her hopes, her doubts, her life, and her love. But he and Deborah never talked. The voice to which he listened in his mind, and

the face he watched with so much love and care, belonged
not to Deborah, but to Esther. Again he felt this strange
chill in him, implying disaster and delight: and then he
hoped that she would not come, that something would
happen that would make it impossible for him ever to
see her again.

She came, however; late, just before the pastor was
about to present the speaker of the hour to the congregation. She did not come alone, but had brought her
mother with her—promising what spectacle Gabriel
could not imagine, nor could he imagine how she had
escaped her young man of the evening. But she had; she
was here; she preferred, then, to hear him preach the
gospel than to linger with others in carnal delight. She
was here, and his heart was uplifted; something exploded
in his heart when the opening door revealed her, smiling
faintly and with eyes downcast, moving directly to a seat
in the back of the congregation. She did not look at him
at all, and yet he knew immediately that she had seen
him. And in a moment he imagined her, because of the
sermon that he would preach, on her knees before the
altar, and then her mother and that gambling, loud-
talking stepfather of hers, brought by Esther into the
service of the Lord. Heads turned when they came in,
and a murmur, barely audible, of astonishment and
pleasure swept over the church. Here were sinners,
come to hear the Word of God.

And, indeed, from their apparel the sinfulness of their
lives was evident: Esther wore a blue hat, trimmed with
many ribbons, and a heavy, wine-red dress; and her
mother, massive, and darker than Esther, wore great
gold ear-rings in her pierced ears and had that air,
vaguely disreputable, and hurriedly dressed, of women
he had known in sporting-houses. They sat in the back,
rigid and uncomfortable, like sisters of sin, like a living
defiance of the drab sanctity of the saints. Deborah

turned to look at them, and in that moment Gabriel saw, as though for the first time, how black and how bony was this wife of his, and how wholly undesirable. Deborah looked at him with a watchful silence in her look; he felt the hand that held his Bible begin to sweat and tremble; he thought of the joyless groaning of their marriage bed; and he hated her.

Then the pastor rose. While he spoke, Gabriel closed his eyes. He felt the words that he was about to speak fly from him; he felt the power of God go out of him. Then the voice of the pastor ceased, and Gabriel opened his eyes in the silence and found that all eyes were on him. And so he rose and faced the congregation.

'Dearly beloved in the Lord,' he began—but her eyes were on him, that strange, that mocking light— 'let us bow our heads in prayer.' And he closed his eyes and bowed his head.

His later memory of this sermon was like the memory of a storm. From the moment that he raised his head and looked out over their faces again, his tongue was loosed and he was filled with the power of the Holy Ghost. Yes, the power of the Lord was on him that night, and he preached a sermon that was remembered in camp-meetings and in cabins, and that set a standard for visiting evangelists for a generation to come. Years later, when Esther and Royal and Deborah were dead, and Gabriel was leaving the South, people remembered this sermon and the gaunt, possessed young man who had preached it.

He took his text from the eighteenth chapter of the second book of Samuel, the story of the young Ahimaaz who ran too soon to bring the tidings of battle to King David. For, before he ran, he was asked by Joab: 'Wherefore wilt thou run, my son, seeing that thou hast no tidings ready?' And when Ahimaaz reached King David, who yearned to know the fate of his headlong son, Absalom, he could only say: 'I saw a great tumult but I knew not what it was.'

And this was the story of all those who failed to wait on the counsel of the Lord; who made themselves wise in their own conceit and ran before they had the tidings ready. This was the story of innumerable shepherds who failed, in their arrogance, to feed the hungry sheep; of many a father and mother who gave to their children not bread but a stone, who offered not the truth of God but the tinsel of this world. This was not belief but unbelief, not humility but pride: there worked in the heart of such a one the same desire that had hurled the son of the morning from Heaven to the depths of Hell, the desire to overturn the appointed times of God, and to wrest from Him who held all power in His hands power not meet for men. Oh, yes, they had seen it, each brother and sister beneath the sound of his voice to-night, and they had seen the destruction caused by a so lamentable unripeness! Babies, bawling, fatherless, for bread, and girls in the gutters, sick with sin, and young men bleeding in the frosty fields. Yes, and there were those who cried—they had heard it, in their homes, and on the street corner, and from the very pulpit—that they should wait no longer, despised and rejected and spat on as they were, but should rise to-day and bring down the mighty, establishing the vengeance that God had claimed. But blood cried out for blood, as the blood of Abel cried out from the ground. Not for nothing was it written: 'He that believeth will not make haste.' Oh, but sometimes the road was rocky. Did they think sometimes that God forgot? Oh, fall on your knees and pray for patience; fall on your knees and pray for faith; fall on your knees and pray for overcoming power to be ready on the day of His soon appearing to receive the crown of life. For God did not forget, no word proceeding from his mouth could fail. Better to wait, like Job, through all the days of our appointed time until our change comes than to rise up, unready, before God speaks. For if we but wait humbly before Him, He will speak glad tidings to our souls; if we but wait our change will come, and that in an instant, in the twinkling of an eye—we will be changed one day from this corruption into incorruptibility forever, caught up with Him beyond the clouds. And these are the tidings we now must bear to all the nations: another son of David has hung from a tree, and he who knows not the meaning of that tumult shall be damned forever in Hell! Brother, sister, you may run, but the day is coming when the King will ask: 'What are the tidings that you bear?' And what will you say on that great day if you know not of the death of His Son?

'Is there a soul here to-night'—tears were on his face and he stood above them with arms outstretched—'who knows not the meaning of that tumult? Is there a soul here to-night who wants to talk to Jesus? Who wants to wait before the Lord, amen, until He speaks? Until He makes to ring in your soul, amen, the glad tidings of salvation? Oh, brothers and sisters'—and still she did not rise; but only watched him from far away—'the time is running out. One day He's coming back to judge the nations, to take His children, hallelujah, to their rest. They tell me, bless God, that two shall be working in the fields, and one shall be taken and the other left. Two shall be lying, amen, in bed, and one shall be taken and the other left. He's coming, beloved, like a thief in the night, and no man knows the hour of His coming. It's going to be too late then to cry: "Lord, have mercy." Now is the time to make yourself ready, now, amen, to-night, before His altar. Won't somebody come to-night? Won't somebody say No to Satan and give their life to the Lord?'

But she did not rise, only looked at him and looked about her with a bright, pleased interest, as though she were at a theatre and were waiting to see what improbable delights would next be offered her. He somehow knew that she would never rise and walk that long aisle to the mercy seat. And this filled him for a moment with a holy rage—that she stood, so brazen, in the congregation of the righteous and refused to bow her head.

He said amen, and blessed them, and turned away, and immediately the congregation began to sing. Now, again, he felt drained and sick; he was soaking wet and he smelled the odour of his own body. Deborah, singing and beating her tambourine in the front of the congregation, watched him. He felt suddenly like a helpless child. He wanted to hide himself for ever and never cease from crying.

Esther and her mother left during the singing—they had come, then, only to hear him preach. He could not imagine what they were saying or thinking now. And he thought of to-morrow, when he would have to see her again.

'Ain't that the little girl what works at the same place with you?' Deborah asked him on the way home.

'Yes,' he said. Now he did not feel like talking. He wanted to get home and take his wet clothes off and sleep.

'She mighty pretty,' said Deborah. 'I ain't never seen her in church before.'

He said nothing.

'Was it you invited her to come out to-night?' she asked, after a bit.

'Yes,' he said. 'I didn't think the Word of God could do her no harm.'

Deborah laughed. 'Don't look like it, does it? She walked out just as cool and sinful as she come in—she and that mother of her'n. And you preached a mighty fine sermon. Look like she just ain't thinking about the Lord.'

'Folks ain't got no time for the Lord,' he said, 'one day *He* ain't going to have no time for *them*.'

When they got home she offered to make him a hot cup of tea, but he refused. He undressed in silence— which she again respected—and got into bed. At length, she lay beside him like a burden laid down at evening which must be picked up once more in the morning.

The next morning Esther said to him, coming into the yard while he was chopping wood for the woodpile: 'Good morning, Reverend. I sure didn't look to see you to-day. I reckoned you'd be all wore out after *that* sermon—does you always preach as hard as that?'

He paused briefly with the axe in the air; then he turned again, bringing the axe down. 'I preach the way the Lord leads me, sister,' he said.

She retreated a little in the face of his hostility. 'Well,' she said in a different tone, 'it was a mighty fine sermon. Me and Mama was mighty glad we come out.'

He left the axe buried in the wood, for splinters flew and he was afraid one might strike her. 'You and your ma—you don't get out to service much?'

'Lord, Reverend,' she wailed, 'look like we just ain't got the time. Mama work so hard all week she just want to lie up in bed on Sunday. And she like me,' she added quickly, after a pause, 'to keep her company.'

Then he looked directly at her. 'Does you really mean to say, sister, that you ain't got no time for the Lord? No time at all?'

'Reverend,' she said, looking at him with the daring defiance of a threatened child, 'I does my best. I really does. Ain't everybody got to have the same spirit.'

And he laughed shortly. 'Ain't but one spirit you got to have—and that's the spirit of the Lord.'

'Well,' she said, 'that spirit ain't got to work in everybody the same, seems to me.'

Then they were silent, each quite vividly aware that they had reached an impasse. After a moment he turned and picked up the axe again. 'Well, you go along, sister. I'm praying for you.'

Something struggled in her face then, as she stood for yet a moment more and watched him—a mixture of fury and amusement; it reminded him of the expression he had often found on the face of Florence. And it was like the look on the faces of the elders during that far-off and so momentous Sunday dinner. He was too angry, while she thus stared at him, to trust himself to speak. Then she shrugged, the mildest, most indifferent gesture he had ever seen, and smiled. 'I'm mighty obliged to you, Reverend,' she said. Then she went into the house.

This was the first time they spoke in the yard, a frosty morning. There was nothing in that morning to warn him of what was coming. She offended him because she was so brazen in her sins, that was all; and he prayed for her soul, which would one day find itself naked and speechless before the judgment bar of Christ. Later, she told him that he had pursued her, that his eyes had left her not a moment's peace. 'That weren't no reverend looking at me them mornings in the yard,' she had said. 'You looked at me just like a man, like a man what hadn't never heard of the Holy Ghost.' But he believed that the Lord had laid her like a burden on his heart. And he carried her in his heart; he prayed for her and exhorted her, while there was yet time to bring her soul to God.

But she had not been thinking about God; though she accused him of lusting after her in his heart, it was she who, when she looked at him, insisted on seeing not God's minister but a 'pretty man.' On her tongue the very title of his calling became a mark of disrespect.

It began on an evening when he was to preach, when they were alone in the house. The people of the house had gone away for three days to visit relatives; Gabriel had driven them to the railroad station after supper, leaving Esther clearing up the kitchen. When he came back to lock up the house, he found Esther waiting for him on the porch steps.

'I didn't think I'd better leave,' she said, 'till you got back. I ain't got no keys to lock up this house, and white folks is so funny. I don't want them blaming me if something's missing.'

He realized immediately that she had been drinking—she was not drunk, but there was whisky on her breath. And this, for some reason, caused a strange excitement to stir in him.

'That was mighty thoughtful, sister,' he said, staring hard at her to let her know that he knew she had been drinking. She met his stare with a calm, bold smile, a smile mocking innocence, so that her face was filled with the age-old cunning of a woman.

He started past her into the house; then, without thinking, and without looking at her, he offered: 'If you ain't got nobody waiting for you I'll walk you a piece on your way home.'

'No,' she said, 'ain't nobody waiting for me this evening, Reverend, thank you kindly.'

He regretted making his offer almost as soon as it was made; he had been certain that she was about to rush off to some trysting-place or other, and he had merely wished to be corroborated. Now, as they walked together into the house, he became terribly aware of her youthful, vivid presence, of her lost condition; and at the same time the emptiness and silence of the house warned him that he was alone with danger.

'You just sit down in the kitchen,' he said. 'I be as quick as I can.'

But his speech was harsh in his own ears, and he could not face her eyes. She sat down at the table, smiling, to wait for him. He tried to do everything as quickly as possible, the shuttering of windows, and locking of doors. But his fingers were stiff and slippery; his heart was in his mouth. And it came to him that he was barring every exit to this house, except the exit through the kitchen, where Esther sat.

When he entered the kitchen again she had moved, and now stood in the doorway, looking out, holding a glass in her hand. It was a moment before he realized that she had helped herself to more of the master's whisky.

She turned at his step, and he stared at her, and at the glass she held, with wrath and horror.

'I just thought,' she said, almost entirely unabashed, 'that I'd have me a little drink while I was waiting, Reverend. But I didn't figure on you catching me at it.'

She swallowed the last of her drink and moved to the sink to rinse out the glass. She gave a little, ladylike cough as she swallowed—he could not be sure whether this cough was genuine or in mockery of him.

'I reckon,' he said, malevolently, 'you is just made up your mind to serve Satan all your days.'

'I done made up my mind,' she answered, 'to live all I can *while* I can. If that's a sin, well, I'll go on down to Hell and pay for it. But don't *you* fret, Reverend—it ain't your soul.'

He moved and stood next to her, full of anger.

'Girl,' he said, 'don't you believe God? God don't lie—and He says, plain as I'm talking to you, the soul that sinneth, it shall *die*.'

She sighed. 'Reverend, look like to me you'd get tired, all the time beating on poor little Esther, trying to make Esther something she ain't. I just don't feel it *here*,' she said, and put one hand on her breast. 'Now, what you going to do? Don't you know I'm a woman grown, and I ain't fixing to change?'

He wanted to weep. He wanted to reach out and hold

her back from the destruction she so ardently pursued—
to fold her in him, and hide her until the wrath of God
was past. At the same time there rose to his nostrils
again her whisky-laden breath, and beneath this, faint,
intimate, the odour of her body. And he began to feel
like a man in a nightmare, who stands in the path of
oncoming destruction, who must move quickly—but who
cannot move. 'Jesus, Jesus, Jesus,' rang over and over
again in his mind, like a bell—as he moved closer to
her, undone by her breath, and her wide, angry, mocking
eyes.

'You know right well,' he whispered, shaking with
fury, 'you know right well why I keep after you—why
I keep after you like I do.'

'No, I don't,' she answered, refusing, with a small
shake of the head, to credit his intensity. 'I sure don't
know why you can't let Esther have her little whisky,
and have her little ways without all the time trying to
make her miserable.'

He sighed with exasperation, feeling himself begin
to tremble. 'I just don't want to see you go down, girl,
I don't want you to wake up one fine morning sorry
for all the sin you done, old, and all by yourself, with
nobody to respect you.'

But he heard himself speaking, and it made him
ashamed. He wanted to have done with talking and
leave this house—in a moment they would leave, and
the nightmare would be over.

'Reverend,' she said, 'I ain't done nothing that I'm
ashamed of, and I hope I *don't* do nothing I'm ashamed
of, ever.'

At the word 'Reverend,' he wanted to strike her; he
reached out instead and took both her hands in his. And
now they looked directly at each other. There was
surprise in her look, and a guarded triumph; he was
aware that their bodies were nearly touching and that

he should move away. But he did not move—he could
not move.

'But I can't help it,' she said, after a moment, maliciously teasing, 'if you done things that *you's* ashamed
of, Reverend.'

He held on to her hands as though he were in the
middle of the sea and her hands were the lifeline that
would drag him in to shore. 'Jesus, Jesus, Jesus,' he
prayed, 'oh, Jesus, Jesus. Help me to stand.' He thought
that he was pulling back against her hands—but he was
pulling her to him. And he saw in her eyes now a look
that he had not seen for many a long day and night, a
look that was never in Deborah's eyes.

'*Yes*, you know,' he said, 'why I'm all the time worrying about you—why I'm all the time miserable when I
look at you.'

'But you ain't never told me none of this,' she said.

One hand moved to her waist, and lingered there. The
tips of her breasts touched his coat, burning in like acid
and closing his throat. Soon it would be too late; he
wanted it to be too late. That river, his infernal need,
rose, flooded, sweeping him forward as though he were
a long-drowned corpse.

'*You* know,' he whispered, and touched her breasts
and buried his face in her neck.

So he had fallen: for the first time since his conversion,
for the last time in his life. Fallen: he and Esther in the
white folks' kitchen, the light burning, the door half-
open, grappling and burning beside the sink. Fallen
indeed: time was no more, and sin, death, Hell, the
judgment were blotted out. There was only Esther, who
contained in her narrow body all mystery and all passion,
and who answered all his need. Time, snarling so swiftly
past, had caused him to forget the clumsiness, and sweat,
and dirt of their first coupling; how his shaking hands
undressed her, standing where they stood, how her dress

fell at length like a snare about her feet; how his hands
tore at her undergarments so that the naked, vivid flesh
might meet his hands; how she protested: 'Not here, not
here'; how he worried, in some buried part of his mind,
about the open door, about the sermon he was to preach,
about his life, about Deborah; how the table got in
their way, how his collar, until her fingers loosened it,
threatened to choke him; how they found themselves
on the floor at last, sweating and groaning and locked
together; locked away from all others, all heavenly or
human help. Only they could help each other. They were
alone in the world.

Had Royal, his son, been conceived that night? Or the
next night? Or the next? It had lasted only nine days.
Then he had come to his senses—after nine days God
gave him the power to tell her this thing could not be.

She took his decision with the same casualness, the
same near-amusement, with which she had taken his fall.
He understood about Esther, during those nine days:
that she considered his fear and trembling fanciful and
childish, a way of making life more complicated than it
need be. She did not think life was like that; she wanted
life to be simple. He understood that she was sorry for
him because he was always worried. Sometimes, when
they were together, he tried to tell her of what he felt,
how the Lord would punish them for the sin they were
committing. She would not listen: 'You ain't in the pulpit
now. You's here with me. Even a Reverend's got the
right to take off his clothes *sometime* and act like a natural
man.' When he told her that he would not see her any
more, she was angry, but she did not argue. Her eyes
told him that she thought he was a fool; but that, even
had she loved him ever so desperately, it would have
been beneath her to argue about his decision—a large
part of her simplicity consisted in determining not to
want what she could not have with ease.

So it was over. Though it left him bruised and frightened, though he had lost the respect of Esther for ever (he prayed that she would never again come to hear him preach) he thanked God that it had been no worse. He prayed that God would forgive him, and never let him fall again.

Yet what frightened him, and kept him more than ever on his knees, was the knowledge that, once having fallen, nothing would be easier than to fall again. Having possessed Esther, the carnal man awoke, seeing the possibility of conquest everywhere. He was made to remember that though he was holy he was yet young; the women who had wanted him wanted him still; he had but to stretch out his hand and take what he wanted—even sisters in the church. He struggled to wear out his visions in the marriage bed, he struggled to awaken Deborah, for whom daily his hatred grew.

He and Esther spoke in the yard again as spring was just beginning. The ground was still with melting snow and ice; the sun was everywhere; the naked branches of the trees seemed to be lifting themselves upward toward the pale sun, impatient to put forth leaf and flower. He was standing at the well in his shirt-sleeves, singing softly to himself—praising God for the dangers he had passed. She came down the porch steps into the yard, and though he heard the soft step, and knew that it was she, it was a moment before he turned round.

He expected her to come up to him and ask for his help in something she was doing in the house. When she did not speak, he turned around. She was wearing a light, cotton dress of light-brown and dark-brown squares, and her hair was braided tightly all around her head. She looked like a little girl, and he almost smiled. Then: 'What's the matter?' he asked her; and felt the heart within him sicken.

'Gabriel,' she said, 'I going to have a baby.'

He stared at her; she began to cry. He put the two pails of water carefully on the ground. She put out her hands to reach him, but he moved away.

'Girl, stop that bellering. What you talking about?'

But, having allowed her tears to begin, she could not stop them at once. She continued to cry, weaving a little where she stood, and with her hands to her face. He looked in panic around the yard and toward the house. 'Stop that,' he cried again, not daring here and now to touch her, 'and tell me what's the matter!'

'I told you,' she moaned, 'I done told you. I going to have a baby.' She looked at him, her face broken up and the hot tears falling. 'It's the Lord's truth. I ain't making up no story, it's the Lord's truth.'

He could not take his eyes from her, though he hated what he saw. 'And when you done find this out?'

'Not so long. I thought maybe I was mistook. But ain't no mistake. Gabriel, what we going to do?'

Then, as she watched his face, her tears began again.

'Hush,' he said, with a calm that astonished him, 'we *going* to do something, just you be quiet.'

'What we going to do, Gabriel? *Tell* me—what you a-fixing in your mind to do?'

'You go on back in the house. Ain't no way for us to talk now.'

'Gabriel——'

'Go on in the house, girl. Go *on!*' And when she did not move, but continued to stare at him: 'We going to talk about it *to-night*. We going to get to the bottom of *this* thing to-night!'

She turned from him and started up the porch steps. 'And dry your *face*,' he whispered. She bent over, lifting the front of her dress to dry her eyes, and stood so for a moment on the bottom step while he watched her. Then she straightened and walked into the house, not looking back.

She was going to have his baby—*his* baby? While Deborah, despite their groaning, despite the humility with which she endured his body, yet failed to be quickened by any coming life. It was in the womb of Esther, who was no better than a harlot, that the seed of the prophet would be nourished.

And he moved from the well, picking up, like a man in a trance, the heavy pails of water. He moved toward the house, which now—high, gleaming roof, and spun-gold window—seemed to watch him and to listen; the very sun above his head and the earth beneath his feet had ceased their turning; the water, like a million warning voices, lapped in the buckets he carried on each side; and his mother, beneath the startled earth on which he moved, lifted up, endlessly, her eyes.

They talked in the kitchen as she was cleaning up.

'How come you'—it was his first question—'to be so sure this here's my baby?'

She was not crying now. 'Don't you start a-talking that way,' she said. 'Esther ain't in the habit of lying to *no*body, and I ain't gone with so many men that I'm subject to get my mind confused.'

She was very cold and deliberate, and moved about the kitchen with a furious concentration on her tasks, scarcely looking at him.

He did not know what to say, how to reach her.

'You tell your mother yet?' he asked, after a pause. 'You been to see a doctor? How come you to be so sure?'

She sighed sharply. 'No, I ain't told my mother, I ain't crazy. I ain't told nobody except you.'

'How come you to be so sure?' he repeated. 'If you ain't seen no doctor?'

'What doctor in this town you want me to go see? I go to see a doctor, I might as well get up and shout it from the housetops. No, I ain't seen no doctor, and I ain't fixing to see one in a hurry. I don't need no doctor to tell me what's happening in my belly.'

'And how long you been knowing about this?'

'I been knowing this for maybe a month—maybe six weeks now.'

'Six weeks? Why ain't you opened your mouth before?'

'Because I wasn't sure. I thought I'd wait and make sure. I didn't see no need for getting all up in the air before I *knew*. I didn't want to get you all upset and scared and evil, like you is now, if it weren't no need.' She paused, watching him. Then: 'And you said this morning we was going to do something. What we going to do? That's what we got to figure out now, Gabriel.'

'What we going to do?' he repeated at last; and felt that the sustaining life had gone out of him. He sat down at the kitchen table and looked at the whirling pattern on the floor.

But the life had not gone out of her; she came to where he sat, speaking softly, with bitter eyes. 'You sound mighty strange to me,' she said. 'Don't look to me like you thinking of nothing but how you can get shut of this —and me, too—quick as you know how. It wasn't like that always, was it, Reverend? Once upon a time you couldn't think of nothing and nobody *but* me. What you thinking about to-night? I be damned if I think it's *me* you thinking of.'

'Girl,' he said, wearily, 'don't talk like you ain't got good sense. You know I got a wife to think about——' and he wanted to say more, but he could not find the words, and, helplessly, he stopped.

'I know that,' she said with less heat, but watching him still with eyes from which the old, impatient mockery was not entirely gone, 'but what I mean is, if you was able to forget her once you ought to be able to forget her twice.'

He did not understand her at once; but then he sat straight up, his eyes wide and angry. 'What you mean, girl? What you trying to say?'

She did not flinch—even in his despair and anger he recognized how far she was from being the frivolous child she had always seemed to him. Or was it that she had been, in so short a space of time, transformed? But he spoke to her at this disadvantage: that whereas he was unprepared for any change in her, she had apparently taken his measure from the first and could be surprised by no change in him.

'You know what I mean,' she said. 'You ain't never going to have no kind of life with that skinny, black woman—and you ain't never going to be able to make her happy—and she ain't never going to have no children. I be blessed, anyway, if I think you was in your right mind when you married her. And it's *me* that's going to have your baby!'

'You want me,' he asked at last, 'to leave my wife— and come with you?'

'*I* thought,' she answered, 'that you had done thought of that yourself, already, many and many a time.'

'You know,' he said, with a halting anger, 'I ain't never said nothing like that. I ain't never told you I wanted to leave my wife.'

'I ain't talking,' she shouted, at the end of patience, 'about nothing you done *said!*'

Immediately, they both looked toward the closed kitchen doors—for they were not alone in the house this time. She sighed, and smoothed her hair with her hand; and he saw then that her hand was trembling and that her calm deliberation was all a frenzied pose.

'Girl,' he said, 'does you reckon I'm going to run off and lead a life of sin with you somewhere, just because you tell me you got my baby kicking in your belly? How many kinds of a fool you think I am? I got God's work to do—my life don't belong to you. Nor to that baby, neither—if it *is* my baby.'

'It's your baby,' she said, coldly, 'and ain't no way in the world to get around *that*. And it ain't been so very long ago, right here in this very *room*, when looked to me like a life of sin was all you was ready for.'

'Yes,' he answered, rising, and turning away, 'Satan tempted me and I fell. I ain't the first man been made to fall on account of a wicked woman.'

'You be careful,' said Esther, 'how you talk to me. I ain't the first girl's been ruined by a holy man, neither.'

'Ruined?' he cried. 'You? How you going to be ruined? When you been walking through this town just like a harlot, and a-kicking up your heels all over the pasture? How you going to stand there and tell me you been *ruined?* If it hadn't been me, it sure would have been somebody else.'

'But it *was* you,' she retorted, 'and what I want to know is what we's going to do about it.'

He looked at her. Her face was cold and hard—ugly; she had never been so ugly before.

'I don't know,' he said, deliberately, 'what *we* is going to do. But I tell you what I think *you* better do: you better go along and get one of these boys you been running around with to marry you. Because I can't go off with you nowhere.'

She sat down at the table and stared at him with scorn and amazement; sat down heavily, as though she had been struck. He knew that she was gathering her forces; and now she said what he had dreaded to hear:

'And suppose I went through town and told your wife, and the churchfolks, and everybody—suppose I did that, Reverend?'

'And who you think,' he asked—he felt himself enveloped by an awful, falling silence—'is going to believe you?'

She laughed. 'Enough folks'd believe me to make it mighty hard on you.' And she watched him. He walked up and down the kitchen, trying to avoid her eyes. 'You just think back,' she said, 'to that first night, right here on this damn white folks' floor, and you'll see it's too late for you to talk to Esther about how holy you is. I don't care if you want to live a lie, but I don't see no reason for you to make me suffer on account of it.'

'You can go around and tell folks if you want to,' he said, boldly, 'but it ain't going to look so good for you neither.'

She laughed again. 'But I ain't the holy one. You's a married man, and you's a preacher—and who you think folks is going to blame most?'

He watched her with a hatred that was mixed with his old desire, knowing that once more she had the victory.

'I can't marry you, you know that,' he said. 'Now, what you want me to do?'

'No,' she said, 'and I reckon you *wouldn't* marry me even if you *was* free. I reckon you don't want no whore like Esther for your wife. Esther's just for the night, for the dark, where won't nobody see you getting your holy self all dirtied up with Esther. Esther's just good enough to go out and have *your* bastard somewhere in the goddamn woods. Ain't that so, Reverend?'

He did not answer her. He could find no words. There was only silence in him, like the grave.

She rose, and moved to the open kitchen door, where she stood, her back to him, looking out into the yard and on the silent streets where the last, dead rays of the sun still lingered.

'But I reckon,' she said slowly, 'that I don't want to be with you no more'n you want to be with me. I don't want no man what's ashamed and scared. Can't do me no good, that kind of man.' She turned in the door and faced him; this was the last time she really looked at him, and he would carry that look to his grave. 'There's just one thing I want you to do,' she said. 'You do that, and we be all right.'

'What you want me to do?' he asked, and felt ashamed.

'I *would* go through this town,' she said, 'and tell everybody about the Lord's anointed. Only reason I don't is because I don't want my mama and daddy to know what a fool I been. I ain't ashamed of *it*—I'm ashamed of *you*—you done made me feel a shame I ain't never felt before. I shamed before my *God*—to let somebody make me cheap, like you done done.'

He said nothing. She turned her back to him again.

'I . . . just want to go somewhere,' she said, '*go* somewhere, and *have* my baby, and think all this out of my mind. I want to go somewhere and get my mind straight. *That's* what I want you to do—and that's pretty cheap. I guess it takes a holy man to make a girl a real whore.'

'Girl,' he said, 'I ain't got no *money*.'

'Well,' she said, coldly, 'you damn well better find some.'

Then she began to cry. He moved toward her, but she moved away.

'If I go out into the field,' he said, helplessly, 'I ought to be able to make enough money to send you away.'

'How long that going to take?'

'A month maybe.'

And she shook her head. 'I ain't going to stay around here that long.'

They stood in silence in the open kitchen door, she struggling against her tears, he struggling against his shame. He could only think: 'Jesus, Jesus, Jesus. Jesus, Jesus.'

'Ain't you got nothing saved up?' she asked at last. 'Look to me like you been married long enough to've saved something!'

Then he remembered that Deborah had been saving
money since their wedding day. She kept it in a tin box
at the top of the cupboard. He thought of how sin led
to sin.

'Yes,' he said, 'a little. I don't know how much.'

'You bring it to-morrow,' she told him.

'Yes,' he said.

He watched her as she moved from the door and went
to the closet for her hat and coat. Then she came back,
dressed for the street and, without a word, passed him,
walking down the short steps into the yard. She opened
the low gate and turned down the long, silent, flaming
street. She walked slowly, head bowed, as though she
were cold. He stood watching her, thinking of the many
times he had watched her before, when her walk had
been so different and her laughter had come ringing back
to mock him.

He stole the money while Deborah slept. And he gave
it to Esther in the morning. She gave notice that same
day, and a week later she was gone—to Chicago, said
her parents, to find a better job and to have a better life.

Deborah became more silent than ever in the weeks
that followed. Sometimes he was certain she had discovered that the money was missing and knew that he
had taken it—sometimes he was certain that she knew
nothing. Sometimes he was certain that she knew everything: the theft, and the reason for the theft. But she did
not speak. In the middle of the spring he went out into
the field to preach, and was gone three months. When he
came back he brought the money with him and put it in
the box again. No money had been added in the meanwhile, so he still could not be certain whether Deborah
knew or not.

He decided to let it all be forgotten, and begin his life
again.

But the summer brought him a letter, with no return name or address, but postmarked from Chicago. Deborah gave it to him at breakfast, not seeming to have remarked the hand or the postmark, along with the bundle of tracts from a Bible house which they both distributed each week through the town. She had a letter, too, from Florence, and it was perhaps this novelty that distracted her attention.

Esther's letter ended:

> *What I think is, I made a mistake, that's true, and I'm paying for it now. But don't you think you ain't going to pay for it—I don't know when and I don't know how, but I know you going to be brought low one of these fine days. I ain't holy like you are, but I know right from wrong.*
>
> *I'm going to have my baby and I'm going to bring him up to be a man. And I ain't going to read to him out of no Bibles and I ain't going to take him to hear no preaching. If he don't drink nothing but moonshine all his natural days he be a better man than his Daddy.*

'What Florence got to say?' he asked dully, crumpling his letter in his fist.

Deborah looked up with a faint smile. 'Nothing much, honey. But she sound like she going to get married.'

Near the end of that summer he went out again into the field. He could not stand his home, his job, the town itself—he could not endure, day in, day out, facing the scenes and the people he had known all his life. They seemed suddenly to mock him, to stand in judgment on him; he saw his guilt in everybody's eyes. When he stood in the pulpit to preach they looked at him, he felt, as though he had no right to be there, as though they condemned him as he had once condemned the twenty-three elders. When souls came weeping to the altar he scarce dared to rejoice, remembering that soul who had not bowed, whose blood, it might be, would be required of him at judgment.

So he fled from these people, and from these silent witnesses, to tarry and preach elsewhere—to do, as it were, in secret, his first works over, seeking again the holy fire that had so transformed him once. But he was to find, as the prophets had found, that the whole earth became a prison for him who fled before the Lord. There was peace nowhere, and healing nowhere, and forgetfulness nowhere. In every church he entered, his sin had gone before him. It was in the strange, the welcoming faces, it cried up to him from the altar, it sat, as he mounted the pulpit steps, waiting for him in his seat. It stared upward from his Bible: there was no word in all that holy book which did not make him tremble. When he spoke of John on the isle of Patmos, taken up in the spirit on the Lord's day, to behold things past, present, and to come, saying: 'he which is filthy, let him be filthy still,' it was he who, crying these words in a loud voice, was utterly confounded; when he spoke of David, the shepherd boy, raised by God's power to be the King of Israel, it was he who, while they shouted: 'Amen!' and: 'Hallelujah!' struggled once more in his chains; when he spoke of the day of Pentecost when the Holy Ghost had come down on the apostles who tarried in the upper room, causing them to speak in tongues of fire, he thought of his own baptism and how he had offended the Holy Ghost. No: though his name was writ large on placards, though they praised him for the great work God worked through him, and though they came, day and night, before him to the altar, there was no word in the Book for him.

And he saw, in this wandering, how far his people had wandered from God. They had all turned aside, and gone out into the wilderness, to fall down before idols of gold and silver, and wood and stone, false gods that could not heal them. The music that filled any town or city he entered was not the music of the saints but another music, infernal, which glorified lust and held righteousness up to scorn. Women, some of whom should have been at home, teaching their grandchildren how to pray, stood, night after night, twisting their bodies into lewd hallelujahs in smoke-filled, gin-heavy dance halls, singing for their 'loving man.' And their loving man was any man, any morning, noon, or night—when one left town they got another—men could drown, it seemed, in their warm flesh and they would never know the difference. 'It's here for you and if you don't get it it ain't no fault of mine.' They laughed at him when they saw him—'a pretty man like you?'—and they told him that they knew a long brown girl who could make him lay his Bible down. He fled from them; they frightened him. He began to pray for Esther. He imagined her standing one day where these women stood to-day.

And blood, in all the cities through which he passed, ran down. There seemed no door, anywhere, behind which blood did not call out, unceasingly, for blood; no woman, whether singing before defiant trumpets or rejoicing before the Lord, who had not seen her father, her brother, her lover, or her son cut down without mercy; who had not seen her sister become part of the white man's great whorehouse, who had not, all too narrowly, escaped that house herself; no man, preaching, or cursing, strumming his guitar in the lone, blue evening, or blowing in fury and ecstasy his golden horn at night, who had not been made to bend his head and drink white men's muddy water; no man whose manhood had not been, at the root, sickened, whose loins had not been dishonoured, whose seed had not been scattered into oblivion and worse than oblivion, into living shame and rage, and into endless battle. Yes, their parts were all cut off, they were dishonoured, their very names were nothing more than dust blown disdainfully across the field of time—to fall where, to blossom where, bringing forth what fruit hereafter, where?—their very names were not their own. Behind them was the darkness, nothing but the darkness, and all around them destruction, and before them nothing but the fire—a bastard people, far from God, singing and crying in the wilderness!

Yet, most strangely, and from deeps not before discovered, his faith looked up; before the wickedness that he saw, the wickedness from which he fled, he yet beheld, like a flaming standard in the middle of the air, that power of redemption to which he must, till death, bear witness; which, though it crush him utterly, he could not deny; though none among the living might ever behold it, *he* had beheld it, and must keep the faith. He would not go back into Egypt for friend, or lover, or bastard son: he would not turn his face from God, no matter how deep might grow the darkness in which God hid His face from him. One day God would give him a sign, and the darkness would all be finished—one day God would raise him, who had suffered him to fall so low.

Hard on the heels of his return that winter, Esther came home too. Her mother and stepfather travelled north to claim her lifeless body and her living son. Soon after Christmas, on the last, dead days of the year, she was buried in the churchyard. It was bitterly cold and there was ice on the ground, as during the days when he had first possessed her. He stood next to Deborah, whose arm in his shivered incessantly with the cold, and watched while the long, plain box was lowered into the ground. Esther's mother stood in silence beside the deep hole, leaning on her husband, who held their grandchild in his arms. 'Lord have mercy, have mercy, have mercy,' someone began to chant; and the old mourning women clustered of a sudden round Esther's mother to hold her up. Then earth struck the coffin; the child awakened and began to scream.

Then Gabriel prayed to be delivered from blood-guiltiness. He prayed to God to give him a sign one day to make him know he was forgiven. But the child who screamed at that moment in the churchyard had cursed, and sung, and been silenced for ever before God gave him a sign.

And he watched this son grow up, a stranger to his father and a stranger to God. Deborah, who became after the death of Esther more friendly with Esther's people, reported to him from the very beginning how shamefully Royal was being spoiled. He was, inevitably, the apple of their eye, a fact that, in operation, caused Deborah to frown, and sometimes, reluctantly, to smile; and, as they said, if there was any white blood in him, it didn't show —he was the spit and image of his mother.

The sun did not rise or set but that Gabriel saw his lost, his disinherited son, or heard of him; and he seemed with every passing day to carry more proudly the doom printed on his brow. Gabriel watched him run headlong, like David's headlong son, towards the disaster that had been waiting for him from the moment he had been conceived. It seemed that he had scarcely begun to walk before he swaggered; he had scarcely begun to talk before he cursed. Gabriel often saw him on the streets, playing on the kerbstone with other boys his age. Once, when he passed, one of the boys had said: 'Here comes Reverend Grimes,' and nodded, in brief, respectful silence. But Royal had looked boldly up into the preacher's face. He said: 'How-de-do, Reverend?' and suddenly, irrepressibly, laughed. Gabriel, wishing to smile down into the boy's face, to pause and touch him on the forehead, did none of these things, but walked on. Behind him, he heard Royal's explosive whisper: 'I bet he got a mighty big one!'—and then all the children laughed. It came to Gabriel then how his own mother must have suffered to watch him in the unredeemed innocence that so surely led to death and Hell.

'I wonder,' said Deborah idly once, 'why she called him Royal? You reckon that's his daddy's name?'

He did not wonder. He had once told Esther that if the Lord ever gave him a son he would call him Royal, because the line of the faithful was a royal line—his son would be a royal child. And this she had remembered as she thrust him from her; with what had perhaps been her last breath she had mocked him and his father with this name. She had died, then, hating him; she had carried into eternity a curse on him and his.

'I reckon,' he said at last, 'it *must* be his daddy's name —less they just given him that name in the hospital up north after . . . she was dead.'

'His grandmama, Sister McDonald'—she was writing a letter, and did not look at him as she spoke—'well, *she* think it must've been one of them boys what's all time passing through here, looking for work, on their way north—you know? Them real shiftless niggers—well, *she* think it must've been one of them got Esther in trouble. She say Esther wouldn't never've gone north if she hadn't been a-trying to find that boy's daddy. Because she was in trouble when she left here'—and she looked up from her letter a moment—'*that's* for certain.'

'I reckon,' he said again, made uncomfortable by her unaccustomed chatter, but not daring, too sharply, to stop her. He was thinking of Esther, lying cold and still in the ground, who had been so vivid and shameless in his arms.

'And Sister McDonald say,' she went on, 'that she left here with just a little *bit* of money; they had to keep a-sending her money all the time she was up there almost, specially near the end. We was just talking

F

about it yesterday—she say, look like Esther just decided over*night* she had to go, and couldn't nothing stop her. And she say she didn't *want* to stand in the girl's way—but if she'd've *known* something was the matter she wouldn't *never*'ve let that girl away from her.'

'Seems funny to *me*,' he muttered, scarcely knowing what he was saying, 'that she didn't think *something*.'

'Why she didn't think nothing, because Esther always *told* her mother everything—weren't no shame between them—they was just like two women together. She say she never *dreamed* that Esther would run away from her if she got herself in trouble.' And she looked outward, past him, her eyes full of a strange, bitter pity. 'That poor thing,' she said, 'she must have suffered *some*.'

'I don't see no need for you and Sister McDonald to sit around and *talk* about it all the time,' he said, then. 'It all been a mighty long time ago; that boy is growing up already.'

'That's true,' she said, bending her head once more, 'but some things, look like, ain't to be forgotten in a hurry.'

'Who you writing to?' he asked, as oppressed suddenly by the silence as he had been by her talk.

She looked up. 'I'm writing to your sister, Florence. You got anything you want me to say?'

'No,' he said. 'Just tell her I'm praying for her.'

When Royal was sixteen the war came, and all the young men, first the sons of the mighty, and then the sons of his own people, were scattered into foreign lands. Gabriel fell on his knees each night to pray that Royal would not have to go. 'But I hear he *want* to go,' said Deborah. 'His grandmama tell me he giving her a *time* because she won't let him go and sign up.'

'Look like,' he said sullenly, 'that won't none of these young men be satisfied till they can go off and get themselves crippled or killed.'

'Well, you know that's the way the young folks is,' said Deborah, cheerfully. 'You can't never tell them nothing—and when they find out it's too late then.'

He discovered that whenever Deborah spoke of Royal, a fear deep within him listened and waited. Many times he had thought to unburden his heart to her. But she gave him no opportunity, never said anything that might allow him the healing humility of confession—or that might, for that matter, have permitted him at last to say how much he hated her for her barrenness. She demanded of him what she gave—nothing—nothing, at any rate, with which she could be reproached. She kept his house and shared his bed; she visited the sick, as she had always done, and she comforted the dying, as she had always done. The marriage for which he had once dreamed the world would mock him had so justified itself—in the eyes of the world—that no one now could imagine, for either of them, any other condition or alliance. Even Deborah's weakness, which grew more marked with the years, keeping her more frequently in her bed, and her barrenness, like her previous dishonour, had come to seem mysterious proofs of how completely she had surrendered herself to God.

He said: 'Amen,' cautiously, after her last remark, and cleared his throat.

'I declare,' she said, with the same cheerfulness, 'sometime he remind me of you when you was a young man.'

And he did not look at her, though he felt her eyes on him; he reached for his Bible and opened it. 'Young men,' he said, 'is all the same, don't Jesus change their hearts.'

Royal did not go to war, but he went away that summer to work on the docks in another town. Gabriel did not see him any more until the war was over.

On that day, a day he was never to forget, he went

when work was done to buy some medicine for Deborah, who was in bed with a misery in her back. Night had not yet fallen and the streets were grey and empty— save that here and there, polished in the light that spilled outward from a pool-room or a tavern, white men stood in groups of half-a-dozen. As he passed each group, silence fell, and they watched him insolently, itching to kill; but he said nothing, bowing his head, and they knew, anyway, that he was a preacher. There were no black men on the streets at all, save him. There had been found that morning, just outside of town, the dead body of a soldier, his uniform shredded where he had been flogged, and, turned upward through the black skin, raw, red meat. He lay face downward at the base of a tree, his fingernails digging into the scuffed earth. When he was turned over, his eyeballs stared upward in amazement and horror, his mouth was locked open wide; his trousers, soaked with blood, were torn open, and exposed to the cold, white air of morning the thick hairs of his groin, matted together, black and rust-red, and the wound that seemed to be throbbing still. He had been carried home in silence and lay now behind locked doors, with his living kinsmen, who sat, weeping, and praying, and dreaming of vengeance, and waiting for the next visitation. Now, someone spat on the pavement at Gabriel's feet, and he walked on, his face not changing, and he heard it reprovingly whispered behind him that he was a good nigger, surely up to no trouble. He hoped that he would not be spoken to, that he would not have to smile into any of these so well-known white faces. While he walked, held by his caution more rigid than an arrow, he prayed, as his mother had taught him to pray, for loving kindness; yet he dreamed of the feel of a white man's forehead against his shoe; again and again, until the head wobbled on the broken neck and his foot encountered nothing but the rushing blood. And he was thinking

that it was only the hand of the Lord that had taken Royal
away, because if he had stayed they would surely have
killed him, when, turning a corner, he looked into Royal's
face.

Royal was now as tall as Gabriel, broad-shouldered,
and lean. He wore a new suit, blue, with broad, blue
stripes, and carried, crooked under his arm, a brown-
paper bundle tied with string. He and Gabriel stared at
one another for a second with no recognition. Royal
stared in blank hostility, before, seeming to remember
Gabriel's face, he took a burning cigarette from between
his lips, and said, with pained politeness: 'How-de-do,
sir.' His voice was rough, and there was, faintly, the
odour of whisky on his breath.

But Gabriel could not speak at once; he struggled to
get his breath. Then: 'How-de-do,' he said. And they
stood, each as though waiting for the other to say something of the greatest importance, on the deserted corner.
Then, just as Royal was about to move, Gabriel remembered the white men all over town.

'Boy,' he cried, 'ain't you got good sense? Don't you
know you ain't got no business to be out here, walking
around like this?'

Royal stared at him, uncertain whether to laugh or to
take offence, and Gabriel said, more gently: 'I just mean
you better be careful, son. Ain't nothing but white folks
in town to-day. They done killed . . . last night . . .'

Then he could not go on. He saw, as though it were a
vision, Royal's body, sprawled heavy and unmoving for
ever against the earth, and tears blinded his eyes.

Royal watched him, a distant and angry compassion in
his face.

'I know,' he said abruptly, 'but they ain't going to
bother me. They done got their nigger for this week. I
ain't going far noway.'

Then the corner on which they stood seemed suddenly

to rock with the weight of mortal danger. It seemed for a moment, as they stood there, that death and destruction rushed towards them: two black men alone in the dark and silent town where white men prowled like lions —what mercy could they hope for, should they be found here, talking together? It would surely be believed that they were plotting vengeance. And Gabriel started to move away, thinking to save his son.

God bless you, boy,' said Gabriel. 'You hurry along now.'

'Yeah,' said Royal, 'thanks.' He moved away, about to turn the corner. He looked back at Gabriel. 'But you be careful, too,' he said, and smiled.

He turned the corner and Gabriel listened as his footfalls moved away. They were swallowed up in silence; he heard no voices raised to cut down Royal as he went his way; soon there was silence everywhere.

Not quite two years later Deborah told him that his son was dead.

And now John tried to pray. There was a great noise of praying all around him, a great noise of weeping and of song. It was Sister McCandless who led the song, who sang it nearly alone, for the others did not cease to moan and cry. It was a song he had heard all his life:

> 'Lord, I'm travelling, Lord,
> I got on my travelling shoes.'

Without raising his eyes, he could see her standing in the holy place, pleading the blood over those who sought there, her head thrown back, eyes shut, foot pounding the floor. She did not look, then, like the Sister McCandless who sometimes came to visit them, like the woman who went out every day to work for the white people downtown, who came home at evening, climbing, with such weariness, the long, dark stairs. No: her face was transfigured now, her whole being was made new by the power of her salvation.

'Salvation is real,' a voice said to him, 'God is real. Death may come soon or late, why do you hesitate? Now is the time to seek and serve the Lord.' Salvation was real for all these others, and it might be real for him. He had only to reach out and God would touch him; he had only to cry and God would hear. All these others, now, who cried so far beyond him with such joy, had once been in their sins, as he was now—and they had cried and God had heard them, and delivered them out of all their troubles. And what God had done for others, He could also do for him.

But—out of *all* their troubles? Why did his mother weep? Why did his father frown? If God's power was so great, why were their lives so troubled?

He had never tried to think of their trouble before; rather, he had never before confronted it in such a narrow place. It had always been there, at his back perhaps, all these years, but he had never turned to face it. Now it stood before him, staring, nevermore to be escaped, and its mouth was enlarged without any limit. It was ready to swallow him up. Only the hand of God could deliver him. Yet, in a moment, he somehow knew from the sound of that storm which rose so painfully in him now, which laid waste—for ever?—the strange, yet comforting landscape of his mind, that the hand of God would surely lead him into this staring, waiting mouth, these distended jaws, this hot breath as of fire. He would be led into darkness, and in darkness would remain; until in some incalculable time to come the hand of God would reach down and raise him up; he, John, who having lain in darkness would no longer be himself but some other man. He would have been changed, as they said, for ever; sown in dishonour, he would be raised in honour: he would have been born again.

Then he would no longer be the son of his father, but the son of his Heavenly Father, the King. Then he need no longer fear his father, for he could take, as it were, their quarrel over his father's head to Heaven—to the Father who loved him, who had come down in the flesh to die for him. Then he and his father would be equals, in the sight, and the sound, and the love of God. Then his father could not beat him any more, or despise him any more, or mock him any more—he, John, the Lord's anointed. He could speak to his father then as men spoke to one another—as sons spoke to their fathers, not in trembling but in sweet confidence, not in hatred but in love. His father could not cast him out, whom God had gathered in.

Yet, trembling, he knew that this was not what he wanted. He did not *want* to love his father; he wanted to hate him, to cherish that hatred, and give his hatred words one day. He did not want his father's kiss—not any more, he who had received so many blows. He could not imagine, on any day to come and no matter how greatly he might be changed, wanting to take his father's hand. The storm that raged in him to-night could not uproot this hatred, the mightiest tree in all John's country, all that remained to-night, in this, John's floodtime.

And he bowed his head yet lower before the altar in weariness and confusion. Oh, that his father would *die!*—and the road before John be open, as it must be open for others. Yet in the very grave he would hate him; his father would but have changed conditions, he would be John's father still. The grave was not enough for punishment, for justice, for revenge. Hell, everlasting, unceasing, perpetual, unquenched for ever, should be his father's portion; with John there to watch, to linger, to smile, to laugh aloud, hearing, at last, his father's cries of torment.

And, even then, it would not be finished. *The everlasting father*.

Oh, but his thoughts were evil—but to-night he did not care. Somewhere, in all this whirlwind, in the darkness of his heart, in the storm—was something—something he must find. He could not pray. His mind was like the sea itself: troubled, and too deep for the bravest man's descent, throwing up now and again, for the naked eye to wonder at, treasure and debris long forgotten on the bottom—bones and jewels, fantastic shells, jelly that had once been flesh, pearls that had once been eyes. And he was at the mercy of this sea, hanging there with darkness all around him.

The morning of that day, as Gabriel rose and started out to work, the sky was low and nearly black and the air too thick to breathe. Late in the afternoon the wind rose, the skies opened, and the rain came. The rain came down as though once more in Heaven the Lord had been persuaded of the good uses of a flood. It drove before it the bowed wanderer, clapped children into houses, licked with fearful anger against the high, strong wall, and the wall of the lean-to, and the wall of the cabin, beat against the bark and the leaves of trees, trampled the broad grass, and broke the neck of the flower. The world turned dark, for ever, everywhere, and windows ran as though their glass panes bore all the tears of eternity, threatening at every instant to shatter inward against this force, uncontrollable, so abruptly visited on the earth. Gabriel walked homeward through this wilderness of water (which had failed, however, to clear the air) to where Deborah waited for him in the bed she seldom, these days, attempted to leave.

And he had not been in the house five minutes before he was aware that a change had occurred in the quality of her silence: in the silence something waited, ready to spring.

He looked up at her from the table where he sat eating the meal that she had painfully prepared. He asked: 'How you feel to-day, old lady?'

'I feel like about the way I always do,' and she smiled. 'I don't feel no better and I don't feel no worse.'

'We going to get the church to pray for you,' he said, 'and get you on your feet again.'

She said nothing and he turned his attention once more to his plate. But she was watching him; he looked up.

'I hear some mighty bad news to-day,' she said slowly.

'What you hear?'

'Sister McDonald was over this afternoon, and Lord knows she was in a pitiful state.' He sat stock-still, staring at her. 'She done got a letter to-day what says her grandson—you know, that Royal—done got hisself killed in Chicago. It sure look like the Lord is put a curse on that family. First the mother, and now the son.'

For a moment he could only stare at her stupidly, while the food in his mouth slowly grew heavy and dry. Outside rushed the armies of the rain, and lightning flashed against the window. Then he tried to swallow, and his gorge rose. He began to tremble. 'Yes,' she said, not looking at him now, 'he been living in Chicago about a year, just a-drinking and a-carrying on—and his grandmama, she tell me that look like he got to gambling one night with some of them northern niggers, and one of them got mad because he thought the boy was trying to cheat him, and took out his knife and stabbed him. Stabbed him in the throat, and she tell me he died right there on the floor in that bar-room, didn't even have time to get him to no hospital.' She turned in bed and looked at him. 'The Lord sure give that poor woman a heavy cross to bear.'

Then he tried to speak; he thought of the churchyard where Esther was buried, and Royal's first, thin cry. 'She going to bring him back home?'

She stared. 'Home? Honey, they done buried him already up there in the potter's field. Ain't nobody never going to look on that poor boy no more.'

Then he began to cry, not making a sound, sitting at the table, and with his whole body shaking. She watched him for a long while and, finally, he put his head on the table, overturning the coffee cup, and wept aloud. Then it seemed that there was weeping everywhere, waters of anguish riding the world; Gabriel weeping, and rain beating on the roof, and at the windows, and the coffee dripping from the end of the table. And she asked at last:

'Gabriel . . . that Royal . . . he were your flesh and blood, weren't he?'

'Yes,' he said, glad even in his anguish to hear the words fall from his lips, 'that was my son.'

And there was silence again. Then: 'And you sent that girl away, didn't you? With the money outen that box?'

'Yes,' he said, 'yes.'

'Gabriel,' she asked, 'why did you do it? Why you let her go off and die, all by herself? Why ain't you never said nothing?'

And now he could not answer. He could not raise his head.

'Why?' she insisted. 'Honey, I ain't never asked you. But I got a right to know—and when you wanted a son so bad?'

Then, shaking, he rose from the table and walked slowly to the window, looking out.

'I asked my God to forgive me,' he said. 'But I didn't want no harlot's son.'

'Esther weren't no harlot,' she said quietly.

'She weren't my wife. I couldn't make her my wife. I already had *you*'—and he said the last words with venom —'Esther's mind weren't on the Lord—she'd of dragged me right on down to Hell with her.'

'She mighty near has,' said Deborah.

'The Lord He held me back,' he said, hearing the thunder, watching the lightning. 'He put out His hand and held me back.' Then, after a moment, turning back into the room: 'I *couldn't* of done nothing else,' he cried, 'what else could I of done? Where could I of gone with Esther, and me a preacher, too? And what could I of done with you?' He looked at her, old and black and patient, smelling of sickness and age and death. 'Ah,' he said, his tears still falling, 'I bet you was mighty happy to-day, old lady, weren't you? When she told you he, Royal, my son, was dead. *You* ain't never had no son.' And he turned again to the window. Then: 'How long you been knowing about this?'

'I been knowing,' she said, 'ever since that evening, way back there, when Esther come to church.'

'You got a evil mind,' he said. 'I hadn't never touched her then.'

'No,' she said slowly, 'but you had already done touched *me*.'

He moved a little from the window and stood looking down at her from the foot of the bed.

'Gabriel,' she said, 'I been praying all these years that the Lord would touch my body, and make me like them women, all them women, you used to go with all the time.' She was very calm; her face was very bitter and patient. 'Look like it weren't His will. Look like I couldn't nohow forget . . . how they done me way back there when I weren't nothing but a girl.' She paused and looked away. 'But, Gabriel, if you'd said something even when that poor girl was buried, if you'd wanted to own that poor boy, I wouldn't nohow of cared what folks said, or where we might of had to go, or nothing. I'd have raised him like my own, I swear to my God I would have—and he might be living now.'

'Deborah,' he asked, 'what you been thinking all this time?'

She smiled. 'I been thinking,' she said, 'how you better commence to tremble when the Lord, He gives you your heart's desire.' She paused. 'I'd been wanting you since I wanted anything. And then I got you.'

He walked back to the window, tears rolling down his face.

'Honey,' she said, in another, stronger voice, 'you better pray God to forgive you. You better not let go until He make you *know* you been forgiven.'

'Yes,' he sighed, 'I'm waiting on the Lord.'

Then there was only silence, except for the rain. The rain came down in buckets; it was raining, as they said, pitchforks and nigger babies. Lightning flashed again across the sky and thunder rolled.

'Listen,' said Gabriel. 'God is talking.'

Slowly now, he rose from his knees, for half the church was standing: Sister Price, Sister McCandless, and Praying Mother Washington; and the young Ella Mae sat in her chair watching Elisha where he lay. Florence and Elizabeth were still on their knees; and John was on his knees.

And, rising, Gabriel thought of how the Lord had led him to this church so long ago, and how Elizabeth, one night after he had preached, had walked this long aisle to the altar, to repent before God her sin. And then they had married, for he believed her when she said that she was changed—and she was the sign, she and her nameless child, for which he had tarried so many dark years before the Lord. It was as though, when he saw them, the Lord had returned to him again that which was lost.

Then, as he stood with the others over the fallen Elisha, John rose from his knees. He bent a dazed, sleepy, frowning look on Elisha and the others, shivering a little as though he were cold; and then he felt his father's eyes and looked up at his father.

At the same moment, Elisha, from the floor, began to speak in a tongue of fire, under the power of the Holy Ghost. John and his father stared at each other, struck dumb and still and with something come to life between them—while the Holy Ghost spoke. Gabriel had never seen such a look on John's face before; Satan, at that moment, stared out of John's eyes while the Spirit spoke; and yet John's staring eyes to-night reminded Gabriel of other eyes: of his mother's eyes when she beat him, of Florence's eyes when she mocked him, of Deborah's eyes when she prayed for him, of Esther's eyes and Royal's eyes, and Elizabeth's eyes to-night before Roy cursed him, and of Roy's eyes when Roy said: 'You black bastard.' And John did not drop his eyes, but seemed to want to stare for ever into the bottom of Gabriel's soul. And Gabriel, scarcely believing that John could have become so brazen, stared in wrath and horror at Elizabeth's presumptuous bastard boy, grown suddenly so old in evil. He nearly raised his hand to strike him, but did not move, for Elisha lay between them. Then he said, soundlessly, with his lips: 'Kneel down.' John turned suddenly, the movement like a curse, and knelt again before the altar.

# 3   ELIZABETH'S PRAYER

*Lord, I wish I had of died*
*In Egypt land!*

WHILE Elisha was speaking, Elizabeth felt that the Lord was speaking a message to her heart, that this fiery visitation was meant for her; and that if she humbled herself to listen, God would give her the interpretation. This certainty did not fill her with exultation, but with fear. She was afraid of what God might say—of what displeasure, what condemnation, what prophesies of trials yet to be endured might issue from His mouth.

Now Elisha ceased to speak, and rose; now he sat at the piano. There was muted singing all around her; yet she waited. Before her mind's eyes wavered, in a light like the light from a fire, the face of John, whom she had brought so unwillingly into the world. It was for his deliverance that she wept to-night: that he might be carried, past wrath unspeakable, into a state of grace.

They were singing:

> '*Must Jesus bear the cross alone,*
> *And all the world go free?*'

Elisha picked out the song on the piano, his fingers seeming to hesitate, almost to be unwilling. She, too, strained against her great unwillingness, but forced her heart to say Amen, as the voice of Praying Mother Washington picked up the response:

> *'No, there's a cross for everyone,*
> *And there's a cross for me.'*

She heard weeping near her—was it Ella Mae? or Florence? or the echo, magnified, of her own tears? The weeping was buried beneath the song. She had been hearing this song all her life, she had grown up with it, but she had never understood it as well as she understood it now. It filled the church, as though the church had merely become a hollow or a void, echoing with the voices that had driven her to this dark place. Her aunt had sung it always, harshly, under her breath, in a bitter pride:

> *'The consecrated cross I'll bear*
> *Till death shall set me free,*
> *And then go home, a crown to wear,*
> *For there's a crown for me.'*

She was probably an old, old woman now, still in the same harshness of spirit, singing this song in the tiny house down home which she and Elizabeth had shared so long. And she did not know of Elizabeth's shame— Elizabeth had not written about John until long after she was married to Gabriel; and the Lord had never allowed her aunt to come to New York City. Her aunt had always prophesied that Elizabeth would come to no good end, proud, and vain, and foolish as she was, and having been allowed to run wild all her childhood days.

Her aunt had come second in the series of disasters that had ended Elizabeth's childhood. First, when she was eight, going on nine, her mother had died, an event not immediately recognized by Elizabeth as a disaster, since she had scarcely known her mother and had certainly never loved her. Her mother had been very fair, and beautiful, and delicate of health, so that she stayed in bed most of the time, reading spiritualist pamphlets concerning the benefits of disease and complaining to Elizabeth's father of how she suffered. Elizabeth remembered of her only that she wept very easily and that she smelled like stale milk—it was, perhaps, her mother's disquieting colour that, whenever she was held in her mother's arms, made Elizabeth think of milk. Her mother did not, however, hold Elizabeth in her arms very often. Elizabeth very quickly suspected that this was because she was so very much darker than her mother and not nearly, of course, so beautiful. When she faced her mother she was shy, downcast, sullen. She did not know how to answer her mother's shrill, meaningless questions, put with the furious affectation of maternal concern; she could not pretend, when she kissed her mother, or submitted to her mother's kiss, that she was moved by anything more than an unpleasant sense of duty. This, of course, bred in her mother a kind of baffled fury, and she never tired of telling Elizabeth that she was an 'unnatural' child.

But it was very different with her father; he was—and so Elizabeth never failed to think of him—young, and handsome, and kind, and generous; and he loved his daughter. He told her that she was the apple of his eye, that she was wound around his heartstrings, that she was surely the finest little lady in the land. When she was with her father she pranced and postured like a very queen: and she was not afraid of anything, save the moment when he would say that it was her bedtime, or that he had to be 'getting along.' He was always buying her things, things to wear and things to play with, and taking her on Sundays for long walks through the country, or to the circus, when the circus was in town, or to

Punch and Judy shows. And he was dark, like Elizabeth, and gentle, and proud; he had never been angry with her, but she had seen him angry a few times with other people—her mother, for example, and later, of course, her aunt. Her mother was always angry and Elizabeth paid no attention; and, later, her aunt was perpetually angry and Elizabeth learned to bear it: but if her father had ever been angry with her—in those days—she would have wanted to die.

Neither had he ever learned of her disgrace; when it happened, she could not think how to tell him, how to bring such pain to him who had had such pain already. Later, when she would have told him, he was long past caring, in the silent ground.

She thought of him now, while the singing and weeping went on around her—and she thought how he would have loved his grandson, who was like him in so many ways. Perhaps she dreamed it, but she did not believe she dreamed when at moments she thought she heard in John echoes, curiously distant and distorted, of her father's gentleness, and the trick of his laugh—how he threw his head back and the years that marked his face fled away, and the soft eyes softened and the mouth turned upward at the corners like a little boy's mouth— and that deadly pride of her father's behind which he retired when confronted by the nastiness of other people. It was he who had told her to weep, when she wept, alone; never to let the world see, never to ask for mercy; if one had to die, to go ahead and die, but never to let oneself be beaten. He had said this to her on one of the last times she had seen him, when she was being carried miles away, to Maryland, to live with her aunt. She had reason, in the years that followed, to remember his saying this; and time, at last, to discover in herself the depths of bitterness in her father from which these words had come.

For when her mother died, the world fell down; her aunt, her mother's older sister, arrived, and stood appalled at Elizabeth's vanity and uselessness; and decided, immediately, that her father was no fit person to raise a child, especially, as she darkly said, an innocent little girl. And it was this decision on the part of her aunt, for which Elizabeth did not forgive her for many years, that precipitated the third disaster, the separation of herself from her father—from all that she loved on earth.

For her father ran what her aunt called a 'house'—not the house where they lived, but another house, to which, as Elizabeth gathered, wicked people often came. And he had also, to Elizabeth's rather horrified confusion, a 'stable.' Low, common niggers, the lowest of the low, came from all over (and sometimes brought their women and sometimes found them there) to eat, and drink cheap moonshine, and play music all night long—and to do worse things, her aunt's dreadful silence then suggested, which were far better left unsaid. And she would, she swore, move Heaven and earth before she would let her sister's daughter grow up with such a man. Without, however, so much as looking at Heaven, and without troubling any more of the earth than that part of it which held the courthouse, she won the day. Like a clap of thunder, or like a magic spell, like light one moment and darkness the next, Elizabeth's life had changed. Her mother was dead, her father banished, and she lived in the shadow of her aunt.

Or, more exactly, as she thought now, the shadow in which she had lived was fear—fear made more dense by hatred. Not for a moment had she judged her father; it would have made no difference to her love for him had she been told, and even seen it proved, that he was first cousin to the Devil. The proof would not have existed for her, and if it had she would not have regretted being his daughter, or have asked for anything better than to suffer at his side in Hell. And when she had been taken from him her imagination had been wholly unable to lend reality to the wickedness of which he stood accused —*she*, certainly, did not accuse him. She screamed in anguish when he put her from him and turned to go, and she had to be carried to the train. And later, when she understood perfectly all that had happened then, still in her heart she could not accuse him. Perhaps his life had been wicked, but he had been very good to her. His life had certainly cost him enough in pain to make the world's judgment a thing of no account. *They* had not known him as she had known him; *they* did not care as she had cared! It only made her sad that he never, as he had promised, came to take her away, and that while she was growing up she saw him so seldom. When she became a young woman she did not see him at all; but that was her own fault.

No, she did not accuse him; but she accused her aunt, and this from the moment she understood that her aunt had loved her mother, but did not love *him*. This could only mean that her aunt could not love *her*, either, and nothing in her life with her aunt ever proved Elizabeth wrong. It was true that her aunt was always talking of how much she loved her sister's daughter, and what great sacrifices she had made on her account, and what great care she took to see to it that Elizabeth should grow up a good, Christian girl. But Elizabeth was not for a moment fooled, and did not, for as long as she lived with her, fail to despise her aunt. She sensed that what her aunt spoke of as love was something else—a bribe, a threat, an indecent will to power. She knew that the kind of imprisonment that love might impose was also, mysteriously, a freedom for the soul and spirit, was water in the dry place, and had nothing to do with the prisons, churches, laws, rewards, and punishments,

that so positively cluttered the landscape of her aunt's
mind.

And yet, to-night, in her great confusion, she wondered
if she had not been wrong; if there had not been something that she had overlooked, for which the Lord had
made her suffer. 'You little miss great-I-am,' her aunt
had said to her in those days, 'you better watch your
step, you hear me? You go walking around with your
nose in the air, the Lord's going to let you fall right on
down to the bottom of the ground. *You* mark my words.
You'll *see.*'

To this perpetual accusation Elizabeth had never
replied; she merely regarded her aunt with a wide-eyed,
insolent stare, meant at once to register her disdain and
to thwart any pretext for punishment. And this trick,
which she had, unconsciously, picked up from her father,
rarely failed to work. As the years went on, her aunt
seemed to gauge in a look the icy distances that Elizabeth
had put between them, and that would certainly never
be conquered now. And she would add, looking down,
and under her breath: ' 'Cause God don't like it.'

'I sure don't care what God don't like, or you, either,'
Elizabeth's heart replied. 'I'm going away from here.
He's going to come and get me, and I'm going away
from here.'

'He' was her father, who never came. As the years
passed, she replied only: 'I'm going away from here.'
And it hung, this determination, like a heavy jewel
between her breasts; it was written in fire on the dark
sky of her mind.

But, yes—there was something she had overlooked.
*Pride goeth before destruction; and a haughty spirit before
a fall.* She had not known this: she had not imagined
that she could fall. She wondered, to-night, how she
could give this knowledge to her son; if she could help
him to endure what could now no longer be changed; if

while life ran, he would forgive her—for her pride, her folly, and her bargaining with God! For, to-night, those years before her fall, in her aunt's dark house—that house which smelled always of clothes kept too long in closets, and of old women; which was redolent of their gossip, and was pervaded, somehow, by the odour of the lemon her aunt took in her tea, and by the odour of frying fish, and of the still that someone kept in the basement—came before her, entire and overwhelming; and she remembered herself, entering any room in which her aunt might be sitting, responding to anything her aunt might say, standing before her, as rigid as metal and cancerous with hate and fear, in battle every hour of every day, a battle that she continued in her dreams. She knew now of what it was that she had so silently and so early accused her aunt: it was of tearing a bewildered child away from the arms of the father she loved. And she knew now why she had sometimes, so dimly and so unwillingly, felt that her father had betrayed her: it was because he had not overturned the earth to take his daughter away from a woman who did not love her, and whom she did not love. Yet she knew to-night how difficult it was to overturn the earth, for she had tried once, and she had failed. And she knew, too—and it made the tears that touched her mouth more bitter than the most bitter herb—that without the pride and bitterness she had so long carried in her heart against her aunt she could never have endured her life with her.

And she thought of Richard. It was Richard who had taken her out of that house, and out of the South, and into the city of destruction. He had suddenly arrived—and from the moment he arrived until the moment of his death he had filled her life. Not even to-night, in the heart's nearly impenetrable secret place, where the truth is hidden and where only the truth can live, could she wish that she had not known him; nor deny that, so long as he was there, the rejoicing of Heaven could have meant nothing to her—that, being forced to choose between Richard and God, she could only, even with weeping, have turned away from God.

And this was why God had taken him from her. It was for all of this that she was paying now, and it was this pride, hatred, bitterness, lust—this folly, this corruption —of which her son was heir.

Richard had not been born in Maryland, but he was working there, the summer that she met him, as a grocery clerk. It was 1919, and she was one year younger than the century. He was twenty-two, which seemed a great age to her in those days. She noticed him at once because he was so sullen and only barely polite. He waited on folks, her aunt said, furiously, as though he hoped the food they bought would poison them. Elizabeth liked to watch him move; his body was very thin, and beautiful, and nervous—*high strung*, thought Elizabeth, wisely. He moved exactly like a cat, perpetually on the balls of his feet, and with a cat's impressive, indifferent aloofness, his face closed, in his eyes no light at all. He smoked all the time, a cigarette between his lips as he added up the figures, and sometimes left burning on the counter while he went to look for stock. When, as someone entered, he said good morning, or good day, he said it barely looking up, and with an indifference that fell just short of insolence. When, having bought what he wanted and counted his change, the customer turned to leave and Richard said: 'Thank you,' it sounded so much like a curse that people sometimes turned in surprise to stare.

'He sure don't like working in that store,' Elizabeth once observed to her aunt.

'He don't like working,' said her aunt, scornfully. 'He just like you.'

On a bright, summer day, bright in her memory

for ever, she came into the store alone, wearing her
best white summer dress and with her hair, newly
straightened and curled at the ends, tied with a scarlet
ribbon. She was going to a great church picnic with her
aunt, and had come in to buy some lemons. She passed
the owner of the store, who was a very fat man, sitting
out on the pavement, fanning himself; he asked her, as
she passed, if it was hot enough for her, and she said
something and walked into the dark, heavy-smelling
store, where flies buzzed, and where Richard sat on the
counter reading a book.

She felt immediately guilty about having disturbed
him, and muttered apologetically that she only wanted
to buy some lemons. She expected him to get them for
her in his sullen fashion and go back to his book, but he
smiled, and said:

'Is that all you want? You better think now. You sure
you ain't forgot nothing?'

She had never seen him smile before, nor had she
really, for that matter, ever heard his voice. Her heart
gave a dreadful leap and then, as dreadfully, seemed to
have stopped for ever. She could only stand there, staring at him. If he had asked her to repeat what she wanted
she could not possibly have remembered what it was.
And she found that she was looking into his eyes and
where she had thought there was no light at all she found
a light she had never seen before—and he was smiling
still, but there was something curiously urgent in his
smile. Then he said: 'How many lemons, little girl?'

'Six,' she said at last, and discovered to her vast relief
that nothing had happened: the sun was still shining, the
fat man still sat at the door, her heart was beating as
though it had never stopped. She was not, however,
fooled; she remembered the instant at which her heart
had stopped, and she knew that it beat now with a
difference.

He put the lemons into a bag and, with a curious diffidence, she came closer to the counter to give him the money. She was in a terrible state, for she found that she could neither take her eyes off him nor look at him.

'Is that your mother you come in with all the time?' he asked.

'No,' she said, 'that's my aunt.' She did not know why she said it, but she did: 'My mother's dead.'

'Oh,' he said. Then: 'Mine, too.' They both looked thoughtfully at the money on the counter. He picked it up, but did not move. 'I didn't think it was your mother,' he said, finally.

'Why?'

'I don't know. She don't look like you.'

He started to light a cigarette, and then looked at her and put the packet in his pocket again.

'Don't mind me,' she said quickly. 'Anyway, I got to go. She's waiting—we going out.'

He turned and banged the cash register. She picked up her lemons. He gave her her change. She felt that she ought to say something else—it didn't seem right, somehow, just to walk out—but she could not think of anything. But he said:

'Then *that's* why you so dressed up to-day. Where you going to go?'

'We going to a picnic—a church picnic,' she said, and suddenly, unaccountably, and for the first time, smiled.

And he smiled, too, and lit his cigarette, blowing the smoke carefully away from her. 'You like picnics?'

'Sometimes,' she said. She was not comfortable with him yet, and still she was beginning to feel that she would like to stand and talk to him all day. She wanted to ask him what he was reading, but she did not dare. Yet: 'What's your name?' she abruptly brought out.

'Richard,' he said.

'Oh,' she said thoughtfully. Then: 'Mine's Elizabeth.'

'I know,' he said. 'I heard her call you one time.'

'Well,' she said helplessly, after a long pause, 'good-bye.'

'Good-*bye?* You ain't going away, is you?'

'Oh, no,' she said, in confusion.

'Well,' he said, and smiled and bowed, 'good *day.*'

'Yes,' she said, 'good day.'

And she turned and walked out into the streets; not the same streets from which she had entered a moment ago. These streets, the sky above, the sun, the drifting people, all had, in a moment, changed, and would never be the same again.

'You remember that day,' he asked much later, 'when you come into the store?'

'Yes?'

'Well, you was mighty pretty.'

'I didn't think you never looked at me.'

'Well, I didn't think you never looked at me.'

'You was reading a book.'

'Yes.'

'What book was it, Richard?'

'Oh, I don't remember. Just a book.'

'You smiled.'

'You did, too.'

'No, I didn't. I remember.'

'Yes, you did.'

'No, I *didn't.* Not till you did.'

'Well, anyway—you was mighty pretty.'

She did not like to think of with what hardness of heart, what calculated weeping, what deceit, what cruelty she now went into battle with her aunt for her freedom. And she won it, even though on certain not-to-be-dismissed conditions. The principal condition was that she should put herself under the protection of a distant, unspeakably respectable female relative of her aunt's, who lived in New York City—for when the summer ended, Richard said that he was going there and he wanted her to come with him. They would get married there. Richard said that he hated the South, and this was perhaps the reason it did not occur to either of them to begin their married life there. And Elizabeth was checked by the fear that if her aunt should discover how things stood between her and Richard she would find, as she had found so many years before in the case of her father, some means of bringing about their separation. This, as Elizabeth later considered it, was the first in the sordid series of mistakes which was to cause her to fall so low.

But to look back from the stony plain along the road which led one to that place is not at all the same thing as walking on the road; the perspective, to say the very least, changes only with the journey; only when the road has, all abruptly and treacherously, and with an absoluteness that permits no argument, turned or dropped or risen is one able to see all that one could not have seen from any other place. In those days, had the Lord Himself descended from Heaven with trumpets telling her to turn back, she could scarcely have heard Him, and could certainly not have heeded. She lived, in those days, in a fiery storm, of which Richard was the centre and the heart. And she fought only to reach him—only that; she was afraid of what might happen if they were kept from one another; for what might come after she had no thoughts or fears to spare.

Her pretext for coming to New York was to take advantage of the greater opportunities the North offered coloured people; to study in a Northern school, and to find a better job than any she was likely to be offered in the South. Her aunt, who listened to this with no diminution of her habitual scorn, was yet unable to deny that from generation to generation, things, as she grudgingly put it, were bound to change—and neither could she quite take the position of seeming to stand in Elizabeth's

way. In the winter of 1920, as the year began, Elizabeth
found herself in an ugly back room in Harlem in the
home of her aunt's relative, a woman whose respecta-
bility was immediately evident from the incense she
burned in her rooms and the spiritualist séances she held
every Saturday night.

The house was still standing, not very far away; often
she was forced to pass it. Without looking up, she was
able to see the windows of the apartment in which she
had lived, and the woman's sign was in the window still:
MADAME WILLIAMS, SPIRITUALIST.

She found a job as chambermaid in the same hotel in
which Richard worked as lift-boy. Richard said that
they would marry as soon as he had saved some money.
But since he was going to school at night and made very
little money, their marriage, which she had thought of as
taking place almost as soon as she arrived, was planned
for a future that grew ever more remote. And this presented her with a problem that she had refused, at home in
Maryland, to think about, but from which, now, she could
not escape: the problem of their life together. Reality, so
to speak, burst in for the first time on her great dreaming, and she found occasion to wonder, ruefully, what
had made her imagine that, once with Richard, she would
have been able to withstand him. She had kept, pre-
cariously enough, what her aunt referred to as her pearl
without price while she had been with Richard down
home. This, which she had taken as witness to her own
feminine moral strength, had been due to nothing more,
it now developed, than her great fear of her aunt, and
the lack, in that small town, of opportunity. Here, in
this great city where no one cared, where people might
live in the same building for years and never speak to
one another, she found herself, when Richard took her in
his arms, on the edge of a steep place: and down she
rushed, on the descent uncaring, into the dreadful sea.

So it began. Had it been waiting for her since the day she had been taken from her father's arms? The world in which she now found herself was not unlike the world from which she had, so long ago, been rescued. Here were the women who had been the cause of her aunt's most passionate condemnation of her father—hard-drinking, hard-talking, with whisky- and cigarette-breath, and moving with the mystic authority of women who knew what sweet violence might be acted out under the moon and stars, or beneath the tigerish lights of the city, in the raucous hay or the singing bed. And was she, Elizabeth, so sweetly fallen, so tightly chained, one of these women now? And here were the men who had come day and night to visit her father's 'stable'—with their sweet talk and their music, and their violence and their sex—black, brown, and beige, who looked on her with lewd, and lustful, and laughing eyes. And these were Richard's friends. Not one of them ever went to Church—one might scarcely have imagined that they knew that churches existed—they all, hourly, daily, in their speech, in their lives, and in their hearts, cursed God. They all seemed to be saying, as Richard, when she once timidly mentioned the love of Jesus, said: 'You can tell that puking bastard to kiss my big black arse.'

She, for very terror on hearing this, had wept; yet she could not deny that for such an abundance of bitterness there was a positive fountain of grief. There was not, after all, a great difference between the world of the North and that of the South which she had fled; there was only this difference: the North promised more. And this similarity: what it promised it did not give, and what it gave, at length and grudgingly with one hand, it took back with the other. Now she understood in this nervous, hollow, ringing city, that nervousness of Richard's which had so attracted her—a tension so total, and so without the hope, or possibility of release, or resolution, that she felt it in his muscles, and heard it in his breathing, even as on her breast he fell asleep.

And this was perhaps why she had never thought to leave him, frightened though she was during all that time, and in a world in which, had it not been for Richard, she could have found no place to put her feet. She did not leave him, because she was afraid of what might happen to him without her. She did not resist him, because he needed her. And she did not press about marriage because, upset as he was about everything, she was afraid of having him upset about her, too. She thought of herself as his strength; in a world of shadows, the indisputable reality to which he could always repair. And, again, for all that had come, she could not regret this. She had tried, but she had never been and was not now, even to-night, truly sorry. Where, then, was her repentance? And how could God hear her cry?

They had been very happy together, in the beginning; and until the very end he had been very good to her, had not ceased to love her, and tried always to make her know it. No more than she had been able to accuse her father had she ever been able to accuse him. His weakness she understood, and his terror, and even his bloody end. What life had made him bear, her lover, this wild, unhappy boy, many another stronger and more virtuous man might not have borne so well.

Saturday was their best day, for they only worked until one o'clock. They had all the afternoon to be together, and nearly all of the night, since Madame Williams had her séances on Saturday night and preferred that Elizabeth, before whose silent scepticism departed spirits might find themselves reluctant to speak, should not be in the house. They met at the service entrance. Richard was always there before her, looking, oddly, much younger and less anonymous without the ugly, tight-fitting, black uniform that he had to wear when working. He would be talking, or laughing with some of the other boys, or shooting dice, and when he heard her step down the long, stone hall he would look up, laughing; and wickedly nudging one of the other boys, he would half shout, half sing: 'He-y! Look-a-there, ain't she pretty?'

She never failed, at this—which was why he never failed to do it—to blush, half-smiling, half-frowning, and nervously to touch the collar of her dress.

'*Sweet* Georgia Brown!' somebody might say.

'*Miss* Brown to you,' said Richard, then, and took her arm.

'Yeah, that's right,' somebody else would say, 'you *better* hold on to little Miss Bright-eyes, don't somebody sure going to take her away from you.'

'Yeah,' said another voice, 'and it might be me.'

'*Oh*, no,' said Richard, moving with her towards the street, 'ain't nobody going to take *my* little Little-bit away from *me*.'

Little-bit: it had been his name for her. And sometimes he called her Sandwich Mouth, or Funnyface, or Frog-eyes. She would not, of course, have endured these names from anyone else, nor, had she not found herself, with joy and helplessness (and a sleeping panic), living it out, would she ever have suffered herself so publicly to become a man's property—'concubine,' her aunt would have said, and at night, alone, she rolled the word, tart like lemon rind, on her tongue.

She was descending with Richard to the sea. She would have to climb back up alone, but she did not know this then. Leaving the boys in the hall, they gained the midtown New York streets.

'And what we going to do to-day, Little-bit?' With that smile of his, and those depthless eyes, beneath the towers of the white city, with people, white, hurrying all around them.

'I don't know, honey. What you want to do?'

'Well, maybe, we go to a *mu*seum.'

The first time he suggested this, she demanded, in panic, if they would be allowed to enter.

'Sure, they let niggers in,' Richard said. 'Ain't we got to be educated, too—to live with the motherf——s?'

He never 'watched' his language with her, which at first she took as evidence of his contempt because she had fallen so easily, and which later she took as evidence of his love.

And when he took her to the Museum of Natural History, or the Metropolitan Museum of Art, where they were almost certain to be the only black people, and he guided her through the halls, which never ceased in her imagination to be as cold as tombstones, it was then she saw another life in him. It never ceased to frighten her, this passion he brought to something she could not understand.

For she never grasped—not at any rate with her mind —what, with such incandescence, he tried to tell her on these Saturday afternoons. She could not find, between herself and the African statuette, or totem pole, on which he gazed with such melancholy wonder, any point of contact. She was only glad that she did not look that way. She preferred to look, in the other museum, at the paintings; but still she did not understand anything he said about them. She did not know why he so adored things that were so long dead; what sustenance they gave him, what secrets he hoped to wrest from them. But she understood, at least, that they *did* give him a kind of bitter nourishment, and that the secrets they held for him were a matter of his life and death. It frightened her because she felt that he was reaching for the moon and that he would, therefore, be dashed down against the rocks; but she did not say any of this. She only listened, and in her heart she prayed for him.

But on other Saturdays they went to see a movie; they
went to see a play; they visited his friends; they walked
through Central Park. She liked the park because, however spuriously, it re-created something of the landscape
she had known. How many afternoons had they walked
there! She had always, since, avoided it. They bought
peanuts and for hours fed the animals at the zoo; they
bought soda pop and drank it on the grass; they walked
along the reservoir and Richard explained how a city
like New York found water to drink. Mixed with her
fear for him was a total admiration: that he had learned
so young, so much. People stared at them but she did
not mind; he noticed, but he did not seem to notice. But
sometimes he would ask, in the middle of a sentence—
concerned, possibly, with ancient Rome:

'Little-bit—d'you love me?'

And she wondered how he could doubt it. She thought
how infirm she must be not to have been able to make
him know it; and she raised her eyes to his, and she said
the only thing she could say:

'I wish to God I may die if I don't love you. There
ain't no sky above us if I don't love you.'

Then he would look ironically up at the sky, and take
her arm with a firmer pressure, and they would walk on.

Once, she asked him:

'Richard, did you go to school much when you was
little?'

And he looked at her a long moment. Then:

'Baby, I done told you, my mama died when I was
born. And my daddy, he weren't nowhere to be found.
Ain't nobody never took care of me. I just moved from
one place to another. When one set of folks got tired of
me they sent me down the line. I didn't hardly go to
school at all.'

'Then how come you got to be so smart? how come
you got to know so much?'

G

And he smiled, pleased, but he said: 'Little-bit, I don't know so much.' Then he said, with a change in his face and voice which she had grown to know: 'I just decided me one day that I was going to get to know everything them white bastards knew, and I was going to get to know it better than them, so could no white son-of-a-bitch *nowhere* never talk *me* down, and never make me feel like *I* was dirt, when I could read him the alphabet, back, front, and sideways. He weren't going to beat my arse, then. And if he tried to kill me, I'd take him with me, I swear to my mother I would.' Then he looked at her again, and smiled and kissed her, and he said: 'That's how I got to know so much, baby.'

She asked: 'And what you going to do, Richard? What you want to be?'

And his face clouded. 'I don't know. I got to find out. Looks like I can't get my mind straight nohow.'

She did not know *why* he couldn't—or she could only dimly face it—but she knew he spoke the truth.

She had made her great mistake with Richard in not telling him that she was going to have a child. Perhaps, she thought now, if she had told him everything might have been very different, and he would be living yet. But the circumstances under which she had discovered herself to be pregnant had been such to make her decide, for his sake, to hold her peace awhile. Frightened as she was, she dared not add to the panic that overtook him on the last summer of his life.

And yet perhaps it was, after all, this—this failure to demand of his strength what it might then, most miraculously, have been found able to bear; by which —indeed, how could she know?—his strength might have been strengthened, for which she prayed to-night to be forgiven. Perhaps she had lost her love because she had not, in the end, believed in it enough.

She lived quite a long way from Richard—four underground stops; and when it was time for her to go home, he always took the underground uptown with her and walked her to her door. On a Saturday when they had forgotten the time and stayed together later than usual, he left her at her door at two o'clock in the morning. They said good night hurriedly, for she was afraid of trouble when she got upstairs—though, in fact, Madame Williams seemed astonishingly indifferent to the hours Elizabeth kept—and he wanted to hurry back home and go to bed. Yet, as he hurried off down the dark, murmuring street, she had a sudden impulse to call him back, to ask him to take her with him and never let her go again. She hurried up the steps, smiling a little at this fancy: it was because he looked so young and defenceless as he walked away, and yet so jaunty and strong.

He was to come the next evening at supper-time, to make at last, at Elizabeth's urging, the acquaintance of Madame Williams. But he did not come. She drove Madame Williams wild with her sudden sensitivity to footsteps on the stairs. Having told Madame Williams that a gentleman was coming to visit her, she did not dare, of course, to leave the house and go out looking for him, thus giving Madame Williams the impression that she dragged men in off the streets. At ten o'clock, having eaten no supper, a detail unnoticed by her hostess, she went to bed, her head aching and her heart sick with fear; fear over what had happened to Richard, who had never kept her waiting before; and fear involving all that was beginning to happen in her body.

And on Monday morning he was not at work. She left during the lunch hour to go to his room. He was not there. His landlady said that he had not been there all week-end. While Elizabeth stood trembling and indecisive in the hall, two white policemen entered.

She knew the moment she saw them, and before they mentioned his name, that something terrible had happened to Richard. Her heart, as on that bright summer day when he had first spoken to her, gave a terrible bound and then was still, with an awful, wounded stillness. She put out one hand to touch the wall in order to keep standing.

'This here young lady was just looking for him,' she heard the landlady say.

They all looked at her.

'You his girl?' one of the policemen asked.

She looked up at his sweating face, on which a lascivious smile had immediately appeared, and straightened, trying to control her trembling.

'Yes,' she said. 'Where is he?'

'He's in jail, honey,' the other policeman said.

'What for?'

'For robbing a white man's store, black girl. That's what for.'

She found, and thanked Heaven for it, that a cold, stony rage had entered her. She would, otherwise, certainly have fallen down, or began to weep. She looked at the smiling policeman.

'Richard ain't robbed no store,' she said. 'Tell me where he is.'

'And *I* tell you,' he said, not smiling, 'that your boy-friend robbed a store and he's in jail for it. He's going to stay there, too—now, what you got to say to that?'

'And he probably did it for you, too,' the other policeman said. 'You look like a girl a man could rob a store for.'

She said nothing; she was thinking how to get to see him, how to get him out.

One of them, the smiler, turned now to the landlady and said: 'Let's have the key to his room. How long's he been living here?'

'About a year,' the landlady said. She looked unhappily at Elizabeth. 'He seemed like a real nice boy.'

'Ah, yes,' he said, mounting the steps, 'they all seem like real nice boys when they pay their rent.'

'You going to take me to see him?' she asked of the remaining policeman. She found herself fascinated by the gun in his holster, the club at his side. She wanted to take that pistol and empty it into his round, red face; to take that club and strike with all her strength against the base of his skull where his cap ended, until the ugly, silky, white man's hair was matted with blood and brains.

'Sure, girl,' he said, 'you're coming right along with us. The man at the station-house wants to ask you some questions.'

The smiling policeman came down again. 'Ain't nothing up there,' he said. 'Let's go.'

She moved between them, out into the sun. She knew that there was nothing to be gained by talking to them any more. She was entirely in their power; she would have to think faster than they could think; she would have to contain her fear and her hatred, and find out what could be done. Not for anything short of Richard's life, and not, possibly, even for that, would she have wept before them, or asked of them a kindness.

A small crowd, children and curious passers-by, followed them as they walked the long, dusty, sunlit street. She hoped only that they would not pass anyone she knew; she kept her head high, looking straight ahead, and felt the skin settle over her bones as though she were wearing a mask.

And at the station she somehow got past their brutal laughter. (*What was he doing with you, girl, until two o'clock in the morning?—Next time you feel like that, girl, you come by here and talk to me.*) She felt that she was about to burst, or vomit, or die. Though the sweat stood out cruelly, like needles on her brow, and she felt herself, from every side, being covered with a stink and filth, she found out, in their own good time, what she wanted to know. He was being held in a prison downtown called the Tombs (the name made her heart turn over), and she could see him to-morrow. The state, or the prison, or someone, had already assigned him a lawyer; he would be brought to trial next week.

But the next day, when she saw him, she wept. He had been beaten, he whispered to her, and he could hardly walk. His body, she later discovered, bore almost no bruises, but was full of strange, painful swellings, and there was a welt above one eye.

He had not, of course, robbed the store, but, when he left her that Saturday night, had gone down into the underground station to wait for his train. It was late, and trains were slow; he was all alone on the platform, only half awake, thinking, he said, of her.

Then, from the far end of the platform, he heard a sound of running; and, looking up, he saw two coloured boys come running down the steps. Their clothes were torn, and they were frightened; they came up the platform and stood near him, breathing hard. He was about to ask them what the trouble was when, running across the tracks towards them, and followed by a white man, he saw another coloured boy; and at the same instant another white man came running down the underground steps.

Then he came full awake, in panic; he knew that whatever the trouble was, it was now his trouble also; for these white men would make no distinction between him and the three boys they were after. They were all coloured, they were about the same age, and here they stood together on the underground platform. And they were all, with no questions asked, herded upstairs, and into the wagon and to the station-house.

At the station Richard gave his name and address and age and occupation. Then for the first time he stated that he was not involved, and asked one of the other boys

to corroborate his testimony. This they rather despair-
ingly did. They might, Elizabeth felt, have done it
sooner, but they probably also felt that it would be useless to speak. And they were not believed; the owner
of the store was being brought there to make the identi-
fication. And Richard tried to relax: the man *could* not
say that he had been there if he had never seen him
before.

But when the owner came, a short man with a bloody
shirt—for they had knifed him—in the company of yet
another policeman, he looked at the four boys before
him and said: 'Yeah, that's them, all right.'

Then Richard shouted: 'But *I* wasn't there! Look at
me, goddammit—I wasn't *there!*'

'You black bastards,' the man said, looking at him,
'you're all the same.'

Then there was silence in the station, the eyes of the
white men all watching. And Richard said, but quietly,
knowing that he was lost: 'But all the same, mister, I
wasn't there.' And he looked at the white man's bloody
shirt and thought, he told Elizabeth, at the bottom of his
heart: 'I wish to God they'd killed you.'

Then the questioning began. The three boys signed a
confession at once, but Richard would not sign. He said
at last that he would die before he signed a confession to
something he hadn't done. 'Well then,' said one of them,
hitting him suddenly across the head, 'maybe you *will*
die, you black son-of-a-bitch.' And the beating began.
He would not, then, talk to her about it; she found that,
before the dread and the hatred that filled her mind, her
imagination faltered and held its peace.

'What we going to do?' she asked at last.

He smiled a vicious smile—she had never seen such a
smile on his face before. 'Maybe you ought to pray to
that Jesus of yours and get Him to come down and tell
these white men something.' He looked at her a long,

dying moment. 'Because I don't know nothing *else* to do,' he said.

She suggested: 'Richard, what about another lawyer?'

And he smiled again. 'I declare,' he said, 'Little-bit's been holding out on me. She got a fortune tied up in a sock, and she ain't never told me nothing about it.'

She had been trying to save money for a whole year, but she had only thirty dollars. She sat before him, going over in her mind all the things she might do to raise money, even to going on the streets. Then, for very helplessness, she began to shake with sobbing. At this, his face became Richard's face again. He said in a shaking voice: 'Now, look here, Little-bit, don't you be like that. We going to work this out all right.' But she could not stop sobbing. 'Elizabeth,' he whispered, 'Elizabeth, Elizabeth.' Then the man came and said that it was time for her to go. And she rose. She had brought two packets of cigarettes for him, and they were still in her bag. Wholly ignorant of prison regulations, she did not dare to give them to him under the man's eyes. And, somehow, her failure to remember to give him the cigarettes, when she knew how much he smoked, made her weep the harder. She tried—and failed—to smile at him, and she was slowly led to the door. The sun nearly blinded her, and she heard him whisper behind her: 'So long, baby. Be good.'

In the streets she did not know what to do. She stood awhile before the dreadful gates, and then she walked and walked until she came to a coffee shop where taxi drivers and the people who worked in nearby offices hurried in and out all day. Usually she was afraid to go into downtown establishments, where only white people were, but to-day she did not care. She felt that if anyone said anything to her she would turn and curse him like the lowest bitch on the streets. If anyone touched her, she would do her best to send his soul to Hell.

But no one touched her; no one spoke. She drank her coffee, sitting in the strong sun that fell through the window. Now it came to her how alone, how frightened she was; she had never been so frightened in her life before. She knew that she was pregnant—knew it, as the old folks said, in her bones; and if Richard should be sent away, what, under Heaven, could she do? Two years, three years—she had no idea how long he might be sent away for—what would she do? And how could she keep her aunt from knowing? And if her aunt should find out, then her father would know, too. The tears welled up, and she drank her cold, tasteless coffee. And what would they do with Richard? And if they sent him away, what would he be like, then, when he returned? She looked out into the quiet, sunny streets, and for the first time in her life, she hated it all—the white city, the white world. She could not, that day, think of one decent white person in the whole world. She sat there, and she hoped that one day God, with tortures inconceivable, would grind them utterly into humility, and make them know that black boys and black girls, whom they treated with such condescension, such disdain, and such good humour, had hearts like human beings, too, more human hearts than theirs.

But Richard was not sent away. Against the testimony of the three robbers, and her own testimony, and, under oath, the storekeeper's indecision, there was no evidence on which to convict him. The courtroom seemed to feel, with some complacency and some disappointment, that it was his great good luck to be let off so easily. They went immediately to his room. And there—she was never all her life long to forget it—he threw himself, face downward, on his bed and wept.

She had only seen one other man weep before—her father—and it had not been like this. She touched him, but he did not stop. Her own tears fell on his dirty, uncombed hair. She tried to hold him, but for a long while he would not be held. His body was like iron; she could find no softness in it. She sat curled like a frightened child on the edge of the bed, her hand on his back, waiting for the storm to pass over. It was then that she decided not to tell him yet about the child.

By and by he called her name. And then he turned, and she held him against her breast, while he sighed and shook. He fell asleep at last, clinging to her as though he were going down into the water for the last time.

And it was the last time. That night he cut his wrists with his razor and he was found in the morning by his landlady, his eyes staring upward with no light, dead among the scarlet sheets.

And now they were singing:

> 'Somebody needs you, Lord,
> Come by here.'

At her back, above her, she heard Gabriel's voice. He had risen and was helping the others to pray through. She wondered if John were still on his knees, or had risen, with a child's impatience, and was staring around the church. There was a stiffness in him that would be hard to break, but that, nevertheless, would one day surely be broken. As hers had been, and Richard's—there was no escape for anyone. God was everywhere, terrible, the living God; and so high, the song said, you couldn't get over Him; so low you couldn't get under Him; so wide you couldn't get around Him; but must come in at the door.

And she, she knew to-day that door: a living, wrathful gate. She knew through what fires the soul must crawl, and with what weeping one passed over. Men spoke of how the heart broke up, but never spoke of how the soul hung speechless in the pause, the void, the terror between the living and the dead; how, all garments rent and cast aside, the naked soul passed over the very mouth of Hell. Once there, there was no turning back; once there, the soul remembered, though the heart sometimes forgot. For the world called to the heart, which stammered to reply; life, and love, and revelry, and, most falsely, hope, called the forgetful, the human heart. Only the soul, obsessed with the journey it had made, and had still to make, pursued its mysterious and dreadful end; and carried, heavy with weeping and bitterness, the heart along.

And, therefore, there was war in Heaven, and weeping before the throne: the heart chained to the soul, and the soul imprisoned within the flesh—a weeping, a confusion, and a weight unendurable filled all the earth. Only the love of God could establish order in this chaos; to Him the soul must turn to be delivered.

But what a turning! How could she fail to pray that He would have mercy on her son, and spare him the sin-born anguish of his father and his mother. And that his heart might know a little joy before the long bitterness descended.

Yet she knew that her weeping and her prayers were in vain. What was coming would surely come; nothing could stop it. She had tried, once, to protect someone and had only hurled him into prison. And she thought to-night, as she had thought so often, that it might have been better, after all, to have done what she had first determined in her heart to do—to have given her son away to strangers, who might have loved him more than Gabriel had ever loved him. She had believed him when he said that God had sent him to her for a sign. He had said that he would cherish her until the grave, and that he would love her nameless son as though he were his own flesh. And he had kept the letter of his promise: he had fed him and clothed him and taught him the Bible— but the spirit was not there. And he cherished—*if* he cherished her—only because she was the mother of his son, Roy. All of this she had through the painful years divined. He certainly did not know she knew it, and she wondered if he knew it himself.

She had met him through Florence. Florence and she had met at work in the middle of the summer, a year after Richard's death. John was then over six months old.

She was very lonely that summer, and beaten down. She was living alone with John in a furnished room even grimmer than the room that had been hers in Madame Williams's apartment. She had, of course, left Madame Williams's immediately upon the death of Richard, saying that she had found a sleep-in job in the country. She had been terribly grateful that summer for Madame Williams's indifference; the woman had simply not seemed to see that Elizabeth, overnight, had become an old woman and was half mad with fear and grief. She wrote her aunt the driest, and briefest, and coldest of notes, not wishing in any way to awaken whatever concern might yet slumber in her breast, telling her the same thing she had told Madame Williams, and telling her not to worry, she was in the hands of God. And she certainly was; through a bitterness that only the hand of God could have laid on her, this same hand brought her through.

Florence and Elizabeth worked as cleaning-women in a high, vast, stony office-building on Wall Street. They arrived in the evening and spent the night going through the great deserted halls and the silent offices with mops and pails and brooms. It was terrible work, and Elizabeth hated it; but it was at night, and she had taken it joyfully, since it meant that she could take care of John herself all day and not have to spend extra money to keep him in a nursery. She worried about him all night long, of course, but at least at night he was sleeping. She could only pray that the house would not burn down, that he would not fall out of bed or, in some mysterious way, turn on the gas-burner, and she had asked the woman next door, who unhappily drank too much, to keep an eye out for him. This woman, with whom she sometimes spent an hour or so in the afternoons, and her landlady, were the only people she saw. She had stopped seeing Richard's friends because, for some reason, she did not want them to know about Richard's child; and because, too, the moment that he was dead it became immediately apparent on both sides how little they had in common. And she did not seek new people; rather, she fled from them. She could not bear, in her changed and fallen state, to submit herself to the eyes of others. The Elizabeth that she had been was buried far away— with her lost and silent father, with her aunt, in Richard's grave—and the Elizabeth she had become she did not recognize, she did not want to know.

But one night, when work was ended, Florence invited her to share a cup of coffee in the all-night coffee shop nearby. Elizabeth had, of course, been invited before by other people—the night watchman, for example—but she had always said no. She pleaded the excuse of her baby, whom she must rush home to feed. She was pretending in those days to be a young widow, and she wore a wedding ring. Very shortly, fewer people asked her, and she achieved the reputation of being 'stuck up.'

Florence had scarcely ever spoken to her before she arrived at this merciful unpopularity; but Elizabeth had noticed Florence. She moved in a silent ferocity of dignity which barely escaped being ludicrous. She was extremely unpopular also and she had nothing whatever to do with any of the women she worked with. She was, for one thing, a good deal older, and she seemed to have nothing to laugh or gossip about. She came to work, and she did her work, and she left. One could not imagine what she was thinking as she marched so grimly down the halls, her head tied up in a rag, a bucket and a mop in her hands. Elizabeth thought that she must once have been very rich, and had lost her money; and she felt for her, as one fallen woman for another, a certain kinship.

A cup of coffee together as day was breaking, became in time their habit. They sat together in the coffee shop, which was always empty when they arrived and was crowded fifteen minutes later when they left, and had their coffee and doughnuts before they took the underground uptown. While they had their coffee, and on the ride uptown, they talked, principally about Florence, how badly people treated her, and how empty her life was now that her husband was dead. He had adored her, she told Elizabeth, and satisfied her every whim, but he had tended to irresponsibility. If she had told him once, she had told him a hundred times: 'Frank, you better take out life insurance.' But he had thought—and wasn't it just like a man!—that he would live for ever. Now here she was, a woman getting along in years, forced to make her living among all the black scum of this wicked city. Elizabeth, a little astonished at the need for confession betrayed by this proud woman, listened, nevertheless, with great sympathy. She was very grateful for Florence's interest. Florence was so much older and seemed so kind.

It was no doubt this, Florence's age and kindness, that led Elizabeth, with no premeditation, to take Florence into her confidence. Looking back, she found it hard to believe that she could have been so desperate, or so childish; though, again, on looking back, she was able to see clearly what she then so incoherently felt: how much she needed another human being, somewhere, who knew the truth about her.

Florence had often said how glad she would be to make the acquaintance of little Johnny; she was sure, she said, that any child of Elizabeth's must be a wonderful child. On a Sunday near the end of that summer,

Elizabeth dressed him in his best clothes and took him to
Florence's house. She was oddly and fearfully depressed
that day; and John was not in a good mood. She found
herself staring at him darkly, as though she were trying
to read his future in his face. He would grow big one
day, he would talk, and he would ask her questions.
What questions would he ask her, what answers would
she give? She surely would not be able to lie to him
indefinitely about his father, for one day he would be old
enough to realize that it was not his father's name he
bore. Richard had been a fatherless child, she helplessly,
bitterly remembered as she carried John through the
busy, summer, Sunday streets. *When one set of folks got
tired of me they sent me down the line.* Yes, down the line,
through poverty, hunger, wandering, cruelty, fear, and
trembling, to death. And she thought of the boys who
had gone to prison. Were they there still? Would John
be one of these boys one day? These boys, now, who
stood before drug-store windows, before pool-rooms, on
every street corner, who whistled after her, whose lean
bodies fairly rang, it seemed, with idleness, and malice,
and frustration. How could she hope, alone, and in famine
as she was, to put herself between him and this so wide
and raging destruction? And then, as though to confirm
her in all her dark imaginings, he began, as she reached
the underground steps, to whimper, and moan, and cry.

And he kept this up, too, all the way uptown—so that,
what with the impossibility of pleasing him that day, no
matter what she did, what with restless weight, and
the heat, and the smiling, staring people, and the strange
dread that weighed on her so heavily, she was nearly
ready to weep by the time she arrived at Florence's door.

He, at that moment, to her exasperated relief, became
the most cheerful of infants. Florence was wearing a
heavy, old-fashioned garnet brooch, which, as she opened
the door, immediately attracted John's eye. He began

reaching for the brooch and babbling and spitting at
Florence as though he had known her all of his short life.

'Well!' said Florence, 'when he get big enough to
*really* go after the ladies you going to have your hands
full, girl.'

'That,' said Elizabeth, grimly, 'is the Lord's truth. He
keep me so busy now I don't know half the time if I'm
coming or going.'

Florence, meanwhile, attempted to distract John's
attention from the brooch by offering him an orange;
but he had seen oranges before; he merely looked at it a
moment before letting it fall to the floor. He began
again, in his disturbingly fluid fashion, to quarrel about
the brooch.

'He like you,' said Elizabeth, finally, calmed a little
by watching him.

'You must be tired,' said Florence, then: 'Put him
down there.' And she dragged one large easy chair to
the table so that John could watch them while they ate.

'I got a letter from my brother the other day,' she said,
bringing the food to the table. 'His wife, poor ailing soul,
done passed on, and he thinking about coming North.'

'You ain't never told me,' said Elizabeth, with a quick
and rather false interest, 'you had a brother! And he
coming up here?'

'So he say. Ain't nothing, I reckon, to keep him down
home no more—now Deborah's gone.' She sat down
opposite Elizabeth. 'I ain't seen him,' she said, musingly,
'for more than twenty years.'

'Then it'll be a great day,' Elizabeth smiled, 'when
you two meet again.'

Florence shook her head, and motioned for Elizabeth
to start eating. 'No,' she said, 'we ain't never got along,
and I don't reckon he's changed.'

'Twenty years is a mighty long time,' Elizabeth said,
'he's bound to have changed *some*.'

'That man,' said Florence, 'would have to do a whole *lot* of changing before him and me hit it off. No,'—she paused, grimly, sadly—'I'm mighty sorry he's coming. I didn't look to see him no more in this world—or in the next one, neither.'

This was not, Elizabeth felt, the way a sister ought to talk about her brother, especially to someone who knew him not at all, and who would, probably, eventually meet him. She asked, helplessly:

'What do he do—your brother?'

'He some kind of preacher,' said Florence. 'I ain't never heard him. When *I* was home he weren't doing nothing but chasing after women and lying in the ditches, drunk.'

'I hope,' laughed Elizabeth, 'he done changed his *ways* at least.'

'Folks,' said Florence, 'can change their ways much as they want to. But I don't care how many times you change your ways, what's in you is in you, and it's got to come out.'

'Yes,' said Elizabeth, thoughtfully. 'But don't you think,' she hesitantly asked, 'that the Lord can change a person's heart?'

'I done heard it said often enough,' said Florence, 'but I got yet to see it. These niggers running around, talking about the Lord done changed their hearts—ain't nothing happened to them niggers. They got the same old black hearts they was born with. I reckon the Lord done give them *those* hearts—and, honey, the Lord don't give out no second helpings, *I'm* here to tell you.'

'No,' said Elizabeth heavily, after a long pause. She turned to look at John, who was grimly destroying the square, tasselled doilies that decorated Florence's easy chair. 'I reckon that's the truth. Look like it go around once, and that's that. You miss it, and you's fixed for fair.'

'Now you sound,' said Florence, 'mighty sad all of a sudden. What's the matter with you?'

'Nothing,' she said. She turned back to the table. Then, helplessly, and thinking that she must not say too much: 'I was just thinking about this boy here, what's going to happen to him, how I'm going to raise him, in this awful city all by myself.'

'But you ain't fixing, is you,' asked Florence, 'to stay single all your days? You's a right young girl, and a right pretty girl. I wouldn't be in no hurry if I was you to find no new husband. I don't believe the nigger's been born what knows how to treat a woman right. You got time, honey, so *take* your time.'

'I ain't,' said Elizabeth, quietly, 'got so much time.' She could not stop herself; though something warned her to hold her peace, the words poured out. 'You see this wedding ring? Well, I bought this ring myself. This boy ain't got no daddy.'

Now she had said it: the words could not be called back. And she felt, as she sat, trembling, at Florence's table, a reckless, pained relief.

Florence stared at her with a pity so intense that it resembled anger. She looked at John, and then back at Elizabeth.

'You poor thing,' said Florence, leaning back in her chair, her face still filled with this strange, brooding fury, 'you *is* had a time, ain't you?'

'I was *scared*,' Elizabeth brought out, shivering, still compelled to speak.

'I ain't never,' said Florence, 'seen it to fail. Look like ain't no woman born what don't get walked over by some no-count man. Look like ain't no woman nowhere but ain't been dragged down in the dirt by some man, and left there, too, while he go on about his business.'

Elizabeth sat at the table, numb, with nothing more to say.

'What he do,' asked Florence, finally, 'run off and leave you?'

'Oh, no,' cried Elizabeth, quickly, and the tears sprang
to her eyes, 'he weren't like that! He died, just like I say
—he got in trouble, and he died—a long time before this
boy was born.' She began to weep with the same helplessness with which she had been speaking. Florence
rose and came over to Elizabeth, holding Elizabeth's
head against her breast. 'He wouldn't never of left me,'
said Elizabeth, 'but he *died*.'

And now she wept, after her long austerity, as though
she would never be able to stop.

'Hush now,' said Florence, gently, 'hush now. You
going to frighten the little fellow. He don't want to see
his mamma cry. All right,' she whispered to John, who
had ceased his attempts at destruction, and stared now
at the two women, 'all right. Everything's all right.'

Elizabeth sat up and reached in her handbag for a
handkerchief, and began to dry her eyes.

'Yes,' said Florence, moving to the window, 'the
menfolk, they die, all right. And it's us women who walk
around, like the Bible says, and mourn. The menfolk,
they die, and its over for them, but we women, we have
to keep on living and try to forget what they done to us.
Yes, Lord——' and she paused; she turned and came
back to Elizabeth. 'Yes, Lord,' she repeated, 'don't *I*
know.'

'I'm mighty sorry,' said Elizabeth, 'to upset your nice
dinner this way.'

'Girl,' said Florence, 'don't you say a word about being
sorry, or I'll show you to this door. You pick up that boy
and sit down there in that easy chair and pull yourself
together. I'm going out in the kitchen and make us something cold to drink. You try not to fret, honey. The Lord,
He ain't going to let you fall but so low.'

Then she met Gabriel, two or three weeks later, at
Florence's house on a Sunday.

Nothing Florence had said had prepared her for him. She had expected him to be older than Florence, and bald, or grey. But he seemed considerably younger than his sister, with all his teeth and hair. There he sat, that Sunday, in Florence's tiny, fragile parlour, a very rock, it seemed to the eye of her confusion, in her so weary land.

She remembered that as she mounted the stairs with John's heavy weight in her arms, and as she entered the door, she heard music, which became perceptibly fainter as Florence closed the door behind her. John had heard it, too, and had responded by wriggling, and moving his hands in the air, and making noises, meant, she supposed, to be taken for a song. 'You's a nigger, all right,' she thought with amusement and impatience—for it was someone's gramophone, on a lower floor, filling the air with the slow, high, measured wailing of the blues.

Gabriel rose, it seemed to her, with a speed and eagerness that were not merely polite. She wondered immediately if Florence had told him about her. And this caused her to stiffen with a tentative anger against Florence, and with pride and fear. Yet when she looked into his eyes she found there a strange humility, an altogether unexpected kindness. She felt the anger go out of her, and her defensive pride; but somewhere, crouching, the fear remained.

Then Florence introduced them, saying: 'Elizabeth, this here's my brother I been telling you so much about. He's a preacher, honey—so we got to be mighty careful what we talk about when *he's* around.'

Then he said, with a smile less barbed and ambiguous than his sister's remark: 'Ain't no need to be afraid of me, sister. I ain't nothing but a poor, weak vessel in the hands of the Lord.'

'You *see!*' said Florence, grimly. She took John from his mother's arms. 'And this here's little Johnny,' she said, 'shake hands with the preacher, Johnny.'

But John was staring at the door that held back the music; towards which, with an insistence at once furious and feeble, his hands were still outstretched. He looked questioningly, reproachfully, at his mother, who laughed, watching him, and said, 'Johnny want to hear some more of that music. He like to started dancing when we was coming up the stairs.'

Gabriel laughed, and said, circling around Florence to look into John's face: 'Got a man in the Bible, son, who like music, too. He used to play on his harp before the king, and he got to dancing one day before the Lord. You reckon you going to dance for the Lord one of these days?'

John looked with a child's impenetrable gravity into the preacher's face, as though he were turning this question over in his mind and would answer when he had thought it out. Gabriel smiled at him, a strange smile— strangely, she thought, loving—and touched him on the crown of the head.

'He a mighty fine boy,' said Gabriel. 'With them big eyes he ought to see everything *in* the Bible.'

And they all laughed. Florence moved to deposit John in the easy chair that was his Sunday throne. And Elizabeth found that she was watching Gabriel, unable to find in the man before her the brother whom Florence so despised.

They sat down at the table, John placed between herself and Florence and opposite Gabriel.

'So,' Elizabeth said, with a nervous pleasantness, it being necessary, she felt, to say something, 'you just getting to this big city? It must seem mighty strange to you.'

His eyes were still on John, whose eyes had not left him. Then he looked again at Elizabeth. She felt that the air between them was beginning to be charged, and she could find no name, or reason, for the secret excitement that moved in her.

'It's mighty big,' he said, 'and looks to me—and *sounds* to me—like the Devil's working every day.'

This was in reference to the music, which had not ceased, but she felt, immediately, that it included her; this, and something else in Gabriel's eyes, made her look down quickly to her plate.

'He ain't,' said Florence, briskly, 'working no harder up here than he worked down home. Them niggers down home,' she said to Elizabeth, 'they think New York ain't nothing but one long, Sunday drunk. They don't *know*. Somebody better tell them—they can get better moonshine right there where they is than they likely to here—and cheaper, too.'

'But I *do* hope,' he said, with a smile, 'that you ain't taken to drinking moonshine, sister.'

'It wasn't never *me*,' she said, promptly, 'had *that* habit.'

'Don't know,' he persisted, still smiling, and still looking at Elizabeth, 'tell me folks do things up North they wouldn't think about doing down home.'

'Folks got their dirt to do,' said Florence. 'They going to do it, no matter where they is. Folks do lots of things down home they don't want nobody to know about.'

'Like my aunt used to say,' Elizabeth said, smiling timidly, 'she used to say, folks sure better not do in the dark what they's scared to look at in the light.'

She had meant it as a kind of joke; but the words were not out of her mouth before she longed for the power to call them back. They rang in her own ears like a confession.

'That's the Lord's truth,' he said, after the briefest pause. 'Does you really believe that?'

She forced herself to look up at him, and felt at that moment the intensity of the attention that Florence fixed on her, as though she were trying to shout a warning. She knew that it was something in Gabriel's voice that had caused Florence, suddenly, to be so wary and so tense. But she did not drop her eyes from Gabriel's eyes. She answered him: 'Yes. That's the way I want to live.'

'Then the Lord's going to bless you,' he said, 'and open up the windows of Heaven for you—for you, and that boy. He going to pour down blessings on you till you won't know where to put them. You mark my words.'

'Yes,' said Florence, mildly, 'you *mark* his words.'

But neither of them looked at her. It came into Elizabeth's mind, filling her mind: *All things work together for good to them that love the Lord.* She tried to obliterate this burning phrase, and what it made her feel. What it made her feel, for the first time since the death of Richard, was hope; his voice had made her feel that she was not altogether cast down, that God might raise her again in honour; his eyes had made her know that she could be—again, this time in honour—a woman. Then, from what seemed to be a great, cloudy distance, he smiled at her—and she smiled.

The distant gramophone stuck now, suddenly, on a grinding, wailing, sardonic trumpet-note; this blind, ugly crying swelled the moment and filled the room. She looked down at John. A hand somewhere struck the gramophone arm and sent the silver needle on its way through the whirling, black grooves, like something bobbing, anchorless, in the middle of the sea.

'Johnny's done fell asleep,' she said.

She, who had descended with such joy and pain, had begun her upward climb—upward, with her baby, on the steep, steep side of the mountain.

She felt a great commotion in the air around her—a great excitement, muted, waiting on the Lord. And the air seemed to tremble, as before a storm. A light seemed to hang—just above, and all around them—about to burst into revelation. In the great crying, the great singing all around her, in the wind that gathered to fill the church, she did not hear her husband; and she thought of John as sitting, silent now and sleepy, far in the back of the church—watching, with that wonder and that terror in his eyes. She did not raise her head. She wished to tarry yet a little longer, that God might speak to her.

It had been before this very altar that she had come to kneel, so many years ago, to be forgiven. When the autumn came, and the air was dry and sharp, and the wind high, she was always with Gabriel. Florence did not approve of this, and Florence said so often; but she never said more than this, for the reason, Elizabeth decided, that she had no evil to report—it was only that she was not fond of her brother. But even had Florence been able to find a language unmistakable in which to convey her prophecies, Elizabeth could not have heeded her because Gabriel had become her strength. He watched over her and her baby as though it had become his calling; he was very good to John, and played with him, and bought him things, as though John were his own. She knew that his wife had died childless, and that he had always wanted a son—he was praying still, he told her, that God would bless him with a son. She thought sometimes, lying on her bed alone, and thinking of all his kindness, that perhaps John was that son, and that he would grow one day to comfort and bless them both. Then she thought how, now, she would embrace again the faith she had abandoned, and walk again in the light from which, with Richard, she had so far fled. Sometimes, thinking of Gabriel, she remembered Richard—his voice, his breath, his arms—with a terrible pain; and then she felt herself shrinking from Gabriel's anticipated touch. But this shrinking she would not countenance. She told herself that it was foolish and sinful to look backward when her safety lay before her, like a hiding-place hewn in the side of the mountain.

'Sister,' he asked one night, 'don't you reckon you ought to give your heart to the Lord?'

They were in the dark streets, walking to church. He had asked her this question before, but never in such a tone; she had never before felt so compelling a need to reply.

'I reckon,' she said.

'If you call on the Lord,' he said, 'He'll lift you up, He'll give you your heart's desire. I'm a witness,' he said, and smiled at her, 'you call on the Lord, you wait on the Lord, He'll answer. God's promises don't never fail.'

Her arm was in his, and she felt him trembling with his passion.

'Till you come,' she said, in a low, trembling voice, 'I didn't never hardly go to church at all, Reverend. Look like I couldn't see my way nohow—I was all bowed down with shame . . . and sin.'

She could hardly bring the last words out, and as she spoke tears were in her eyes. She had told him that John was nameless; and she had tried to tell him something of her suffering, too. In those days he had seemed to understand, and he had not stood in judgment on her. When had he so greatly changed? Or was it that he had not changed, but that her eyes had been opened through the pain he had caused her?

'Well,' he said, 'I done come, and it was the hand of the Lord what sent me. He brought us together for a sign. You fall on your knees and see if that ain't so—you fall down and ask Him to speak to you to-night.'

Yes, a sign, she thought, a sign of His mercy, a sign of His forgiveness.

When they reached the church doors he paused, and looked at her and made his promise.

'Sister Elizabeth,' he said, 'when you go down on your knees to-night, I want you to ask the Lord to speak to your heart, and tell you how to answer what I'm going to say.'

She stood a little below him, one foot lifted to the short, stone step that led to the church entrance, and looked up into his face. And looking into his face, which burned—in the dim, yellow light that hung about them there—like the face of a man who has wrestled with angels and demons and looked on the face of God, it came to her, oddly, and all at once, that she had become a woman.

'Sister Elizabeth,' he said, 'the Lord's been speaking to my heart, and I believe it's His will that you and me should be man and wife.'

And he paused; she said nothing. His eyes moved over her body.

'I know,' he said, trying to smile, and in a lower voice, 'I'm a lot older than you. But that don't make no difference. I'm a mighty strong man yet. I done been down the line, Sister Elizabeth, and maybe I can keep you from making . . . some of my mistakes, bless the Lord . . . maybe I can help keep your foot from stumbling . . . again . . . girl . . . for as long as we's in this world.'

Still she waited.

'And I'll love you,' he said, 'and I'll honour you . . . until the day God calls me home.'

Slow tears rose to her eyes; of joy, for what she had come to; of anguish, for the road that had brought her here.

'And I'll love your son, your little boy,' he said at last, 'just like he was my own. He won't never have to fret or worry about nothing; he won't never be cold or hungry as long as I'm alive and I got my two hands to work with. I swear this before my God,' he said, 'because He done give me back something I thought was lost.'

Yes, she thought, a sign—a sign that He is mighty to save. Then she moved and stood on the short step, next to him, before the doors.

'Sister Elizabeth,' he said—and she would carry to the grave the memory of his grace and humility at that moment, 'will you pray?'

'Yes,' she said. 'I been praying. I'm going to pray.'

They had entered this church, these doors; and when the pastor made the altar call, she rose, while she heard them praising God, and walked down the long church aisle; down this aisle, to this altar, before this golden cross; to these tears, into this battle—would the battle end one day? When she rose, and as they walked once more through the streets, he had called her God's daughter, handmaiden to God's minister. He had kissed her on the brow, with tears, and said that God had brought them together to be each other's deliverance. And she had wept, in her great joy that the hand of God had changed her life, had lifted her up and set her on the solid rock, alone.

She thought of that far-off day when John had come into the world—that moment, the beginning of her life and death. Down she had gone that day, alone, a heaviness intolerable at her waist, a secret in her loins, down into the darkness, weeping and groaning and cursing God. How long she had bled, and sweated, and cried, no language on earth could tell—how long she had crawled through darkness she would never, never know. There, her beginning, and she fought through darkness still; towards that moment when she would make her peace with God, when she would hear Him speak, and He would wipe all tears from her eyes; as, in that other darkness, after eternity, she had heard John cry.

As now, in the sudden silence, she heard him cry: not the cry of the child, newborn, before the common light of earth; but the cry of the man-child, bestial, before the light that comes down from Heaven. She opened her eyes and stood straight up; all of the saints surrounded her; Gabriel stood staring, struck rigid as a pillar in the temple. On the threshing-floor, in the centre of the crying, singing saints, John lay astonished beneath the power of the Lord.

# THE
# THRESHING-
# FLOOR

*Then said I, Woe is me! for I am
undone; because I am a man of unclean
lips, and I dwell in the midst of a
people of unclean lips; for mine eyes
have seen the King, the Lord of hosts.*

Part Three

# THE
# THRESHING-
# FLOOR

*Then I buckled up my shoes,*
*And I started.*

HE KNEW, without knowing how it had happened, that he lay on the floor, in the dusty space before the altar which he and Elisha had cleaned; and knew that above him burned the yellow light which he had himself switched on. Dust was in his nostrils, sharp and terrible, and the feet of saints, shaking the floor beneath him, raised small clouds of dust that filmed his mouth. He heard their cries, so far, so high above him— he could never rise that far. He was like a rock, a dead man's body, a dying bird, fallen from an awful height; something that had no power of itself, any more, to turn.

And something moved in John's body which was not John. He was invaded, set at naught, possessed. This power had struck John, in the head or in the heart; and, in a moment, wholly, filling him with an anguish that he could never in his life have imagined, that he surely could not endure, that even now he could not believe, had opened him up; had cracked him open, as wood beneath the axe cracks down the middle, as rocks break up; had ripped him and felled him in a moment, so that John had not felt the wound, but only the agony, had not felt the fall, but only the fear; and lay here, now, helpless, screaming, at the very bottom of darkness.

He wanted to rise—a malicious, ironic voice insisted that he rise—and, at once, to leave this temple and go out into the world.

He wanted to obey the voice, which was the only voice that spoke to him; he tried to assure the voice that he would do his best to rise; he would only lie here a moment, after his dreadful fall, and catch his breath. It was at this moment, precisely, that he found he could not rise; something had happened to his arms, his legs, his feet—ah, something had happened to John! And he began to scream again in his great, bewildered terror, and felt himself, indeed, begin to move—not upward, toward the light, but down again, a sickness in his bowels, a tightening in his loin-strings; he felt himself turning, again and again, across the dusty floor, as though God's toe had touched him lightly. And the dust made him cough and retch; in his turning the centre of the whole earth shifted, making of space a sheer void and a mockery of order, and balance, and time. Nothing remained: all was swallowed up in chaos. And: *Is this it?* John's terrified soul inquired —*What is it?*—to no purpose, receiving no answer. Only the ironic voice insisted yet once more that he rise from that filthy floor if he did not want to become like all the other niggers.

Then the anguish subsided for a moment, as water withdraws briefly to dash itself once more against the rocks: he knew that it subsided only to return. And he coughed and sobbed in the dusty space before the altar, lying on his face. And still he was going down, farther and farther from the joy, the singing, and the light above him.

He tried, but in such despair!—the utter darkness does not present any point of departure, contains no beginning, and no end—to rediscover, and, as it were, to trap and hold tightly in the palm of his hand, the moment

preceding his fall, his change. But that moment was also
locked in darkness, was wordless, and would not come
forth. He remembered only the cross: he had turned
again to kneel at the altar, and had faced the golden
cross. And the Holy Ghost was speaking—seeming to
say, as John spelled out the so abruptly present and
gigantic legend adorning the cross: *Jesus Saves*. He had
stared at this, an awful bitterness in his heart, wanting to
curse—and the Spirit spoke, and spoke in him. Yes: there
was Elisha, speaking from the floor, and his father, silent,
at his back. In his heart there was a sudden yearning
tenderness for holy Elisha; desire, sharp and awful as a
reflecting knife, to usurp the body of Elisha, and lie where
Elisha lay; to speak in tongues, as Elisha spoke, and, with
that authority, to confound his father. Yet this had not
been the moment; it was as far back as he could go, but
the secret, the turning, the abysmal drop was farther
back, in darkness. As he cursed his father, as he loved
Elisha, he had, even then, been weeping; he had already
passed his moment, was already under the power, had
been struck, and was going down.

Ah, down!—and to what purpose, where? To the
bottom of the sea, the bowels of the earth, to the heart of
the fiery furnace? Into a dungeon deeper than Hell, into
a madness louder than the grave? What trumpet sound
would awaken him, what hand would lift him up? For he
knew, as he was struck again, and screamed again, his
throat like burning ashes, and as he turned again, his body
hanging from him like a useless weight, a heavy, rotting
carcass, that if he were not lifted he would never rise.

His father, his mother, his aunt, Elisha—all were far
above him, waiting, watching his torment in the pit. They
hung over the golden barrier, singing behind them, light
around their heads, weeping, perhaps, for John, struck
down so early. And, no, they could not help him any
more—nothing could help him any more. He struggled,

H

struggled to rise up, and meet them—he wanted wings to fly upward and meet them in that morning, that morning where they were. But his struggles only thrust him downward, his cries did not go upward, but rang in his own skull.

Yet, though he scarcely saw their faces, he knew that they were there. He felt them move, every movement causing a trembling, an astonishment, a horror in the heart of darkness where he lay. He could not know if they wished him to come to them as passionately as he wished to rise. Perhaps they did not help him because they did not care—because they did not love him.

Then his father returned to him, in John's changed and low condition; and John thought, but for a moment only, that his father had come to help him. In the silence, then, that filled the void, John looked on his father. His father's face was black—like a sad, eternal night; yet in his father's face there burned a fire—a fire eternal in an eternal night. John trembled where he lay, feeling no warmth for him from this fire, trembled, and could not take his eyes away. A wind blew over him, saying:'Whosoever loveth and maketh a lie.' Only: 'Whosoever loveth and maketh a lie.' And he knew that he had been thrust out of the holy, the joyful, the blood-washed community, that his father had thrust him out. His father's will was stronger than John's own. His power was greater because he belonged to God. Now, John felt no hatred, nothing, only a bitter, unbelieving despair: all prophecies were true, salvation was finished, damnation was real!

Then Death is real, John's soul said, and Death will have his moment.

'Set thine house in order,' said his father, 'for thou shalt die and not live.'

And then the ironic voice spoke again, saying: 'Get up, John. Get up, boy. Don't let him keep you here. You got everything your daddy got.'

John tried to laugh—John thought that he was laughing—but found, instead, that his mouth was filled with
salt, his ears were full of burning water. Whatever was
happening in his distant body now, he could not change
or stop; his chest heaved, his laughter rose and bubbled
at his mouth, like blood.

And his father looked on him. His father's eyes looked
down on him, and John began to scream. His father's eyes
stripped him naked, and hated what they saw. And as he
turned, screaming, in the dust again, trying to escape his
father's eyes, those eyes, that face, and all their faces,
and the far-off yellow light, all departed from his vision as
though he had gone blind. He was going down again. There
is, his soul cried out again, no bottom to the darkness!

He did not know where he was. There was silence
everywhere—only a perpetual, distant, faint trembling
far beneath him—the roaring, perhaps, of the fires of
Hell, over which he was suspended, or the echo, per-
sistent, invincible still, of the moving feet of the saints.
He thought of the mountain-top, where he longed to be,
where the sun would cover him like a cloth of gold,
would cover his head like a crown of fire, and in his
hands he would hold a living rod. But this was no mountain where John lay, here, no robe, no crown. And the
living rod was uplifted in other hands.

'I'm going to beat sin out of him. I'm going to beat it
out.'

Yes, he had sinned, and his father was looking for him.
Now, John did not make a sound, and did not move at
all, hoping that his father would pass him by.

'Leave him be. Leave him alone. Let him pray to the
Lord.'

'Yes, Mama. I'm going to try to love the Lord.'

'He done run off somewhere. I'm going to find him.
I'm going to beat it out.'

Yes, he had sinned: one morning, alone, in the dirty

bathroom, in the square, dirt-grey cupboard room that was filled with the stink of his father. Sometimes, leaning over the cracked, 'tattle-tale grey' bath-tub, he scrubbed his father's back; and looked, as the accursed son of Noah had looked, on his father's hideous nakedness. It was secret, like sin, and slimy, like the serpent, and heavy, like the rod. Then he hated his father, and longed for the power to cut his father down.

Was this why he lay here, thrust out from all human or heavenly help to-night? This, and not that other, his deadly sin, having looked on his father's nakedness and mocked and cursed him in his heart? Ah, that son of Noah's had been cursed, down to the present groaning generation: *A servant of servants shall he be unto his brethren.*

Then the ironic voice, terrified, it seemed, of no depth, no darkness, demanded of John, scornfully, if he believed that he was cursed. All niggers had been cursed, the ironic voice reminded him, all niggers had come from this most undutiful of Noah's sons. How could John be cursed for having seen in a bath-tub what another man—*if* that other man had ever lived—had seen ten thousand years ago, lying in an open tent? Could a curse come down so many ages? Did it live in time, or in the moment? But John found no answer for this voice, for he was in the moment, and out of time.

And his father approached. 'I'm going to beat sin out of him. I'm going to beat it out.' All the darkness rocked and wailed as his father's feet came closer; feet whose tread resounded like God's tread in the garden of Eden, searching the covered Adam and Eve. Then his father stood just above him, looking down. Then John knew that a curse was renewed from moment to moment, from father to son. Time was indifferent, like snow and ice; but the heart, crazed wanderer in the driving waste, carried the curse for ever.

'John,' said his father, 'come with me.'

Then they were in a straight street, a narrow, narrow way. They had been walking for many days. The street stretched before them, long, and silent, going down, and whiter than the snow. There was no one on the street, and John was frightened. The buildings on this street, so near that John could touch them on either side, were narrow, also, rising like spears into the sky, and they were made of beaten gold and silver. John knew that these build-ings were not for him—not to-day—*no, nor to-morrow, either!* Then, coming up this straight and silent street, he saw a woman, very old and black, coming toward them, staggering on the crooked stones. She was drunk, and dirty, and very old, and her mouth was bigger than his mother's mouth, or his own; her mouth was loose and wet, and he had *never* seen anyone so black. His father was astonished to see her, and beside himself with anger; but John was glad. He clapped his hands, and cried:

'See! She's uglier than Mama! She's uglier than me!'

'You mighty proud, ain't you,' his father said, 'to be the Devil's son?'

But John did not listen to his father. He turned to watch the woman pass. His father grabbed his arm.

'You see that? That's sin. That's what the Devil's son runs after.'

'Whose son are you?' John asked.

His father slapped him. John laughed, and moved a little away.

'I seen it. I seen it. I ain't the Devil's son for nothing.'

His father reached for him, but John was faster. He moved backward down the shining street, looking at his father—his father who moved toward him, one hand out-stretched in fury.

'And I *heard* you—all the night-time long. I know what you do in the dark, black man, when you think the Devil's son's asleep. I heard you, spitting, and groaning, and choking—and I *seen* you, riding up and down, and going in and out. I ain't the Devil's son for nothing.'

The listening buildings, rising upward yet, leaned, closing out the sky. John's feet began to slip; tears and sweat were in his eyes; still moving backward before his father, he looked about him for deliverance; but there was no deliverance in this street for him.

'And I hate you. I hate you. I don't care about your golden crown. I don't care about your long white robe. I seen you under the robe, I seen you!'

Then his father was upon him; at his touch there was singing, and fire. John lay on his back in the narrow street, looking up at his father, that burning face beneath the burning towers.

'I'm going to beat it out of you. I'm going to beat it out.'

His father raised his hand. The knife came down. John rolled away, down the white, descending street, screaming:

'*Father! Father!*'

These were the first words he uttered. In a moment there was silence, and his father was gone. Again, he felt the saints above him—and dust was in his mouth. There was singing somewhere; far away, above him; singing slow and mournful. He lay silent, racked beyond endurance, salt drying on his face, with nothing in him any more, no lust, no fear, no shame, no hope. And yet he knew that it would come again—the darkness was full of demons crouching, waiting to worry him with their teeth again.

*Then I looked in the grave and I wondered.*

Ah, down!—what was he searching here, all alone in darkness? But now he knew, for irony had left him, that he was searching something, hidden in the darkness, that must be found. He would die if it was not found; or, he was dead already, and would never again be joined to the living, if it was not found.

*And the grave looked so sad and lonesome.*

In the grave where he now wandered—he knew it was the grave, it was so cold and silent, and he moved in icy mist—he found his mother and his father, his mother dressed in scarlet, his father dressed in white. They did not see him: they looked backward, over their shoulders, at a cloud of witnesses. And there was his Aunt Florence, gold and silver flashing on her fingers, brazen ear-rings dangling from her ears; and there was another woman, whom he took to be that wife of his father's, called Deborah—who had, as he had once believed, so much to tell him. But she, alone, of all that company, looked at him and signified that there was no speech in the grave. He was a stranger there—they did not see him pass, they did not know what he was looking for, they could not help him search. He wanted to find Elisha, who knew, perhaps, who would help him—but Elisha was not there. There was Roy: Roy also might have helped him, but he had been stabbed with a knife, and lay now, brown and silent, at his father's feet.

Then there began to flood John's soul the waters of despair. *Love is as strong as death, as deep as the grave.* But love, which had, perhaps, like a benevolent monarch, swelled the population of his neighbouring kingdom, Death, had not himself descended: they owed him no allegiance here. Here there was no speech or language, and there was no love; no one to say: You are beautiful, John; no one to forgive him, no matter what his sin; no one to heal him, and lift him up. No one: father and mother looked backward, Roy was bloody, Elisha was not here.

Then the darkness began to murmur—a terrible sound —and John's ears trembled. In this murmur that filled the grave, like a thousand wings beating on the air, he recognized a sound that he had always heard. He began, for terror, to weep and moan—and this sound was swallowed up, and yet was magnified by the echoes that filled the darkness.

This sound had filled John's life, so it now seemed, from the moment he had first drawn breath. He had heard it everywhere, in prayer and in daily speech, and wherever the saints were gathered, and in the unbelieving streets. It was in his father's anger, and in his mother's calm insistence, and in the vehement mockery of his aunt; it had rung, so oddly, in Roy's voice this afternoon, and when Elisha played the piano it was there; it was in the beat and jangle of Sister McCandless's tambourine, it was in the very cadence of her testimony, and invested that testimony with a matchless, unimpeachable authority. Yes, he had heard it all his life, but it was only now that his ears were opened to this sound that came from darkness, that could only come from darkness, that yet bore such sure witness to the glory of the light. And now in his moaning, and so far from any help, he heard it in himself—it rose from his bleeding, his cracked-open heart. It was a sound of rage and weeping which filled the grave, rage and weeping from time set free, but bound now in eternity; rage that had no language, weeping with no voice—which yet spoke now, to John's startled soul, of boundless melancholy, of the bitterest patience, and the longest night; of the deepest water, the strongest chains, the most cruel lash; of humility most wretched, the dungeon most absolute, of love's bed defiled, and birth dishonoured, and most bloody, unspeakable, sudden death. Yes, the darkness hummed with murder: the body in the water, the body in the fire, the body on the tree. John looked down the line of these armies of darkness, army upon army, and his soul whispered: *Who are these? Who are they?* And wondered: *Where shall I go?*

There was no answer. There was no help or healing in the grave, no answer in the darkness, no speech from all that company. They looked backward. And John looked back, seeing no deliverance.

*I, John, saw the future, way up in the middle of the air.*

Were the lash, the dungeon, and the night for him? And the sea for him? And the grave for him?

*I, John, saw a number, way in the middle of the air.*

And he struggled to flee—out of this darkness, out of this company—into the land of the living, so high, so far away. Fear was upon him, a more deadly fear than he had ever known, as he turned and turned in the darkness, as he moaned, and stumbled, and crawled through darkness, finding no hand, no voice, finding no door. *Who are these? Who are they?* They were the despised and rejected, the wretched and the spat upon, the earth's offscouring; and he was in their company, and they would swallow up his soul. The stripes they had endured would scar his back, their punishment would be his, their portion his, his their humiliation, anguish, chains, their dungeon his, their death his. *Thrice was I beaten with rods, once I was stoned, thrice I suffered shipwreck, a night and a day I have been in the deep.*

And their dread testimony would be his!

*In journeyings often, in perils of waters, in perils of robbers, in perils by mine own countrymen, in perils by the heathen, in perils in the city, in perils in the wilderness, in perils in the sea, in perils among false brethren.*

And their desolation, his:

*In weariness and painfulness, in watchings often, in hunger and thirst, in fastings often, in cold and nakedness.*

And he began to shout for help, seeing before him the lash, the fire, and the depthless water, seeing his head bowed down for ever, he, John, the lowest among these lowly. And he looked for his mother, but her eyes were fixed on this dark army—she was claimed by this army. And his father would not help him, his father did not see him, and Roy lay dead.

Then he whispered, not knowing that he whispered: 'Oh, Lord, have mercy on me. Have mercy on me.'

And a voice, for the first time in all his terrible journey, spoke to John, through the rage and weeping, and fire, and darkness, and flood:

'Yes,' said the voice, 'go through. Go through.'

'Lift me up,' whispered John, 'lift me up. I can't go through.'

'Go through,' said the voice, 'go through.'

Then there was silence. The murmuring ceased. There was only this trembling beneath him. And he knew there was a light somewhere.

'Go through.'

'Ask Him to take you through.'

But he could never go through this darkness, through this fire and this wrath. He never could go through. His strength was finished, and he could not move. He belonged to the darkness—the darkness from which he had thought to flee had claimed him. And he moaned again, weeping, and lifted up his hands.

'Call on Him. Call on Him.'

'Ask Him to take you through.'

Dust rose again in his nostrils, sharp as the fumes of Hell. And he turned again in the darkness, trying to remember something he had heard, something he had read.

*Jesus saves.*

And he saw before him the fire, red and gold, and waiting for him—yellow, and red, and gold, and burning in a night eternal, and waiting for him. He must go through this fire, and into this night.

*Jesus saves.*

*Call on Him.*

*Ask Him to take you through.*

He could not call, for his tongue would not unlock, and his heart was silent, and great with fear. In the darkness, how to move?—with death's ten thousand jaws agape,

and waiting in the darkness. On any turning whatsoever
the beast may spring—to move in the darkness is to move
into the waiting jaws of death. And yet, it came to him that
he must move; for there was a light somewhere, and life,
and joy, and singing—somewhere, somewhere above him.

And he moaned again: 'Oh, Lord, have mercy. Have
mercy, Lord.'

There came to him again the communion service at
which Elisha had knelt at his father's feet. Now this
service was in a great, high room, a room made golden
by the light of the sun; and the room was filled with a
multitude of people, all in long, white robes, the women
with covered heads. They sat at a long, bare, wooden
table. They broke at this table flat, unsalted bread, which
was the body of the Lord, and drank from a heavy silver
cup the scarlet wine of His blood. Then he saw that they
were barefoot, and that their feet were stained with this
same blood. And a sound of weeping filled the room as
they broke the bread and drank the wine.

Then they rose, to come together over a great basin
filled with water. And they divided into four groups,
two of women and two of men; and they began, woman
before woman, and man before man, to wash each other's
feet. But the blood would not wash off; many washings
only turned the crystal water red; and someone cried:
'*Have you been to the river?*'

Then John saw the river, and the multitude was there.
And now they had undergone a change; their robes were
ragged, and stained with the road they had travelled, and
stained with unholy blood; the robes of some barely
covered their nakedness; and some indeed were naked.
And some stumbled on the smooth stones at the river's
edge, for they were blind; and some crawled with a
terrible wailing, for they were lame; some did not cease
to pluck at their flesh, which was rotten with running
sores. All struggled to get to the river, in a dreadful

hardness of heart: the strong struck down the weak, the ragged spat on the naked, the naked cursed the blind, the blind crawled over the lame. And someone cried: *'Sinner, do you love my Lord?'*

Then John saw the Lord—for a moment only; and the darkness, for a moment only, was filled with a light he could not bear. Then, in a moment, he was set free; his tears sprang as from a fountain; his heart, like a fountain of waters, burst. Then he cried: 'Oh, blessed Jesus! Oh, Lord Jesus! Take me through!'

Of tears there was, yes, a very fountain—springing from a depth never sounded before, from depths John had not known were in him. And he wanted to rise up, singing, singing in that great morning, the morning of his new life. Ah, how his tears ran down, how they blessed his soul!—as he felt himself, out of the darkness, and the fire, and the terrors of death, rising upward to meet the saints.

'Oh, yes!' cried the voice of Elisha. 'Bless our God for ever!'

And a sweetness filled John as he heard this voice, and heard the sound of singing: the singing was for him. For his drifting soul was anchored in the love of God; in the rock that endured for ever. The light and the darkness had kissed each other, and were married now, for ever, in the life and the vision of John's soul.

*I, John, saw a city, way in the middle of the air,*
*Waiting, waiting, waiting up there.*

He opened his eyes on the morning, and found them, in the light of the morning, rejoicing for him. The trembling he had known in darkness had been the echo of their joyful feet—these feet, bloodstained for ever, and washed in many rivers—they moved on the bloody road for ever, with no continuing city, but seeking one to come: a city out of time, not made with hands, but eternal in the heavens. No power could hold this army back, no water disperse them, no fire consume them. One day they would compel the earth to heave upward, and surrender the waiting dead. They sang, where the darkness gathered, where the lion waited, where the fire cried, and where blood ran down:

*My soul, don't you be uneasy!*

They wandered in the valley for ever; and they smote the rock, for ever; and the waters sprang, perpetually, in the perpetual desert. They cried unto the Lord for ever, and lifted up their eyes for ever, they were cast down for ever, and He lifted them up for ever. No, the fire could not hurt them, and yes, the lion's jaws were stopped; the serpent was not their master, the grave was not their resting-place, the earth was not their home. Job bore them witness, and Abraham was their father, Moses had elected to suffer with them rather than glory in sin for a season. Shadrach, Meshach, and Abednego had gone before them into the fire, their grief had been sung by David, and Jeremiah had wept for them. Ezekiel had prophesied upon them, these scattered bones, these slain, and, in the fullness of time, the prophet, John, had come out of the wilderness, crying that the promise was for them. They were encompassed with a very cloud of witnesses: Judas, who had betrayed the Lord; Thomas, who had doubted Him; Peter, who had trembled at the crowing of a cock; Stephen, who had been stoned; Paul, who had been bound; the blind man crying in the dusty road, the dead man rising from the grave. And they looked unto Jesus, the author and the finisher of their faith, running with patience the race He had set before them; they endured the cross, and they despised the shame, and waited to join Him, one day, in glory, at the right hand of the Father.

*My soul! don't you be uneasy!*
*Jesus going to make up my dying bed!*

'Rise up, rise up, Brother Johnny, and talk about the Lord's deliverance.'

It was Elisha who had spoken; he stood just above John, smiling; and behind him were the saints—Praying Mother Washington, and Sister McCandless, and Sister Price. Behind these, he saw his mother, and his aunt; his father, for the moment, was hidden from his view.

'Amen!' cried Sister McCandless, 'rise up, and praise the Lord!'

He tried to speak, and could not, for the joy that rang in him this morning. He smiled up at Elisha, and his tears ran down; and Sister McCandless began to sing:

> 'Lord, I ain't
> No stranger now!'

'Rise up, Johnny,' said Elisha, again. 'Are you saved, boy?'

'Yes,' said John, 'oh, yes!' And the words came upward, it seemed, of themselves, in the new voice God had given him. Elisha stretched out his hand, and John took the hand, and stood—so suddenly, and so strangely, and with such wonder!—once more on his feet.

> 'Lord, I ain't
> No stranger now!'

Yes, the night had passed, the powers of darkness had been beaten back. He moved among the saints, he, John, who had come home, who was one of their company now; weeping, he yet could find no words to speak of his great gladness; and he scarcely knew how he moved, for his hands were new, and his feet were new, and he moved in a new and Heaven-bright air. Praying Mother Washington took him in her arms, and kissed him, and their tears, his tears and the tears of the old, black woman, mingled.

'God bless you, son. Run on, honey, and don't get weary!'

*'Lord, I been introduced,*
*To the Father and the Son,*
*And I ain't*
*No stranger now!'*

Yet, as he moved among them, their hands touching, and tears falling, and the music rising—as though he moved down a great hall, full of a splendid company—something began to knock in that listening, astonished, newborn, and fragile heart of his; something recalling the terrors of the night, which were not finished, his heart seemed to say; which, in this company, were now to begin. And, while his heart was speaking, he found himself before his mother. Her face was full of tears, and for a long while they looked at each other, saying nothing. And once again, he tried to read the mystery of that face —which, as it had never before been so bright and pained with love, had never seemed before so far from him, so wholly in communion with a life beyond his life. He wanted to comfort her, but the night had given him no language, no second sight, no power to see into the heart of any other. He knew only—and now, looking at his mother, he knew that he could never tell it—that the heart was a fearful place. She kissed him, and she said: 'I'm mighty proud, Johnny. You keep the faith. I'm going to be praying for you till the Lord puts me in my grave.'

Then he stood before his father. In the moment that he forced himself to raise his eyes and look into his father's face, he felt in himself a stiffening, and a panic, and a blind rebellion, and a hope for peace. The tears still on his face, and smiling still, he said: 'Praise the Lord.'

'Praise the Lord,' said his father. He did not move to touch him, did not kiss him, did not smile. They stood before each other in silence, while the saints rejoiced; and John struggled to speak the authoritative, the living word that would conquer the great division between his father and himself. But it did not come, the living word; in the silence something died in John, and something came alive. It came to him that he must testify: his tongue only could bear witness to the wonders he had seen. And he remembered, suddenly, the text of a sermon he had once heard his father preach. And he opened his mouth, feeling, as he watched his father, the darkness roar behind him, and the very earth beneath him seem to shake; yet he gave to his father their common testimony. 'I'm saved,' he said, 'and I know I'm saved.' And then, as his father did not speak, he repeated his father's text: 'My witness is in Heaven and my record is on high.'

'It come from your mouth,' said his father then. 'I want to see you live it. It's more than a notion.'

'I'm going to pray God,' said John—and his voice shook, whether with joy or grief he could not say—'to keep me, and make me strong . . . to stand . . . to stand against the enemy . . . and against everything and everybody . . . that wants to cut down my soul.'

Then his tears came down again, like a wall between him and his father. His Aunt Florence came and took him in her arms. Her eyes were dry, and her face was old in the savage, morning light. But her voice, when she spoke, was gentler than he had ever known it to be before.

'You fight the good fight,' she said, 'you hear? Don't you get weary, and don't you get scared. Because I *know* the Lord's done laid His hands on you.'

'Yes,' he said, weeping, 'yes. I'm going to serve the Lord.'

'Amen!' cried Elisha. 'Bless our God!'

The filthy streets rang with the early-morning light as they came out of the temple.

They were all there, save young Ella Mae, who had departed while John was still on the floor—she had a bad cold, said Praying Mother Washington, and needed to have her rest. Now, in three groups, they walked the long, grey, silent avenue: Praying Mother Washington with Elizabeth and Sister McCandless and Sister Price, and before them Gabriel and Florence, and Elisha and John ahead.

'You know, the Lord is a wonder,' said the praying mother. 'Don't you know, all this week He just burdened my soul, and kept me a-praying and a-weeping before Him? Look like I just couldn't get no ease nohow—and I *know* He had me a-tarrying for that boy's soul.'

'Well, amen,' said Sister Price. 'Look like the Lord just wanted this church to *rock*. You remember how He spoke through Sister McCandless Friday night, and told us to pray, and He'd work a mighty wonder in our midst? And He done *moved*—hallelujah—He done troubled *everybody's* mind.'

'I just tell you,' said Sister McCandless, 'all you got to do is *listen* to the Lord; He'll lead you right every *time*; He'll move every *time*. Can't nobody tell me *my* God ain't real.'

'And you see the way the Lord worked with young Elisha there?' said Praying Mother Washington, with a calm, sweet smile. 'Had that boy down there on the floor a-prophesying in *tongues*, amen, just the very *minute* before Johnny fell out a-screaming, and a-crying before the Lord. Look like the Lord was using Elisha to say: "It's time, boy, come on home." '

'Well, He *is* a wonder,' said Sister Price. 'And Johnny's got *two* brothers now.'

Elizabeth said nothing. She walked with her head bowed, hands clasped lightly before her. Sister Price turned to look at her, and smiled.

'I know,' she said, 'you's a mighty happy woman this morning.'

Elizabeth smiled and raised her head, but did not look directly at Sister Price. She looked ahead, down the long avenue, where Gabriel walked with Florence, where John walked with Elisha.

'Yes,' she said, at last, 'I been praying. And I ain't stopped praying yet.'

'Yes, Lord,' said Sister Price, 'can't none of us stop praying till we see His blessed face.'

'But I bet you didn't never think,' said Sister McCandless, with a laugh, 'that little Johnny was going to jump up so soon, and get religion. *Bless* our God!'

'The Lord's going to bless that boy, you mark my words,' said Praying Mother Washington.

*'Shake hands with the preacher, Johnny.'*

*'Got a man in the Bible, son, who liked music, too. And he got to dancing one day before the Lord. You reckon you going to dance before the Lord one of these days?'*

'Yes, Lord,' said Sister Price, 'the Lord done raised you up a holy son. He going to comfort your grey hairs.'

Elizabeth found that her tears were falling, slowly, bitterly, in the morning light. 'I pray the Lord,' she said, 'to bear him up on every side.'

'Yes,' said Sister McCandless, gravely, 'it's more than a notion. The Devil rises on every hand.'

Then, in silence, they came to the wide crossing where the tramline ran. A lean cat stalked the gutter and fled as they approached; turned to watch them, with yellow, malevolent eyes, from the ambush of a dustbin. A grey bird flew above them, above the electric wires for the tram line, and perched on the metal cornice of a roof. Then, far down the avenue, they heard a siren, and the clanging of a bell, and looked up to see the ambulance speed past them on the way to the hospital that was near the church.

'Another soul struck down,' murmured Sister McCandless. 'Lord have mercy.'

'He said in the last days evil would abound,' said Sister Price.

'Well, yes, He *did* say it,' said Praying Mother Washington, 'and I'm so glad He told us He wouldn't leave us comfortless.'

'When ye see all these things, know that your salva-tion is at hand,' said Sister McCandless. 'A thousand shall fall at thy side, and ten thousand at thy right hand —but it ain't going to come nigh thee. So glad, amen, this morning, bless my Redeemer.'

*'You remember that day when you come into the store?'*

*'I didn't think you never looked at me.'*

*'Well—you was mighty pretty.'*

'Didn't little Johnny never say nothing,' asked Praying Mother Washington, 'to make you think the Lord was working in his heart?'

'He always kind of quiet,' said Elizabeth. 'He don't say much.'

'No,' said Sister McCandless, 'he ain't like all these rough young ones nowadays—*he* got some respect for his elders. You done raised him mighty well, Sister Grimes.'

'It was his birthday yesterday,' Elizabeth said.

'No!' cried Sister Price. 'How old he got to be yesterday?'

'He done made fourteen,' she said.

'You hear that?' said Sister Price, with wonder. 'The Lord done saved that boy's soul on his birthday!'

'Well, he got two birthdays now,' smiled Sister McCandless, 'just like he got two brothers—one in the flesh, and one in the Spirit.'

'Amen, bless the Lord!' cried Praying Mother Washington.

*'What book was it, Richard?'*

*'Oh, I don't remember. Just a book.'*

*'You smiled.'*

*'You was mighty pretty.'*

She took her sodden handkerchief out of her bag, and dried her eyes; and dried her eyes again, looking down the avenue.

'Yes,' said Sister Price, gently, 'you just *thank* the Lord. You just *let* the tears fall. I know your heart is full this morning.'

'The Lord's done give you,' said Praying Mother Washington, 'a mighty blessing—and what the Lord gives, can't no man take away.'

'I open,' said Sister McCandless, 'and no man can shut. I shut, and no man can open.'

'Amen,' said Sister Price. 'Amen.'


'Well, I reckon,' Florence said, 'your soul is praising God this morning.'

He looked straight ahead, saying nothing, holding his body more rigid than an arrow.

'You always been saying,' Florence said, 'how the Lord would answer prayer.' And she looked sideways at him, with a little smile.

'He going to learn,' he said at last, 'that it ain't all in the singing and the shouting—the way of holiness is a hard way. He got the steep side of the mountain to climb.'

'But he got you there,' she said, 'ain't he, to help him when he stumbles, and to be a good example?'

'I'm going to see to it,' he said, 'that he walks right before the Lord. The Lord's done put his soul in *my* charge—and I ain't going to have that boy's blood on my hands.'

'No,' she said, mildly, 'I reckon you don't want that.'

Then they heard the siren, and the headlong, warning bell. She watched his face as he looked outward at the silent avenue and at the ambulance that raced to carry someone to healing, or to death.

'Yes,' she said, 'that wagon's coming, ain't it, one day for everybody?'

'I pray,' he said, 'it finds you ready, sister.'

'Is it going to find you ready?' she asked.

'I know my name is written in the Book of Life,' he said. 'I know I'm going to look on my Saviour's face in glory.'

'Yes,' she said, slowly, 'we's all going to be together there. Mama, and you, and me, and Deborah—and what was the name of that little girl who died not long after I left home?'

'What little girl who died?' he asked. 'A *lot* of folks died after *you* left home—you left your *mother* on her dying bed.'

'This girl was a mother, too,' she said. 'Look like she went north all by herself, and had her baby, and died—weren't nobody to help her. Deborah wrote me about it. Sure, you ain't forgotten that girl's name, Gabriel!'

Then his step faltered—seemed, for a moment, to drag. And he looked at her. She smiled, and lightly touched his arm.

'You ain't forgotten her name,' she said. 'You can't tell me you done forgot her name. Is you going to look on her face, too? Is her name written in the Book of Life?'

In utter silence they walked together, her hand still under his trembling arm.

'Deborah didn't never write,' she at last pursued, 'about what happened to the baby. Did you ever see him? You going to meet him in Heaven, too?'

'The Word tell us,' he said, 'to let the dead bury the dead. Why you want to go rummaging around back there, digging up things what's all forgotten now? The Lord, He knows my life—He done forgive me a long time ago.'

'Look like,' she said, 'you think the Lord's a man like you; you think you can fool Him like you fool men, and you think He forgets, like men. But God don't forget nothing, Gabriel—if your name's down there in the Book, like you say, it's got all what you done right down there with it. And you going to answer for it, too.'

'I done answered,' he said, 'already before my God. I ain't got to answer now, in front of you.'

She opened her handbag, and took out the letter.

'I been carrying this letter now,' she said, 'for more

than thirty years. And I been wondering all that time if I'd ever talk to you about it.'

And she looked at him. He was looking, unwillingly, at the letter, which she held tightly in one hand. It was old, and dirty, and brown, and torn; he recognized Deborah's uncertain, trembling hand, and he could see her again in the cabin, bending over the table, laboriously trusting to paper the bitterness she had not spoken. It had lived in her silence, then, all of those years? He could not believe it. She had been praying for him as she died—she had sworn to meet him in glory. And yet, this letter, her witness, spoke, breaking her long silence, now that she was beyond his reach for ever.

'Yes,' said Florence, watching his face, 'you didn't give her no bed of roses to sleep on, did you?—poor, simple, ugly, black girl. And you didn't treat that other one no better. Who is you met, Gabriel, all your holy life long, you ain't made to drink a cup of sorrow? And you doing it still—you going to be doing it till the Lord puts you in your grave.'

'God's way,' he said, and his speech was thick, his face was slick with sweat, 'ain't man's way. I been doing the will of the Lord, and can't nobody sit in judgment on me but the Lord. The Lord called me out, He chose *me*, and I been running with Him ever since I made a start. You can't keep your eyes on all this foolishness here below, all this wickedness here below—you got to lift up your eyes to the hills and run from the destruction falling on the earth, you got to put your hand in Jesus' hand, and go where *He* says go.'

'And if you been but a stumbling-stone here below?' she said. 'If you done caused souls right and left to stumble and fall, and lose their happiness, and lose their souls? What then, prophet? What then, the Lord's anointed? Ain't no reckoning going to be called of *you?* What you going to say when the wagon comes?'

He lifted up his head, and she saw tears mingled with his sweat. 'The Lord,' he said, 'He sees the heart—He sees the heart.'

'Yes,' she said, 'but I done read the Bible, too, and it tells me you going to know the tree by its fruit. What fruit I seen from you if it ain't been just sin and sorrow and shame?'

'You be careful,' he said, 'how you talk to the Lord's anointed. 'Cause my life ain't in that letter—you don't know my life.'

'Where *is* your life, Gabriel?' she asked, after a despairing pause. 'Where *is* it? Ain't it all done gone for nothing? Where's your branches? Where's your fruit?'

He said nothing; insistently, she tapped the letter with her thumbnail. They were approaching the corner where she must leave him, turning westward to take her underground home. In the light that filled the streets, the light that the sun was now beginning to corrupt with fire, she watched John and Elisha just before them, John's listening head bent, Elisha's arm about his shoulder.

'I got a son,' he said at last, 'and the Lord's going to raise him up. I know—the Lord has promised—His word is true.'

And then she laughed. '*That* son,' she said, 'that Roy. You going to weep for many a eternity before you see him crying in front of the altar like Johnny was crying to-night.'

'God sees the heart,' he repeated, 'He sees the heart.'

'Well, He ought to see it,' she cried, 'He made it! But don't nobody else see it, not even your own self! *Let* God see it—He sees it all right, and He don't say nothing.'

'He speaks,' he said, 'He speaks. All you got to do is listen.'

'I been listening many a night-time long,' said Florence, then, 'and He ain't never spoke to me.'

'He ain't never spoke,' said Gabriel, 'because you ain't

never wanted to hear. You just wanted Him to tell you your way was right. And that ain't no way to wait on God.'

'Then tell me,' said Florence, 'what He done said to you—that you didn't want to hear?'

And there was silence again. Now they both watched John and Elisha.

'I going to tell you something, Gabriel,' she said. 'I know you thinking at the bottom of your heart that if you just make *her*, her and her bastard boy, pay enough for her sin, *your* son won't have to pay for yours. But I ain't going to let you do that. You done made enough folks pay for sin, it's time you started paying.'

'What you think,' he asked, 'you going to be able to do—against me?'

'Maybe,' she said, 'I ain't long for this world, but I got this letter, and I'm sure going to give it to Elizabeth before I go, and if she don't want it, I'm going to find *some* way—some way, I don't know how—to rise up and tell it, tell *everybody*, about the blood the Lord's anointed is got on his hands.'

'I done told you,' he said, 'that's all done and finished; the Lord done give me a sign to make me know I been forgiven. What good you think it's going to do to start talking about it now?'

'It'll make Elizabeth to know,' she said, 'that she ain't the only sinner . . . in your holy house. And little Johnny, there—he'll know he ain't the only bastard.'

Then he turned again, and looked at her with hatred in his eyes.

'You ain't never changed,' he said. 'You still waiting to see my downfall. You just as wicked now as you was when you was young.'

She put the letter in her bag again.

'No,' she said, 'I ain't changed. You ain't changed neither. You still promising the Lord you going to do better—and you think whatever you done already, whatever you doing right at that *minute*, don't count. Of all the men I *ever* knew, you's the man who ought to be hoping the Bible's all a lie—'cause if that trumpet ever sounds, you going to spend eternity talking.'

They had reached her corner. She stopped, and he stopped with her, and she stared into his haggard, burning face.

'I got to take my underground,' she said. 'You got anything you want to say to me?'

'I been living a long time,' he said, 'and I ain't never seen nothing but evil overtake the enemies of the Lord. You think you going to use that letter to hurt me—but the Lord ain't going to let it come to pass. You going to be cut down.'

The praying women approached them, Elizabeth in the middle.

'Deborah,' Florence said, 'was cut down—but she left word. She weren't no enemy of *nobody*—and she didn't see nothing but evil. When I go, brother, you better tremble, 'cause I ain't going to go in silence.'

And, while they stared at each other, saying nothing more, the praying women were upon them.

Now the long, the silent avenue stretched before them like some grey country of the dead. It scarcely seemed that he had walked this avenue only (as time was reckoned up by men) some few hours ago; that he had known this avenue since his eyes had opened on the dangerous world; that he had played here, wept here, fled, fallen down, and been bruised here—in that time, so far behind him, of his innocence and anger.

Yes, on the evening of the seventh day, when, raging, he had walked out of his father's house, this avenue had been filled with shouting people. The light of the day had begun to fail—the wind was high, and the tall lights, one by one, and then all together, had lifted up their heads against the darkness—while he hurried to the temple. Had he been mocked, had anyone spoken, or laughed, or called? He could not remember. He had been walking in a storm.

Now the storm was over. And the avenue, like any landscape that has endured a storm, lay changed under Heaven, exhausted and clean, and new. Not again, for ever, could it return to the avenue it once had been. Fire, or lightning, or the latter rain, coming down from these skies which moved with such pale secrecy above him now, had laid yesterday's avenue waste, had changed it in a moment, in the twinkling of an eye, as all would be changed on the last day, when the skies would open up once more to gather up the saints.

Yet the houses were there, as they had been; the windows, like a thousand, blinded eyes, stared outward at the morning—at the morning that was the same for them as the mornings of John's innocence, and the mornings before his birth. The water ran in the gutters with a small, discontented sound; on the water travelled paper, burnt matches, sodden cigarette-ends; gobs of spittle, green-yellow, brown, and pearly; the leavings of a dog, the vomit of a drunken man, the dead sperm, trapped in rubber, of one abandoned to his lust. All moved slowly to the black grating where down it rushed, to be carried to the river, which would hurl it into the sea.

Where houses were, where windows stared, where gutters ran, were people—sleeping now, invisible, private, in the heavy darknesses of these houses, while the Lord's day broke outside. When John should walk these streets again, they would be shouting here again; the roar of children's roller skates would bear down on him from behind; little girls in pigtails, skipping rope, would establish on the pavement a barricade through which he must stumble as best he might. Boys would be throwing ball in these streets again—they would look at him, and call:

'Hey, Frog-eyes!'

Men would be standing on corners again, watching him pass, girls would be sitting on stoops again, mocking his walk. Grandmothers would stare out of windows, saying:

'That sure is a sorry little boy.'

He would weep again, his heart insisted, for now his weeping had begun; he would rage again, said the shifting air, for the lions of rage had been unloosed; he would be in darkness again, in fire again, now that he had seen the fire and the darkness. He was free—*whom the Son sets free is free indeed*—he had only to stand fast in his liberty. He was in battle no longer, this unfolding Lord's day, with this avenue, these houses, the sleeping, staring, shouting people, but had entered into battle with Jacob's angel, *with the princes and the powers of the air*. And he was filled with a joy, a joy unspeakable, whose roots, though he would not trace them on this new day of his life, were nourished by the wellspring of a despair not yet discovered. *The joy of the Lord is the strength of His people.* Where joy was, there strength followed; where strength was, sorrow came—for ever? For ever and for ever, said the arm of Elisha, heavy on his shoulder. And John tried to see through the morning wall, to stare past the bitter houses, to tear the thousand grey veils of the sky away, and look into that heart—the monstrous heart which beat for ever, turning the astounded universe, commanding the stars to flee away before the sun's red sandal, bidding the moon to wax and wane, and disappear, and come again; with a silver net holding back the sea, and, out of mysteries abysmal, re-creating, each day, the earth. That heart, that breath, without which *was not anything made which was made*. Tears came into his eyes again, making the avenue shiver, causing the houses to shake—

his heart swelled, lifted up, faltered, and was dumb. Out
of joy strength came, strength that was fashioned to bear
sorrow: sorrow brought forth joy. For ever? This was
Ezekiel's wheel, in the middle of the burning air for
ever—and the little wheel ran by faith, and the big wheel
ran by the grace of God.

'Elisha?' he said.

'If you ask Him to bear you up,' said Elisha, as though
he had read his thoughts, 'He won't never let you fall.'

'It was you,' he said, 'wasn't it, who prayed me
through?'

'We was all praying, little brother,' said Elisha, with
a smile, 'but yes, I was right over you the whole time.
Look like the Lord had put you like a burden on my
soul.'

'Was I praying long?' he asked.

Elisha laughed. 'Well, you started praying when it
was night and you ain't stopped praying till it was
morning. That's a right smart time, it seems to me.'

John smiled, too, observing with some wonder that a
saint of God could laugh.

'Was you glad,' he asked, 'to see me at the altar?'

Then he wondered why he had asked this, and hoped
Elisha would not think him foolish.

'I was mighty glad,' said Elisha soberly, 'to see little
Johnny lay his sins on the altar, lay his *life* on the altar
and rise up, praising God.'

Something shivered in him as the word *sin* was spoken.
Tears sprang to his eyes again. 'Oh,' he said, 'I pray
God, I *pray* the Lord . . . to make me strong . . . to
sanctify me wholly . . . and keep me saved!'

'Yes,' said Elisha, 'you keep that spirit, and I know
the Lord's going to see to it that you get home all right.'

'It's a long way,' John said slowly, 'ain't it? It's a hard
way. It's uphill all the way.'

'You remember Jesus.' Elisha said. 'You keep your

mind on Jesus. *He* went that way—up the steep side of the mountain—and He was carrying the cross, and didn't nobody help Him. He went that way for us. He carried that cross for us.'

'But He was the Son of God,' said John, 'and He knew it.'

'He knew it,' said Elisha, 'because He was willing to pay the price. Don't you know it, Johnny? Ain't you willing to pay the price?'

'That song they sing,' said John, finally, '*if it costs my life*—is that the price?'

'Yes,' said Elisha, 'that's the price.'

Then John was silent, wanting to put the question another way. And the silence was cracked, suddenly, by an ambulance siren, and a crying bell. And they both looked up as the ambulance raced past them on the avenue on which no creature moved, save for the saints of God behind them.

'But that's the Devil's price, too,' said Elisha, as silence came again. 'The Devil, he don't ask for nothing less than your life. And he take it, too, and it's lost for ever. For ever, Johnny. You in darkness while you living and you in darkness when you dead. Ain't nothing but the love of God can make the darkness light.'

'Yes,' said John, 'I remember. I remember.'

'Yes,' said Elisha, 'but you got to remember when the evil day comes, when the flood rises, boy, and look like your soul is going under. You got to remember when the Devil's doing all he can to make you forget.'

'The Devil,' he said, frowning and staring, 'the Devil. How many faces is the Devil got?'

'He got as many faces,' Elisha said,' as you going to see between now and the time you lay your burden down. And he got a lot more than that, but ain't nobody seen them all.'

'Except Jesus,' John said then. 'Only Jesus.'

'Yes,' said Elisha, with a grave, sweet smile, 'that's the Man you got to call on. That's the Man who knows.'

They were approaching his house—his father's house. In a moment he must leave Elisha, step out from under his protecting arm, and walk alone into the house— alone with his mother and his father. And he was afraid. He wanted to stop and turn to Elisha, and tell him . . . something for which he found no words.

'Elisha——' he began, and looked into Elisha's face. Then: 'You pray for me? Please pray for me?'

'I been praying, little brother,' Elisha said, 'and I sure ain't going to stop praying now.'

'For me,' persisted John, his tears falling, 'for *me*.'

'You know right well,' said Elisha, looking at him, 'I ain't going to stop praying for the brother what the Lord done give me.'

Then they reached the house, and paused, looking at each other, waiting. John saw that the sun was beginning to stir, somewhere in the sky; the silence of the dawn would soon give way to the trumpets of the morning. Elisha took his arm from John's shoulder and stood beside him, looking backward. And John looked back, seeing the saints approach.

'Service is going to be mighty late *this* morning,' Elisha said, and suddenly grinned and yawned.

And John laughed. 'But you be there,' he asked, 'won't you? This morning?'

'Yes, little brother,' Elisha laughed, 'I'm going to be there. I see I'm going to have to do some running to keep up with *you*.'

And they watched the saints. Now they all stood on the corner, where his Aunt Florence had stopped to say good-bye. All the women talked together, while his father stood a little apart. His aunt and his mother kissed each other, as he had seen them do a hundred times, and then his aunt turned to look for them, and waved.

They waved back, and she started slowly across the street, moving, he thought with wonder, like an old woman.

'Well, *she* ain't going to be out to service this morning, I tell you that,' said Elisha, and yawned again.

'And look like *you* going to be half asleep,' John said.

'Now don't you *mess* with me this morning,' Elisha said, 'because you ain't *got* so holy I can't turn you over my knee. I's your *big* brother in the Lord—you just remember *that*.'

Now they were on the near corner. His father and mother were saying good-bye to Praying Mother Washington, and Sister McCandless, and Sister Price. The praying woman waved to them, and they waved back. Then his mother and his father were alone, coming toward them.

'Elisha,' said John, 'Elisha.'

'Yes,' said Elisha, 'what you want now?'

John, staring at Elisha, struggled to tell him something more—struggled to say—all that could never be said. Yet: 'I was down in the valley,' he dared, 'I was by myself down there. I won't never forget. May God forget me if I forget.'

Then his mother and his father were before them. His mother smiled, and took Elisha's outstretched hand.

'Praise the Lord this morning,' said Elisha. 'He done give us something to praise Him for.'

'Amen,' said his mother, 'praise the Lord!'

John moved up to the short, stone step, smiling a little, looking down on them. His mother passed him, and started into the house.

'You better come on upstairs,' she said, still smiling, 'and take off them wet clothes. Don't want you catching cold.'

And her smile remained unreadable; he could not tell what it hid. And to escape her eyes, he kissed her, saying: 'Yes, Mama. I'm coming.'

She stood behind him, in the doorway, waiting.

'Praise the Lord, Deacon,' Elisha said. 'See you at the morning service, Lord willing.'

'Amen,' said his father, 'praise the Lord.' He started up the stone steps, staring at John, who blocked the way. 'Go on upstairs, boy,' he said, 'like your mother told you.'

John looked at his father and moved from his path, stepping down into the street again. He put his hand on Elisha's arm, feeling himself trembling, and his father at his back.

'Elisha,' he said, 'no matter what happens to me, where I go, what folks say about me, no matter what *any*body says, you remember—please remember—I was saved. I was *there*.'

Elisha grinned, and looked up at his father.

'He come through,' cried Elisha, 'didn't he, Deacon Grimes? The Lord done laid him out, and turned him around and wrote his *new* name down in glory. Bless our God!'

And he kissed John on the forehead, a holy kiss.

'Run on, little brother,' Elisha said. 'Don't you get weary. God won't forget you. You won't forget.'

Then he turned away, down the long avenue, home. John stood still, watching him walk away. The sun had come full awake. It was waking the streets, and the houses, and crying at the windows. It fell over Elisha like a golden robe, and struck John's forehead, where Elisha had kissed him, like a seal ineffaceable for ever.

And he felt his father behind him. And he felt the March wind rise, striking through his damp clothes, against his salty body. He turned to face his father—he found himself smiling, but his father did not smile.

They looked at each other a moment. His mother stood in the doorway, in the long shadows of the hall.

'I'm ready,' John said, 'I'm coming. I'm on my way.'

**THE END**